Dear Reader

The ***Scarlet*** ... month offer very different ... the world and heroines with a range ... ging and unusual jobs. I do hope you'll find these brand new stories as interesting to read as I have!

Kathryn Bellamy's *Summer of Secrets* gives us a heroine who's an interior designer mixing with jet-setters in the enthralling world of tennis (including some old friends from Kathryn's first two very popular ***Scarlet*** titles!). *Return to Opal Reach* by Clarissa Garland features an equally glamorous background – the international modelling circuit. But it's an artificial world which Clarissa's heroine rejects in an attempt to find happiness in the Australian Outback. Julie Garratt's heroine in *The Name of the Game* certainly isn't afraid to get her hands dirty: she's a car mechanic! And last but not least we have *Hidden Embers* by Angie Gaynor. Angie's heroine combines two challenging careers (accountancy and running a lodging house) with motherhood!

As always, I've tried to find something to suit everyone this month. Let me know if I've succeeded!

Till next month,

Sally Cooper

SALLY COOPER,
Editor-in-Chief – ***Scarlet***

About the Author

Clarissa Garland's first romantic story was published in an Australian women's magazine when she was sixteen. She has had more than fifty full-length contemporary and regency romances published with several publishers under other names. Her books have frequently featured on romance and mass market best-seller lists in the US. In 1996 one of these ranked #22 on the Waldenbooks mass market top 50 in the month of publication, and stayed high on the romance best-seller list for 3 weeks. It was nominated for a Romance Writers of America RITA award. In the same year, one of her books was a finalist in the Coeur de Bois RWA Chapter Heart of Romance Award. In 1997 she was again a finalist for this award.

Short stories, poetry and articles have been published in New Zealand, Australia, Britain and North America. Some of these have won literary awards. Clarissa is a trained librarian and has found this useful for researching her books. She loves to travel and has recently become an aficionado of the Internet.

The author loves to hear from her readers, so please drop her a line, c/o ***Scarlet***, and we'll happily pass your letter on.

CLARISSA GARLAND

RETURN TO OPAL REACH

Enquiries to:
Robinson Publishing Ltd
7 Kensington Church Court
London W8 4SP

First published in the UK by Scarlet, 1998

Cover photography by Colin Thomas

A copy of the British Library Cataloguing in Publication data is available from the British Library

ISBN 1–85487–884–0

Printed and bound in the EC

10 9 8 7 6 5 4 3 2 1

CHAPTER 1

The horseman seemed to have come from the sea, appearing distantly along the beach, a blurred figure emerging from the mist that drifted and eddied over the water.

The little peaks and hillocks of sand above the tideline were dusted with icy particles of frost, and down where the low, slow waves smoothed the shore and then receded, steam rose in their wake, while the golden disk of the rising sun burned through the mist on the horizon.

Skye's bare feet halted as she walked the darkened edge of firm sand. A shallow, glassy wave yearned and hissed about her ankles, dampening the hem of her white dress, and quickly retreated. Glancing back the way she had come, she saw the uneven trail of her footprints, some already erased by the incoming tide.

The horse came galloping silently towards

her, no longer a shadowy figure of the mist, the man on its back leaning slightly forward, the folds of his faded shirt riffling with the speed of their approach, his face unseen under a stockman's wide-brimmed hat, the man and the horse like one entity – one magnificent, dangerous, powerful creature.

Skye's hands gripped at the fullness of her skirt, ready for flight. She could hear the dull beating of her heart, or perhaps it was the thud of the approaching hooves as horse and rider drew near.

Then they were so close she could see that the horse's sleek coat was a deep, glossy brown, darkened with sweat – or the sea? She smelled its warm, zesty odour and the scent of oiled leather as the rider pulled it to a halt, its hooves raising eddies of sand.

The big animal huffed a small cloud of steam into the frosty air, and briefly showed a crescent of white about a long-lashed eye. There was a faint jingle of metal and the horse's gaunt, imperious head turned aside, the curve of its sinewy body following, presenting at eye level a masculine thigh encased in fabric so well fitted that she could see the muscles contract as the rider signalled the horse to his will. Man and horse circled her, splashing into a shallow wave and out again, while she pivoted instinctively to follow them with her eyes, her body. Her loose hair fanned out, throwing fine black strands across her vision before falling about her shoulders.

'What are you doing?' Her chin lifted, all her nerves contracting.

'Looking at you.' His voice had the voluptuous velvety texture and underlying bite of dark burgundy wine, sending a strangely pleasurable sensation feathering down her spine. 'You're beautiful. Midnight hair and midsummer eyes. You must be accustomed to being looked at.' He had halted the horse, his hands on the shortened reins strong and tanned, controlling the huge beast with ease.

As she watched he gathered the reins into one hand and held the other out towards her, bending slightly in invitation. 'Come here.'

Skye realised her feet were numbed. Why had she come walking on the beach in bare feet and a flimsy white dress? It was winter. She shook her head, clasping her arms about herself. Another wave washed over her feet. The water was warmer than the air, but she shivered.

'You're cold,' he said. 'Let me warm you.'

Her eyes closed. 'Oh,' she said softly, 'will you warm me?'

'I promise. I will.'

She opened her eyes and the beckoning hand

was still there. She took one step towards it, held out her own, felt his strong fingers fasten about hers.

He drew her closer. 'Put your foot on mine.'

The leather boot was smooth and hard under the curve of her bare instep. Then he swung her up before him, settling her sideways with her legs resting over his thigh.

The horse shifted, and the rider released her hand to deal with it. She slid her arms about his waist to keep her balance. He felt rock solid and smelled salty and fresh and earthy.

He quieted the horse and transferred the reins again to one hand while the other arm held Skye snug against him, and his jaw lightly brushed her temple.

Skye laid her cheek to his shoulder, savouring the heat and vitality of his skin through the fabric. She was pierced by a tremendous sense of longing.

His fingers were in her hair, stroking the night-black satin skein, then gently tugging until she had to raise her face and look at him.

Under the wide-brimmed hat his brows were black and straight, his eyes the grey-green of a eucalyptus leaf, turned silvery in the morning light. What little she could see of his hair was the same dark sable as the horse's coat. His nose might have been chiselled by a Roman sculptor;

his taut cheeks were faintly blurred with a morning beard. And his mouth was the sculptor's masterpiece – alluringly masculine, with the potential for ruthlessness or tenderness, perhaps even humour. But about the chin there was no possibility of compromise. It was granite-hard, square-jawed and authoritative.

'Why are you here?' she asked him, wonder lacing her voice.

The silver-gilt eyes lanced into the intensely blue depths of hers. She felt his breath on her lips. His eyelids lowered, the thick lashes veiling the sudden brilliance of his eyes as he looked at her parted mouth, and then the shadow of the broad-brimmed stockman's hat came over them both. His powerful arm tightened about her waist and brought her closer, until his mouth was only a whisper away from hers. 'I've come to take you home,' he said.

And she began to fight him . . .

Skye woke tangled in the bedclothes, panting with fright. The sheet had parted company with the mattress and her feet were icy.

She stopped fighting the blankets and tucked her feet under them, turning on her side to stare out of the window, keeping her eyes wide to dispel the remnants of her dream.

The house was built so that the two bedrooms

and the big living room faced the sea, with the kitchen, laundry and bathroom overlooking the road on the other side. Every night she pulled the curtains back before turning out the light, so that she'd wake to the sun as it crested the horizon.

The clouds hovering above the sweeping curve of the sea were etched with orange flame, and in the half light of dawn a writhing mist over the water obscured the line between sea and sky.

She could still feel the imprint of the hand at her waist holding her to a hard male body. Her breasts tingled where they'd been crushed against him, and her lips burned with the memory of his mouth barely touching hers.

Impatiently she twisted and sat up in one jerky movement, closing her eyes to rest her head on her upraised knees, her cheek laid against the fuzzy wool of the blanket.

It recalled to her mind an unshaven chin rasping her skin, the remembered strength of the horseman's hold, the flexing of masculine thigh muscles under her own, the shape of his body when she slid her arms about him, her fingers finding through the cloth of his shirt the indentation of his spine. The warmth . . .

Her eyes snapped open. Dreams. Nonsense. Slow-motion shampoo-commercial stuff, designed to tap into deep-rooted female fantasies. She'd starred in too many of them. They were coming back to haunt her.

She threw off the covers and slipped out of the bed, ignoring the goose pimples that rose immediately all over her skin under the brushed cotton nightshirt.

In the bathroom she splashed her face with cold water and dried it. Returning to the bedroom, she removed the nightshirt and pulled on trackpants and a matching sweatshirt and thick socks, grabbed a brush from the dressing table to give her hair a few cursory swipes and wrested the thick, glossy strands back into an elastic band.

She padded into the big, timber-lined main room.

Her sneakers, coated with pale sand, were on the broad deck outside the glass sliding door. She pulled back the door, put the shoes on and viciously tightened the laces. Bare feet and white dresses were for dreams.

At the top of the wide wooden steps she stood for a moment, breathing in the cold, crisp air. The morning fog was drifting away, revealing the broad blue expanse of the Pacific. There was nothing between New Zealand's east coast and the distant shores of South America but a vast stretch of ocean, and the horizon curving around a hundred and sixty degrees.

The feathery toe-toe and dry, colourless spinifex on the foreshore were still with morning as she brushed by them. The crust of frost that whitened the beach crunched beneath her shoes as she ran across it to the firmer swath of sand below the tideline. She turned to jog her usual two-mile route, her breath making little clouds ahead of her.

One fading star still clung to the pale sky behind a row of houses straggling along the low, scrubby bank above the beach. Early though it was, the imprints of booted feet and the clear pawprints of a large dog sullied the surface, and someone on a motorbike had left a single long tyre track.

At this time of the year many of the houses were empty. More often than not Skye had the beach to herself, but amateur fishermen often set their lines overnight and checked them for catches early in the morning.

She swerved to avoid a wave that tongued foamily to the still-dry sand, her shoes raising salty splashes at the edge of it.

Then she saw the hoofprints – deep and unmistakable – coming out of the waterline, as if the unseen horse had emerged from the sea. She came to an abrupt halt, staring for several seconds with disbelief, then shaking her head, impatient with her own stupid imagination.

So what if someone had been riding a horse along the sand? It wasn't the first time. Perhaps her subconscious had heard the beat of hooves and manufactured the dream from the sound.

'Are you all right, Skye?'

'Of course I'm all right, Mum.' Skye deliberately loosened her grip on the telephone handpiece and kept any hint of impatience from her voice. She sat down on the chair by the wall-hung phone, waiting for her heart to stop its unwarranted pounding. 'I'm fine,' she lied.

'What are you *doing* with yourself down there?' Genelle Taylor worried. 'Are you sure you don't want me to come and keep you company?'

'Thank you, but no,' Skye said firmly. 'Truly, I'm better on my own for a while. I'm . . . I'm getting back in shape.' Physically and mentally, she hoped. Yes, she was, she told herself. 'Exercising,' she said. 'Enjoying the beach.'

'In winter?' Genelle queried doubtfully. Then, 'You're not *swimming*?'

Skye's laugh sounded almost natural. 'No, I'm not swimming.' She'd thought of it, thought of braving the winter waves, being buffeted by salt water, letting the coldness numb her physically as she was numbed emotionally. But some shred of self-preservation had warned her that if she gave herself up to the chill, impersonal embrace of the sea she might not have the will to leave it.

'I wish you'd stayed here in Auckland and let us look after you,' her mother said.

Skye had tried that, and felt both smothered and ungrateful. And it hadn't helped. She lifted one foot onto the chair, curved a hand about her ankle below the band of her trackpants, and let her head droop. 'I know,' she said softly. 'But that isn't what I need.'

'Are you sure that what you need is to be alone?' Genelle asked bluntly. 'You're not the only one who's grieving, you know.'

Skye closed her eyes. Her throat had closed up too. She couldn't answer.

'Skye? Darling, I didn't mean to hurt you, believe me – I know you're hurting enough already. And I don't want to interfere, but it seems to me – '

'Mum, don't!' Skye interrupted. 'Please. I know you're trying to help, but . . . no one can.'

'You're *not* all right,' her mother wailed. 'If only you'd let us – '

'I will be.' Skye gritted her teeth. 'I'm still a bit raw. That's natural, isn't it?'

'Yes, of course,' her mother said. 'Have . . . have you heard from Jarrah?'

Skye swallowed. 'Yes.' Not for over a week

now, but he'd been punctilious before that. 'Yes, he's . . . he's kept in touch.' She'd thought it might be him when the phone had burred its imperative message. That was why her heart had been working overtime and her palms damp when she'd picked up the receiver.

There was a short, anxious silence from Genelle. 'Well, Dad sends his love. If there's anything you need, anything we can do . . . you will let us know?'

'Yes,' Skye said. 'But you've already done a lot.'

They loved her and they would have done almost anything for her to make her happy again – but no one could give back what she had lost.

After hanging up she dropped her face into her hands and took several deep, ragged breaths, then clamped her teeth shut and stared into space for a few seconds. Finally she pushed back her shoulders and headed for the internal stairs down from the living room.

Twice a day she worked out on the exercise machine in the basement. She had never really enjoyed exercising, but it had been a routine part of her day for a long time, and was the kind of mindless, blessedly tiring activity that she needed most right now.

Her father had bought the beach property partly as an investment and partly as a base for the family when the service sent him home on furlough from his various minor postings in the New Zealand diplomatic service.

Here her father had lived in shorts and bare feet, and spent his days fishing, while her mother sat under a beach umbrella sketching, or set up her easel and paints just inside the big glass door of the living room, surfacing now and then to make a quick meal.

As they grew older Skye and her brother had learned largely to fend for themselves. Mark had developed a taste for cooking in his mid-teens and was now a successful chef in a London restaurant.

Her parents had talked of retiring to live at the beach, but when the early retirement came about they had admitted after only nine months that the tiny community was too quiet and isolated for permanent residence. Genelle missed art galleries and Michael theatres. They bought a house in Auckland and kept the beach house for occasional holidays and for renting out in the summer.

The muscles in Skye's legs ached as she lifted her feet against the weights and felt her abdominal muscles tighten, and sweat moistened her forehead and upper lip. She thought of the other exercises she had done religiously for months, and grimly shook away the shaft of memory.

Lift. Come on, concentrate.

After an hour she picked up a towel and blotted the perspiration from her face before doing a few gentle stretches. Slinging the towel about her shoulders, she headed for the nearby downstairs shower.

Ten minutes later she rubbed excess water from her freshly shampooed hair, pulled on a towelling robe, and dumped her clothes in the hamper near the washing machine before going upstairs.

She was on the way to her bedroom when someone knocked on the wooden door that faced the road.

Skye froze, pulling the edges of the robe together. If she pretended the place was empty perhaps whoever it was would go away.

The knocking came again – loud, determined.

Probably a sales person or a canvasser. So long as she was quiet they'd never know there was anyone home. She continued into the bedroom, pushing the door almost shut, and turned to the built-in drawers, taking out navy leggings and a soft cream woollen jersey. And heard footfalls on the steps that led down from the door to the white pumice-stone car park area.

Then she stiffened at the unmistakable clink of the side gate being opened and closed again, the crunch of footsteps on the crushed shell path.

Her unwelcome visitor might be a burglar targeting empty houses. It was common enough in places like this, where many of the houses were holiday homes, intermittently occupied.

In the wake of the morning's frost the day had turned clear and sunny, the rolling waves outside a pure sea-blue edged with white. After her meagre lunch she had left the glass slider in the living room open to the salty air. An opportunist could slip inside, thinking she'd gone for a walk.

Skye whirled, flinging open the bedroom door and darting across the main room.

Her fingers closed on the handle, ready to draw the door shut, as a tall figure rounded the corner of the house and turned to bound up the steps to the deck.

She stood with her hand clamped about the sunwarmed metal, and the intruder came to a dead stop.

He wore jeans and a grey, flecked-wool pullover, the colour making his light eyes look darker, like a stormy sea.

'You didn't answer your door,' he said.

'I . . . was in the shower.'

He looked her over slowly, noting the tousled dampness of her hair, the pale oval face totally free of make-up, the loose folds of the hurriedly fastened robe revealing the tender skin between her breasts. Then his gaze returned to her face and he regarded her with the intense concentration that she'd come to dread. 'How are you, Skye?' he said, with a rough edge to his deep, dusky voice.

'All right. Why . . . why are you here?'

And Jarrah said, 'I've come to take you home.'

CHAPTER 2

Skye had known the very first time she laid eyes on him that Jarrah Kaine wasn't a man who could be trifled with.

Not that she was in the habit of using men and discarding them – quite the opposite. Skye had been called a snow queen on several occasions, sometimes to her face. Despite the fascination that her classic features, and her pencil-slim but feminine curved figure and long, racy legs held for so many men, she had managed to keep herself aloof from all of them.

It wasn't that she'd never felt sexual desire, only that she was wary of where it might lead. And before that evening she had never seriously regretted making her head rule her hormones.

But she had never been so instantly and strongly attracted to a man as she was to Jarrah Kaine.

They'd met at a charity ball in Sydney. Even

in formal evening clothes, Jarrah had carried an indefinable air of the outdoors with him. It was in his tan which owed nothing to artificial sunning machines, in the way he moved – that lengthy, confident stride belonging to the outback, to wide open spaces – and in his eyes, those striking gum-leaf eyes that appeared so light against his brown skin, and that seemed to look beyond the confines of the opulent ballroom until they were consciously focused on some nearer object.

As they'd focused on Skye when her escort of the evening had introduced them.

On her face first, his eyes meeting hers with an impact that startled her, so that she blinked in self-defence.

His gaze had moved to the mouth carefully outlined with a lip pencil and filled in with rose pink. Then, lightning-fast, he assessed the low-cut, shimmering midnight blue gown, from the narrow straps on her shoulders to the hem that brushed her ankles.

Her spike-heeled shoes increased her not insignificant height only enough to bring her eyes level with his beautifully carved mouth as it quirked in a faint smile.

Skye held her hand out to him in automatic courtesy. Disconcertingly, he first took her narrow fingers and held them on his upturned palm, examining her hand as if it interested him. Then he fleetingly clasped it and let her go.

She turned from him to reply to some remark made to her by a woman nearby, and he spoke to the man at her side, but she knew his attention was on her, as hers was on him.

The man she was with asked her to dance, and she allowed him to take her in his arms. As they glided away she found her gaze colliding with Jarrah Kaine's unsparing silvery glance, and a shiver ran over her.

'Are you cold?' her partner asked in surprise.

'No.' She smiled at him as he turned them. 'I'm not cold.' Her back was bare to just below the waist except for a complex interweaving of three thin straps between her shoulder blades, and she would swear she could feel Jarrah Kaine's gaze on her skin. It burned.

She had the oddest feeling that she would never be cold again.

Surprisingly, it was some time after their initial introduction before he approached her. Skye was on the fringe of another group when a warm hard hand lightly settled on her skin at waist level, just above the edge of the daring dress. She knew who it was even before he murmured, 'Miss Taylor – would you care to dance?'

Turning to him was as natural as taking her

next breath. When they reached the dance floor he kept his right hand on her spine and tucked hers into his left one, bringing it to his chest. But instead of clasping her fingers he pressed them against the soft fabric of his evening shirt, pushing aside the silk lapels of his jacket so that her palm recognized the steady beat of his heart.

Startled, she looked up at him with widened eyes, her left hand resting on his shoulder as he moved into a smooth dance step. Not just a nightclub shuffle, but a real rhythm. Somewhere he'd learned to do this properly.

His hold was firm but he didn't pull her close, keeping their bodies inches apart to touch fleetingly, tantalizingly, when he guided her into a turn or momentarily tightened his grip to adroitly avoid other dancers. She followed his subtle signals with a rare sense of confidence in giving herself up to his lead.

He never shifted his right hand, didn't try taking advantage of the low-cut dress as some men would have. Yet she was terribly conscious of the intimate way he still held her palm over the beat of his heart. And each time her breasts brushed his jacket, or his thigh briefly intruded between hers, she was assailed by a breathtaking awareness that heated her cheeks and made her skin extra-sensitive. When his thumb began to rove gently over the hand that he held inside his jacket, she felt the small caress in every inch of her body.

They hadn't spoken, but in the centre of the floor he suddenly increased the space between them to arm's length, circling dizzily while his gaze dropped over her.

'What are you doing?' she asked him, unsettled by the blatant appraisal.

His eyes lit with amusement. 'Looking at you. You must be accustomed to being looked at.'

'I'm not working tonight,' she protested.

Dark brows lifted. The silvery-green gaze chilled. 'I'm supposed to pay for the privilege?'

A pulse beat angrily in her throat. 'That isn't what I meant!'

'What did you mean?'

'I'm not on display now.'

The faint tilt of his brows expressed his opinion. The dress she wore was clearly meant to showcase the body that had been sought after by top designers to exhibit their clothes; her make-up discreetly highlighted the cobalt eyes, the lushly curved mouth, the blessedly clear, fine skin that had adorned the covers of the world's glossiest fashion magazines.

'You're very beautiful,' he said. His tone implied she must expect men to enjoy staring at her.

Yet she wanted to force this man to see the person behind the shiny surface, the person she would still be when she cleansed off the make-up and removed the dress to get into the old cotton nightshirt that she liked to wear in bed. The person she would always be, even when inevitably she lost the glow of youth and her face was lined, her body no longer slim and supple, her breasts less high and firm.

The words wouldn't come, and even if she'd said them, they were too silly. Of course he'd been lured by her looks. He had only just met her and they'd barely exchanged two words. And for that matter, surely it was *his* looks that had drawn that unprecedented response from her.

Instant attraction. Many people might mistake it for love at first sight. Only Skye didn't believe in that. And something about this tough, enigmatic man assured her he didn't either.

He drew her to him again, and this time he held her closer, their bodies in contact from breast to thigh. 'I'm sorry if I offended you.'

Of course he was sorry. It wasn't a wise move to offend a woman you hoped to get into bed, Skye thought cynically, and offered him a meaningless smile. 'It's all right.' She removed her gaze from his to stare over his shoulder.

'Please don't do that.'

'What?' Startled, she looked at him again.

'I'd rather you were angry than indifferent,' he said.

'I'm not angry.'

'Nor indifferent?' he queried softly.

Skye didn't answer. This was too precipitate for her, his bluntness disconcerting. She schooled her face to the distant, composed mask that some photographers liked her to wear.

'Are you with someone?' Jarrah asked her.

'You know I am. You met him just now – '

'Permanently?' he pressed her. 'Or just for the evening?'

'We're good friends.'

He searched her face, then seemed to take that at face value, giving a small nod. 'I'm with someone else tonight too.' He paused. 'Where can I contact you?'

Skye felt her pulse rate accelerate. The power of whatever was drawing them to each other was almost frightening, her emotions a confusing mixture of excitement and apprehension.

She gave him the name of her Sydney agent. If she came to her senses in the morning she needn't do anything. He would receive the standard agency statement that their models' addresses and telephone numbers were not available to enquirers. And if she decided she wanted hers to be available after all, she'd ask the receptionist to pass on any message from him.

The music changed to a slow, dreamy number. Jarrah eased her still closer, and she felt the faint rasp of his cheek against her temple, like the finest sandpaper. He smelled of soap rather than cologne, with an underlying musky maleness.

When he spoke his breath stirred the wisps of hair that had been allowed to escape from the elaborate knot fastened on top of her head. 'Do you do other things as well as you dance?'

'Other things?' She lifted her head, her direct look challenging any double meaning.

His mouth curved, and she felt the silent laughter that shook his chest. 'Your job, for instance.'

'Some people seem to think so.'

'I've seen your picture, I think, on the covers of the magazines my mother and sisters read. I suppose they'd know your name.'

'If they're interested in fashion.'

'They're women,' he said simply.

She eyed him thoughtfully. 'What about you, Mr Kaine? What do you do for a living?'

'I run a family property in Queensland. Cattle, primarily – and a few thousand sheep.'

'A grazier?' Born in the neighbouring islands of New Zealand, Skye didn't know a lot about Australia's pastoral industry, but her impression was that the owners of vast outback properties were the landed gentry of the island continent.

Maybe that background explained his ease in the sophisticated surroundings of an expensive society occasion, so at odds with his indefinable air of belonging to the outdoors, to wide open spaces. 'What brings you to Sydney?'

'Business.'

It was on the tip of her tongue to ask what kind of business a cattleman from the outback had in the city, but she refrained.

As though he'd read her mind, he said, 'It isn't enough to rely on livestock alone nowadays. A few years of drought can wipe out the entire profits of the good years. We've had to diversify and find other ventures that will see us through the lean times.'

'Like cash crops?'

He looked at her with a hint of surprise. 'That's one way. While I'm here in Sydney I'll be attending a seminar on new crop varieties for tropical conditions. But plants are at the mercy of weather patterns too.'

'So what else is there?'

'We have shares in a couple of mining companies, and we own rural land in New South Wales that's leased out. I'm looking into the property market in Sydney while I'm here. They say commercial property is a sound investment if you choose wisely.'

'We . . .'

'The family.'

'Do your sisters work on the property?'

'Beth is married, and working as a fabric designer in Brisbane. Kelly's a jillaroo on the station.'

'The female equivalent of a jackeroo? A stockman – stockperson?'

He grinned. 'More or less. Jackeroos used to be trainee managers, but now the term's pretty much applied to anyone who works cattle.'

'Do you have any brothers?'

'Two. Erik's our resident mechanic and drives our heavy machinery. And young Dale is studying veterinary science at the University of Queensland.'

'And your father?'

Jarrah shook his head. 'My father died nearly ten years ago.'

'I'm sorry . . . Does that make you the head of the family?'

A smile lurked momentarily about his mouth. 'My mother is that. But I manage the station.' He did a swift turn out of the path of a large man pushing his partner around the floor, and she felt the slight increased pressure of his fingers against her spine. 'What about you?' he asked. 'Are you a Sydneysider?'

'Sydney is my base now. I lived in New York until I established my reputation on the international scene. That gave me an edge with the Australian industry when I decided to move back down under.'

'You prefer to live here, then?'

'I'd rather be here than London or New York. It feels more like home somehow.'

'You're Australian, then? Your accent is . . . hard to place.'

Skye smiled. She'd lived in so many places, worked in so many, meeting people from all over the globe, she supposed she didn't have a true native accent. 'I'm a New Zealander by birth, but the fashion industry over there isn't big enough to keep me in full-time work. My parents are in Auckland – my father's retired from the diplomatic service – and I like being close enough to visit.'

'You get enough work here in Australia?'

'There's plenty of editorial and catalogue work in Sydney and Melbourne – '

'*Vogue* and that sort of thing?'

'Yes. Editorial doesn't pay much, but it gets your face out there, and gives you prestige that can lead to catalogue and advertising jobs.'

'What about haute couture? Or do you specialize in photographic work?'

'I do catwalk stuff sometimes. Most models do all kinds of jobs now, you need to be versatile and able to do anything, but I actually prefer the photographic side of it. I don't do the European shows any more, or work much in New York.' The seasonal schedule was hectic, and increasingly models were expected to be outrageously underweight and often to parade semi-nude. The quest for a fresh new 'look' had brought in girls Skye thought privately were almost freakish, many of them very young, and she'd been uneasy at the pressure being put on some teenagers. Having made her name on the runways, she could command good money for often less demanding photographic work.

'So most of the time you're here?'

'I spend a few weeks in LA and San Francisco during the ready-to-wear season. And I've worked in Japan and New Caledonia, as well as New Zealand.'

'What are you doing tomorrow?'

'Tomorrow I walk for Carlton.'

'A live fashion show?'

Skye nodded. 'That's right.'

'Is it open to the public?' he asked her.

'Most of the seats will be reserved for store buyers and the press. There may be some standing tickets available.'

The music came to an end with a flourish, and he led her from the floor and back to her escort's side.

She hadn't asked if any of his family had

accompanied him on this trip to Sydney, but the honey-tanned blonde who hooked her hand into his arm as he joined a group on the other side of the room was smiling at him in a way that was far from sisterly.

He smiled back, bending his sleek sable-dark head to answer something she said, and although Skye would have sworn he was aware of her own gaze, he never once looked in her direction.

CHAPTER 3

The climax of Carlton's show was an evening dress, and Skye had been chosen to wear it. The gown was fashioned of heavy ruby-red lace with a wide neckline that dipped between her breasts and left her shoulders bare. Over a flesh-coloured lining, the lace hugged her body to the hips, and from there layers of silver-dusted fishnet ruby tulle flared dramatically and trailed in a demi-train behind. It was a classic design with modern flair. The dresser draped a matching drift of tulle over her coiffed hair and arranged it about her shoulders.

She swept out into the spotlight that stayed on her all the way down the raised runway. The photographers lining it on either side, and the spectators on their gilt and velvet chairs, were an anonymous, darkened blur.

Reaching the end, she lifted the swathe of gleaming tulle from her hair, allowing it to slide down and reveal her bare shoulders, the gauzy fabric looping over her hips. And, gazing over the rows of spectators, she saw Jarrah Kaine.

One shoulder was propped against the frame of the double doors facing her, his hand in the trouser pocket of a charcoal business suit worn with a white shirt and dark tie. The casual, almost bored stance didn't disguise the intense fascination with which he was studying her.

Skye was too well disciplined to allow the serene smile on her face to slip, but when her eyes met his metallic stare she missed a beat of the music, holding her pose a fraction longer than she should have.

She moved into her half turns, making up the time before she started back down the runway, paused on cue for another turn, and finished the routine flawlessly.

The next day Jarrah sent her flowers at the agency – half a dozen exquisite deepest red roses. And a note with only his name and the telephone number of his hotel.

Skye waited until the end of the day and phoned him from the tiny flat she called home. 'Thank you for the roses,' she said simply. 'They're very beautiful, and they have a wonderful scent.'

'They reminded me of you.'

Absurdly pleased that he'd chosen them personally, not just given the florist the order, Skye found herself twisting the phone cord about her finger.

'I know this is short notice,' he said, 'but I hoped you might be able to have dinner with me tonight, if you're free?'

'As it happens I am. But I don't want to be out late,' she warned him. 'I have another show tomorrow.'

'My hotel has a restaurant, no fancy cuisine but they do a good dinner. I could book a table for seven-thirty,' he said, 'unless you'd prefer somewhere else.'

'No,' she assured him. 'That sounds fine.'

He offered to pick her up, but didn't insist when she said she'd rather meet him at the hotel.

He was waiting for her in the lobby, striding towards her the moment she entered, the quick light in his eyes so openly sexual that she stopped short, her breath caught in her throat and heat stinging her cheeks.

She was wearing a simple ruched chiffon black sheath and had draped a patterned silk scarf casually about her shoulders. Jarrah stopped two feet away and smiled at her, and the fierce desire in his eyes faded, perhaps deliberately doused. He raised a hand and touched a soft tendril of hair that lay against her cheek, his finger barely grazing her skin before it fell back to his side. Yet she had to clench her teeth to suppress a shudder of sheer pleasure.

She'd met film stars and billionaires and politicians and minor royalty; some of them had even pursued her. None of them had made her feel as Jarrah Kaine did on the barest acquaintance.

Jarrah guided her with the lightest of touches on her arm to their table. Accustomed to garnering attention, Skye was scarcely aware of the stares that followed her progress across the room alongside the tall, striking man who drew stares of his own.

The table was a corner one, with an illusion at least of some kind of privacy, and she chose to sit with her back to the rest of the room.

'What would you like to drink?' Jarrah asked her as he signalled the wine waiter.

She requested bitter lemon with ice, and thought she saw a flash of surprise in his eyes, but he didn't comment before ordering a glass of beer for himself. 'We'll order wine after we've decided on what we're eating,' he told the waiter.

Seated as she was, Skye had nowhere to look but at the man across the table. Not that there was anything to complain about – he was good to look at, and he made no secret of the fact that the feeling was reciprocated. 'I'm flattered,' he said, 'that you agreed to this at such short notice. Did you stand someone up for me?'

Her slightly raised brows chided him for the assumption. 'I don't stand people up without good reason.'

'So how come you were free tonight?'

'Models don't live it up as much as people imagine. If I partied every night I'd have bags under my eyes and no energy to give to my job.'

'How much energy do you need?'

Her chin lifted defensively. 'The pace can be killing, with shows back to back in the season, and bookings in different countries often entail travelling through time zones. At the end of an overnight flight I might have to hit the catwalk within hours, or go to a photo shoot that involves anything from looking as though I'm having fun splashing around in swimwear in the middle of winter to spending hours twirling and jumping and running in forty-degree heat so the photographer can get movement into the clothes for a fashion layout.'

'Sounds like hell,' Jarrah commented, 'but I take it the money's good.'

'It can be very good. And of course it isn't all hell – but it is work.'

'Point taken.' He glanced up as their drinks arrived, and nodded at the waiter before opening the dinner menu. 'But you said you're not doing the European circuit now?'

'No,' she said. 'Only I have to take some overseas work to keep my name in the top magazines. If I don't do that I'll be seen as someone who can't make it any more, and the assignments – and money – will dry up.'

When she had ordered a Caesar salad, he asked her, 'Do you diet?' His gaze, with a slight hint of criticism, ran over her slight figure.

'I stay away from pastries and greasy food, but I don't go hungry. Starving is unhealthy, and doesn't do your skin any good. I exercise or jog every day, and three times a week I go to a gym for a proper work-out.'

'That must take some discipline.' He leaned back in his chair, one strong brown hand curled around the cold beer glass frosted with condensation.

'The job takes a lot of discipline,' she agreed. Too many people equated the illusory glamour of the result with the process and, by association, with the people taking part.

'But you enjoy it?'

'You get to see a lot of interesting places, meet talented people, and wear fabulous clothes.'

'What time is the show tomorrow?'

'It's an afternoon one.'

He raised his brows in surprise. 'You need an early night for that?'

'I'll have to be there at least five or six hours before the show to have fittings and get my make-up done and hair styled, and rehearse my entrances and exits with the show director.'

'You don't rehearse before the day?'

'Often there isn't time, and most directors want a spontaneous effect, so they don't like to over-rehearse.'

He asked more questions, seeming content to listen to her describe her life. Once or twice he laughed, when she mentioned catwalk disasters that in retrospect were funny, or mimicked some of the more flamboyant characters who inhabited the fashion world. He acted so fascinated that she went on talking, stimulated by his blatant interest in her, in everything she said.

She became conscious that her gestures were more extravagant than usual, her smile wider. The salad was only half finished and her glass of white wine barely touched, while Jarrah had emptied his plate of the pork cutlets in orange sauce and pushed it aside.

'I'm talking too much,' she said with abrupt dismay.

He smiled. 'Not at all. But I've asked too many questions and not allowed you to finish your dinner.'

Skye forked up a piece of lettuce. 'Tell me about your cattle station,' she said. 'I've heard that some properties in the outback are the size of a small country. Is it true, or is that an exaggeration?'

'Most of those really large properties are owned by companies now, or they've been broken up,' he told her. 'Opal Reach is one of the few big family-owned properties left. We have close to a couple of thousand square miles in Queensland, bordering the Gulf Country.'

'That's pretty big, all right. You have opals there?'

Jarrah smiled, shaking his head. 'We've never seen any. My grandfather named the place for a water-hole near the homestead. In certain lights the sun reflects colours off the water.'

'Sounds pretty.'

'It's rather beautiful,' he agreed. 'More important though, it's never been known to dry up, even in drought years. We're fortunate in having a well-watered property with several creeks, though we've put down bores as well.'

'And you've lived there all your life?'

'I went to school and university here in Sydney.'

'Isn't that a long way from Queensland?'

'Yes. It's a family tradition, but something of a culture shock for a kid from the outback.'

Skye eyed him curiously. Perhaps he hadn't always carried his present air of assurance. 'How did you feel about going back after that?'

'About going home? I could hardly wait.'

'You didn't like Sydney?'

Jarrah shrugged. 'I belong at Opal Reach.'

Skye felt a surprising pang of envy. She thought of herself as a New Zealander, and had an affection for her country, but she had never had that sense of permanence, of knowing exactly where home was, a true sense of belonging. 'You must love it,' she said.

A smile curled his mouth. 'I suppose I do. You might call it a love-hate relationship. The land is like a wayward mistress – challenging, exciting, and maddening. It's a constant battle, but we can't live without each other.'

'Do you have a mistress?' Skye asked him. She met his eyes, wanting to know the answer. 'Or a wife?'

The smile faded. 'If I had a wife I wouldn't be here with you.' He paused. 'I don't have a mistress either. Do you have a lover?'

It was a fair question, Skye thought. And she'd given him the right to ask it. 'No.'

'Good.' His expression didn't alter, but she felt her pulses accelerate. She seemed unable to drag her gaze away from the grey-green eyes. 'Finish your salad,' he said prosaically. 'Are you sure you eat enough?'

Skye turned her attention to her plate and

speared a crouton with her fork. 'I'm very healthy,' she said. 'You needn't worry about me.' But she felt a ridiculous glow of warmth at his concern.

She had fresh fruit salad without cream, but when Jarrah offered her carte blanche of his cheeseboard she nibbled on a piece of fetta, confessing to loving the pale, salty stuff.

Jarrah shook his head. 'Never acquired the taste myself. Give me a good hearty matured cheddar every time. Something with a bit of bite.'

'You haven't told me much about Opal Reach,' she reminded him.

He cut himself a small wedge of Stilton. 'What do you want to know? We run mainly Brahmans.'

'Indian cattle?'

He nodded. 'Brahmans stand dry conditions better than the British Herefords and Shorthorns. They're fertile breeders too, but on the minus side, a bit hard to handle. We crossbreed for a more manageable herd. And for other traits.'

'Like what?'

'Heavier animals, with plenty of lean meat on them.'

Skye nodded, and returned to her cheese. 'It must be hard work.'

'Uh-huh. And dirty.'

He was looking at her hands as she spread a bit of fetta over a cracker. Her skin was white and smooth, the nails perfectly oval and sheened with pale pink polish. She wondered if he was contrasting his notion of work with hers.

After coffee Jarrah signed for the meal and asked her, 'Would you like a nightcap in the lounge?'

She had a liqueur, and then said she had to go. Jarrah didn't try to detain her, but walked her out to the lobby and asked, 'Do you have a car here?'

'No. I used to have one but I gave it up. In the city it's hard to get parking near where you want to go, and I'm away a lot, so paying for garaging didn't seem worth it.'

Jarrah nodded, and asked the doorman to get her a taxi.

'I know you're working tomorrow,' he said. 'Is it too much to hope we could have dinner again, if I promise not to keep you up late?'

'I'm expected to attend the after-show function. It'll go on into the evening, and there'll be food served.'

'Perhaps a drink or coffee afterwards?' he pressed. 'Or will you be too tired?'

'I'd like that.' She'd be tired, but she would also need to unwind, and a quiet drink with a sexy, interesting man able to talk about something other than haute couture, fashion photography and who was sleeping with whom sounded like just the thing to help her do that.

'I've found a nice little bistro bar overlooking the harbour. Can I pick you up from the function?' he suggested.

'I'd want to go home, have a shower and change.' After the briefest hesitation she said, 'You could pick me up there if you like – at eight-thirty?' She gave him the address as the cab drew up beside them, and he bent to press his lips briefly against hers before opening the door.

When he arrived next evening she had changed into easy-fitting ice-blue silk trousers and a cool matching shirt, used a comb to sweep her hair back from her face but left it loose down her back, and slipped into a pair of comfortable sandals before using a light make-up with a touch of lip gloss and eye shadow.

Jarrah was dressed casually too, in an open-necked shirt and jeans. When she opened the door to him the familiar desire appeared in his eyes, quickly masked as he smiled at her. 'You're ready?'

She had a slim purse in her hand. 'Ready,' she confirmed.

'I paid the cab driver off. Should I have told him to wait?'

'Can't we walk?' Her flat was an inner city one

in an old building, conveniently near the shops and harbour.

He cast a glance at her feet in their pretty but comfortable sandals. 'We could.'

'I can do with some fresh air.'

'Fresh?' Jarrah queried as they reached the street and its growling traffic.

'Comparatively speaking,' Skye conceded. 'I don't suppose it compares with your wide open spaces.'

Despite the probably polluted air, by the time they reached the bar she had shaken off some of her tiredness and a faint flush warmed her cheeks.

Jarrah found them a window table overlooking the water, still tinged with pink in the aftermath of the sunset but rapidly darkening in the gathering dusk. 'Bitter lemon?' he asked her. 'Or something stronger? And anything to eat?'

'I won't have alcohol,' she said. 'But you can get me a plate of corn chips with light sour cream if you like.' If he wanted something to eat she ought to go through the motions of joining him.

As they sipped their drinks he looked at her speculatively. 'How was the show?'

'Okay, I guess. Tomorrow is the last one.'

'And after that?'

'I have an assignment in Melbourne and then a three-day shoot for a TV commercial.'

'I'll watch for it. When will it be shown?'

'Probably within the next couple of months. You have television up there?'

'We do now. Every modern convenience. Even fax machines.'

'I had the impression it was all radiotelephones and diesel generators.'

'They still exist.' He paused. 'Maybe you can come and see for yourself some day.'

Some day. It wasn't an invitation, was it? Just a throwaway remark. 'Maybe,' she agreed lightly. 'If I ever get the time.'

'How far ahead are you booked up?' Jarrah enquired.

'Two or three months.'

'And how long will you be in Melbourne?'

'A couple of days. It's an editorial shoot for the launch issue of a new fashion magazine. They're all very nervous about how it will sell.'

'You'll be on the cover?'

'That's the idea.'

'Then they have nothing to worry about.'

Skye flashed him a smile. 'I hope you're right.'

She nibbled on the corn chips while he demolished a substantial sandwich. Leaning back in her chair, she surveyed the harbour, watching a ferry hurry past a cruise ship anchored by the wharf.

When Jarrah made some remark about the

view, she smiled at him dreamily and he smiled back, the glitter in his eyes softening. 'You're out on your feet, aren't you?' he said. 'I had no right to drag you here like this.'

'I wanted to come. But I should go home and get some sleep now.'

'This time we take a cab,' he promised.

At her door he said, 'Can I see you again tomorrow evening?'

She hardly hesitated. 'Yes, all right.'

'Where would you like to go?'

'Surprise me?'

'All right. On your head be it.'

'I promise not to complain.' She fished in her purse for her key and pulled it out. But as she turned to insert it in the door warm, hard fingers folded about hers, and she felt Jarrah move closer, his breath brushing her temple.

'Last time,' he said, 'I wondered if I'd made a mistake.'

'Mistake?' Skye tilted her head to meet his eyes.

'Putting you in a cab and sending you home alone. Had I missed a cue?'

'You didn't miss anything.' Did he believe that because she was a model she would willingly fall into bed with anyone who bought her dinner? Lots of men did, only she'd hoped he was different.

'That's okay then,' he said calmly, and with a tug on her captured hand, turned her to face him, his arm sliding about her waist.

She lifted her face to his kiss, her lips slightly parted. This time it was more than a light farewell. It was a fully fledged, very satisfying kiss, and when he let her go she felt breathless and bright-eyed.

He removed the key from her fingers and unlocked the door, pushing it open. 'Have a good sleep.'

He took her on the ferry to Manly, the beachside resort half an hour across the harbour. The sea breeze blew tendrils of hair from the coil she'd pinned on top of her head, and flirted with the short flared skirt of her pink cotton dress.

On shore Jarrah took her hand and they strolled along the Corso on the narrow strip of land between harbour and ocean, debating whether to eat Thai, Italian, French or Indian.

They opted for French cuisine and a beach-front table. After a leisurely meal they went for a walk on the foreshore and kissed in the shadow of a tall, spreading Norfolk pine before returning to board the ferry.

He kissed her again at her door, his arms gathering her tightly against him, and her mouth softened and parted for him as he explored deeper, until a long shudder passed through her body and she clutched at his shoulders, giving a little moan.

Jarrah lifted his mouth, breathing harshly. 'Did I hurt you?'

Dizzily, Skye shook her head. She was terribly conscious of the size and strength of him, of the power of the arms that held her. He made her feel small and fragile – no common experience for a woman of her height. Despite the singing in her blood, she wasn't sure she liked it.

When she stirred in his hold he loosened his arms. 'What is it?'

She knew that if she stepped away he would let her go altogether. The thought was both a comfort and a disappointment. 'I'm not ready to . . .'

His hands locked at her waist. 'To make love to me?' His lowered voice, with a raspy edge to it, sent shivers of sheer delight down her spine. 'I'm not going to force it, Skye.'

She nodded. 'I know.' Instinct told her she could trust him. 'I had a lovely time tonight.'

His hands shifted to cup her face between them. 'Thank you.' He kissed her again, soft, sweet and all too brief this time. 'Tomorrow?'

'I'm going down to Melbourne.'

'Ah, yes. The magazine cover.' He eyed her thoughtfully. 'When you get back, then?'

'Will you still be in Sydney?'

'I expect to be.' He smiled. 'I'll make a point of it.'

'Neglecting your stock?' she teased.

'This is the wet season, when it's too hot for animals to be moved about and too wet for outdoor work.'

'So do you usually spend that time in the city?'

'Rarely, when business demands it. Though, actually this time I'm killing two birds with one stone. I came down with my mother – she's visiting her sister in Adelaide. My aunt's recently had an operation for cancer.'

'Is it bad?'

'The surgeon is optimistic.'

'Oh, that's good.'

'She'll have a six-week course of therapy to follow up, then they'll assess the results, and my mother wants to be with her at least until then. We flew down together from Queensland, and once the operation was over I left her there while I took the chance to attend to business.' He paused. 'I have a cattle breeders' and exporters' conference on the twentieth and twenty-first of this month. There's a dinner the final evening. Would you like to come to that with me?'

As his partner she would go anywhere. But she said, 'I'll have to check my diary. Come inside and I'll find it.'

She seldom invited men inside the apartment. It was her own private space that she preferred to keep severely separated from her professional life. Most of her dates, she was well aware, looked on her as a trophy, an accessory to their public image, like their Armani suits and Porsche cars. And it wasn't all one way. Her first agent had explained to her that being seen with the right men, getting her name in the right gossip columns and society pages, was part of building her career.

'Not that you want to earn yourself a reputation for being anyone's girl,' she was warned. 'Don't get involved in a scandal. Keep away from married men, drugs, and people in trouble with the law. And go easy on the drink. Any of those could send your career down the tubes.'

It was advice she'd had little trouble heeding. A few of the publicity-hungry actors, businessmen and politicians she'd been out with had been surprised or disgruntled when she made it clear that her body was not part of the implicit quid pro quo, but most had accepted with good grace that the pleasure of her company did not extend to the bedroom.

She unlocked the door and Jarrah followed her inside when she switched on the light.

It wasn't a big place, but she liked the cosy feel of the modest living room and one bedroom, the galley kitchen and an unexpectedly roomy bathroom with a separate shower.

Although the old building had been refurbished, the original windows with their fan-shaped tops and the pressed-steel ceilings had been retained, and from her living room she could walk onto a narrow balcony guarded by lacy wrought-iron railings.

Skye had pictured the balcony decorated with flowering pot-plants, but she was away so much those she had bought died, and now it held only a tiny wrought-iron table and one matching chair where she often ate in the summer.

'Sit down,' she invited Jarrah, and crossed to a functional desk under a window looking out on the quiet side street.

He took a seat on the wide, linen-cushioned sofa where she liked to stretch out and watch TV, and when she turned from the desk with a thick black diary in her hand he was surveying the room.

The old floorboards had been stripped and polished, and she'd added a Turkish rug patterned in gold and black. Tasselled floor cushions were heaped together in a corner. Brass-trimmed teak side tables stood at either end of the sofa, and an eclectic mixture of posters, prints and photographs crowded the walls.

Skye leafed through the diary. There was an

industry party pencilled in for the twenty-first, but it wasn't an RSVP affair and no one would miss her. 'I can make it on that date,' Skye said, drawing Jarrah's attention from his contemplation of a poster depicting a proud African woman wearing an array of brass and beadwork. 'How formal is this dinner? What should I wear?'

'Something glamorous. It's a fairly dressy affair. When you get back from Melbourne, are you free for the weekend?'

'Yes, I am,' she said, glancing at the diary.

'Not any more.' The lift of his brows made it a question. 'Okay?'

She nodded and closed the diary.

'Aren't you going to write it in?'

Skye shook her head. She wasn't likely to forget. 'Would you like a coffee?' she asked him.

'I would, thanks. Black, two sugars.'

When she had made it and carried it from the kitchen into the other room, he was standing by the French doors to the balcony, in his hand a paperback taken from her bookcase. 'I hope you don't mind,' he said.

'No.'

'Japanese?' he queried, inspecting the cover with interest.

'We spent three years in Japan when my father was in the diplomatic service, and I've modelled there.'

'Yes, I remember you mentioned that. What's this about?'

'It's a love story.'

'You've read it, then.'

'I don't buy books I can't read.'

Jarrah came over and she handed him one of the coffee mugs, then he waited for her to sit down before he took a place beside her, dropped the book between them, and stretched out his legs. 'Then you read French too?' He indicated the bookcase.

'Languages have been useful for my career.'

'I'm impressed. You have a pretty varied collection there.'

Her modest bookcase held a mix of art, biography and travel books, alongside a few hardback classics, some recent best-sellers and paperback fiction.

She sipped at her coffee. 'Do you read?' He seemed such an outdoors person, she could scarcely imagine him sitting with a book for any length of time.

'At Opal Reach we have a fairly good library. I haven't worked my way through it entirely yet. And of course we keep adding to it.'

'A private library?'

'My grandparents had a lot of books, and we still have most of them, plus those my parents collected, and the rest of us buy quite a lot.

There's no public library handy. We were pretty isolated before satellites brought modern telecommunications to the outback. In the Wet there wasn't a lot to do in the evenings.'

Jarrah drank some coffee, his eyes lazily regarding her. Skye wondered if she'd made a mistake inviting him in. Somehow he had already stamped his presence on the room so strongly that she was afraid she would never be able to erase it – if she wanted to.

'Having second thoughts?' he asked her softly.

Skye looked at him directly. 'About what?'

'Inviting me here. Offering me . . . coffee.'

His questioning tone asked if she might have decided to offer more.

'I'm not having second thoughts about anything.'

Jarrah laughed gently, then shrugged. 'A man can hope.' He finished his coffee and turned aside to put the cup on one of the teak tables, then stood up. 'I wouldn't want to outstay my welcome.'

He looked very big, looming over her, his eyes holding both laughter and something much more disturbing. 'Don't get up,' he said. 'I can see myself out.' He bent to brush his lips across her cheek, the merest touch.

After he'd closed the door behind him she could still feel the fleeting kiss on her skin.

CHAPTER 4

Waiting for the art director to set up the cover shoot in Melbourne, Skye finished the paperback novel she had packed into her bag along with her make-up and a change of underwear, and was idly scanning the business section of a newspaper when the words *Jarrah Kaine* caught her eye, under a blurry photograph of a bunch of men seated around a long table.

Apparently he was a member of a producer board concerned with beef exports. She read the brief article accompanying the photograph, absorbing all the information she could about the board and its activities.

When she saw Jarrah on Friday night, she mentioned the article and questioned him over dinner at a downtown restaurant about his work with the producer board.

He seemed mildly amused at her interest, but answered her questions readily enough.

In the taxi on the way back to her flat he captured her hand in his and ran his thumb across her knuckles. 'You have amazing skin,' he murmured. 'So satiny.'

A faint thrill of excitement shivered through her at his touch. The pad of his thumb was warm and slightly roughened. Unlike most of the men she had dated in the past, he was accustomed to using his hands in hard physical work.

He paid off the cab outside the door of her building and followed her up the stairs.

As she fumbled with the key Jarrah took it from her and unlocked the door.

Skye turned to him. 'Thank you for dinner, I enjoyed it.'

'Thank you for your company.' He smiled. 'Tomorrow?'

'Do you have something planned?'

'What about a picnic?'

'Sounds good. Shall I bring something?'

'No, don't bother.' He raised a leisurely hand and cupped her cheek with his big palm. 'Good-night, Skye.'

She met his kiss tentatively, and as if acknowledging her hesitation he kept it restrained, but satisfying. Afterwards he released her slowly and stepped back. 'I'll pick you up about ten. Sweet dreams.'

Skye smiled muzzily, sure they would be. She

didn't close her door until she heard his footsteps going down the stairs.

He called for her next day with a rental car, and drove her to the Hunter Valley where they visited vineyards and sampled wines – although Jarrah did so sparingly – wandered through vineyards, and picnicked at an outdoor table. Jarrah had provided smoked chicken, avocados and crusty French bread. He'd even brought along wine glasses. They finished the meal with cheeses and a shared bunch of grapes.

Skye pulled a grape from its stem and it rolled onto the table. Jarrah picked it up and held it to her mouth, smiling as he slid the cool sphere between her lips.

Silly to feel this fluttering sensation in her chest, the increased flow of blood in her veins. She looked away.

Jarrah gave a small laugh, and said curiously, 'You know, sometimes you seem almost shy.'

Skye lifted a shoulder. 'Maybe I am.'

'With *your* job?' he queried sceptically.

She'd made a career of flaunting her body, allowing it to be used as a clothes hanger, a selling tool, a focus of male fantasies. 'It's like acting. You project a certain mood or persona.'

'You mean what people see on the catwalk and the magazine covers isn't real?'

'Did you think it was?' she challenged him.

He looked thoughtful. 'I didn't imagine that's all there is.'

She wondered just how interested he was in the rest. On past experience, not many men cared about the person inside the glamorous outer shell.

'What are you thinking?' he enquired softly.

'Nothing.' She drained her glass, shaking her head when he lifted the bottle silently and offered her more wine. 'I've had enough.'

'Want to move on?'

'If you're ready.'

'Whenever you are,' he assured her, and started packing up the remains of the food.

She tried to shake off her slight, unreasonable depression, smiled a lot and made light small talk on the way back to Sydney. Acted, in fact, the way she knew the majority of her dates had wanted her to.

Jarrah offered only superficial, courteous responses, his face growing more and more expressionless. But as they left the Pacific Highway he said, 'Shall we stop for dinner in the city or do you want to go back to your flat first?'

'You don't need to take me to dinner.'

'Is that a polite way of saying you're sick of my company?'

Skye bit into her lip. 'I thought you might be sick of mine.'

Jarrah cast her a glance of humorous disbelief, his gaze slipping over her, his mouth curving. 'You're kidding.'

'I've been talking too much.'

He didn't contradict her. 'Why?'

Surprised at the direct question, Skye didn't answer.

'Do I make you nervous?'

Not him so much as her unprecedented reaction to him. She was afraid that this man could change her life. And she wasn't sure that she wanted it changed. 'Most men expect me to entertain them. I have a feeling you don't . . . appreciate a chattering woman.'

He turned his head to her as he stopped for a red light. 'Let's get one thing straight right now,' he said. 'I don't *expect* anything from you, Skye. I would *like* the pleasure of your company this weekend, if that's still all right with you.'

'But is that all you want?' She twisted in her seat to look at him.

'You know better than that.' A spark showed briefly in his eyes. 'But it'll do for now.' The lights changed and he looked away from her as the car glided forward. 'You're discriminating, and I like that.'

'What about you?' she asked. 'Are you . . . discriminating?'

'I'm not in the habit of bedding every woman

who crosses my path,' he said casually, 'if that's what bothers you?'

It would, she thought, if she'd imagined he was.

He grinned suddenly. 'For one thing, there aren't too many of them about where I come from.'

'Who was the blonde woman you were with at the ball?' she asked.

'No one who need concern you.'

He wasn't going to tell her, then. Skye stared out of the side window. Presumably it was over between them, whoever she had been, however close they might have become. She said, 'My partner that night –' He had been simply a casual escort, someone who wanted to be seen with her.

'I don't have any interest in your past lovers, Skye,' Jarrah said. 'Only in your future one.'

Skye hesitated, then closed her lips. Her future lover – singular. He had left her no doubt that he meant that lover to be himself.

They ate at a café bar overlooking the Opera House, lingering over pasta and wine, making it last. When the waiter offered coffee Skye said on impulse, 'We can have it at my place.'

Jarrah looked at her quickly, and nodded. 'Okay. If that's what you'd like.'

They went back to her flat and he sat on her

sofa while she made the coffee, and when they had emptied their cups he took hers and placed it with his on one of the side tables, and reached for her.

Her hand on his chest, she said, 'Jarrah?'

'I told you I'm not going to rush you into anything,' he said. 'But I do want to kiss you.'

She wanted him to kiss her too. She wanted to kiss him back, and did, with a passion that surprised herself and perhaps Jarrah. After a while he leaned into the corner of the sofa, taking her with him so that her body was half across his, and his hands in her hair held her while he teased her mouth to open to the erotic exploration of his tongue. Then he turned, so that she lay against the cushions and her legs were trapped between his. His hand intruded beneath the cotton shirt and found her breast under the flimsy satin of her bra.

Skye made a small sound, and his hand stilled where it was. He raised his head a little. 'What?' he whispered.

She fought a short, furious struggle within herself. Part of her wanted to say, *Go on, please don't stop, don't let me think.* A more rational, cautious corner of her brain was warning that she hardly knew this man, and that she'd promised herself never to lose her head this way. Or anything else . . .

'I . . . think we should stop.' She had to force the words out.

Jarrah momentarily closed his eyes, heaving a breath into his lungs. 'Damn.'

'I'm sorry.'

Jarrah's mouth twisted wryly. 'Your prerogative,' he said. His hand reluctantly left her breast, sliding on the skin over her ribs and shaping her hip before he withdrew it altogether and sat up, allowing her to do the same. 'It isn't because you weren't enjoying it?' he asked.

Skye shook her head. He wasn't stupid enough to believe that, and why should she lie?

'What would you like to do tomorrow?' Jarrah asked. His gaze strayed to her bookcase. 'There's an exhibition of new Australian work at the art gallery. Have you seen it?'

'I haven't had time, but I'd like to.'

'Good. Let's do that, then.'

Skye wondered if he was consulting her taste rather than his own.

She had been educated by her mother about art, taken to the great galleries of the world. But on Sunday she was surprised at the scope of Jarrah's knowledge and interest.

'I had a crush on the art teacher at my boarding school,' he told her. 'We have a few paintings at Opal Reach, but I never really appreciated them until then. I've added a few more to the collection myself, since. What do you think of that one? Ah – I see it's sold.'

'Would you have bought it?'

'Maybe. Would you?'

Skye inspected the work carefully. 'Don't think so.'

'Why not?'

She told him, and they had a thoroughly enjoyable time arguing the merits of that and the other various works, continuing the discussion over a lengthy lunch in a nearby café.

When he left her at the door of her flat he caught both her hands in his. 'Can we do this again?'

'Yes,' she said, smiling. 'Yes, please.'

He laughed softly, and bent to press a light kiss on her lips. His mouth lingered, and grew firmer, asking for her response – and getting it. Finally he drew her into his arms and made a thorough job of it.

When he slowly released her she knew her cheeks were flushed, and her eyes betrayed her emotion. He left with obvious reluctance, and she walked dreamily into the flat and found herself gazing unseeingly into a mirror, with a remembering smile on her face.

Over the next few weeks Jarrah's kisses became increasingly passionate, his touch more intimate.

When he'd left her she would dreamily prepare for bed alone but with the imprint of his lips on hers, the intoxicating male scent of him still in her nostrils. Sometimes he smiled at her with a mixture of amusement and confidence that told her he knew she was close to allowing him into her bed. It was only her innate caution and long habit that delayed the inevitable.

When he came for her the night of the cattle industry dinner she was waiting for him, dressed in a clinging silver-and-white knit dress that moulded her slender curves but covered her from neck to knee, leaving her shoulders bare, and although the high collar encircled her throat, the back was slit from nape to waist.

His mouth curved in approval as he studied her, and she felt almost despairing, looking back at him in his evening clothes. Other men might be more handsome, but none of those she knew approached his rare combination of genuine bred-to-the-land toughness and self-assured sophistication. She smiled at him with helpless fascination.

'You're ready,' he said.

'Yes.' Skye knew he could read her feelings in her face. And didn't care. She picked up her bag and a light wrap and walked by him, then waited while he closed the door. When she went ahead of him along the narrow passageway she heard the audible intake of his breath as he took in the back view of her dress.

Skye glanced over her shoulder. 'You don't approve?'

'It's sensational,' he said. 'I may have to beat off the competition with a cattle prod.'

'Do you have one with you?' Skye started down the stairs and he caught her up.

'I'll get one from somewhere if I have to.'

He wouldn't have to. As far as she was concerned, she could have told him, he didn't have any competition. And if he had, she was sure he wouldn't have needed technological help to defeat it.

The confidence with which he ushered her into the big reception hall, and the proprietorial hand that remained lightly at her waist as he introduced her to his colleagues would have been enough, she thought, to warn them off.

Some of the men who hopefully approached obviously knew her face, and a couple of them ogled her openly, casting looks of conspiratorial envy at the man by her side, until a certain grim note in Jarrah's voice made them blink and back away.

At dinner she astonished the middle-aged producer board member sitting next to her by greeting his avuncular efforts at conversation with a penetrating question about the

Asian beef market, and she saw Jarrah slant her a grin.

Going back to her flat afterwards, he said, 'Old Bernie seemed pretty surprised at how much you seemed to know about live beef exports to the Philippines.'

'I only know what I've read in that article I mentioned to you, and what you've told me. But I suppose Bernie expected a model to lack any brain at all.'

'Does that happen often?'

'Yes. A lot of people are convinced that brains and my profession are mutually exclusive.'

'I don't believe that, but I don't suppose a cattle conference is of consuming interest to someone in your field. Was the evening very boring for you?'

'Not at all.' Not with Jarrah at her side, his sleeve occasionally brushing against her bare arm, his eyes watching her with lazy, slightly amused approval as she fended compliments, turned her warmest smiles on women who regarded her with undisguised envy, and exchanged conversational ping-pong. 'I had a delicious dinner and there were some interesting people there. Thank you for taking me.'

'You're not a diplomat's daughter for nothing, are you?'

'It was a very pleasant evening.'

'Well, the conference is over now. Do you have any plans for tomorrow?'

'Not yet.'

'Any suggestions?'

She thought for a moment. 'Have you ever been to the weekend Paddy's markets? There are some very good ones.'

'Sounds like fun.'

'They are – if you like bargain hunting. You never know what you might find.'

'I'll look forward to it.'

When the cab stopped at her flat Jarrah got out and opened the door for Skye, taking her hand to help her to the pavement before paying the driver.

They didn't touch on the way up the dimly lit stairs, but she was very conscious of him at her side, and then walking behind her along the passageway to her door.

As she opened it with her key she felt the warm tip of his finger below the fastened collar of her dress, and stiffened as he drew it slowly down her spine, on the bare skin revealed by the slit back.

'I've been dying to do that all evening,' he murmured in her ear.

The key turned under her fingers and Skye opened the door. She stepped away from him into the room, lit by a glow from the streetlights outside, and he came after her and pushed the door decisively shut, leaned against it and reached for her, pulling her into his arms.

She went willingly, the tension melting from her body as it curved, pliant as a willow branch, into his.

His hand had slipped inside her dress and was splayed on the skin of her waist, holding her to him while his mouth parted hers and tasted her with frank sensual enjoyment.

After a long time he swung away from the door, turning her with him, and his hands shaped her shoulders, pushing the strap of her bag away so that it fell onto the oriental rug.

He lifted his head at the muted thud, and Skye whispered, 'It doesn't matter.'

Jarrah made a low sound and swept his hands down her arms to her wrists. He was still close, still touching her, body to body, making her heart beat faster with a mixture of nervousness and excitement.

He took one of her hands and pressed his mouth to the smooth skin, then he placed her palm against his heart, under his open jacket, the way he had when they had first met and danced together. 'Can you feel what you're doing to me?' he asked her, his voice deep and harsh.

'The same as you're doing to me.'

'Good.' He released her hands and then his

were gliding over her hips and behind her, while he looked into her face, his own naked and taut with desire and sexual challenge.

Both palms on his chest, she stared back at him, mesmerized by the blaze of his eyes, the naked hunger of his expression.

'If you're going to send me away tonight,' he said, 'you'd better do it now.'

But behind her his hands were moving persuasively on the inviting curves, cupping them, and she felt her own hands creep up over his shirt and lock about his neck, her head tipping back, her mouth parting. One big hand gripped her more firmly, and he moved against her slowly, teasing. The other hand travelled up her spine, exploring the warm skin of her back. 'I knew you weren't wearing a bra,' he muttered. 'It's been driving me crazy for hours.' His thumb discovered the softer flesh under her arm.

Her eyes half-closed, she allowed her head to fall back, and his mouth crashed down on hers, making her gasp, the sound lost as he kissed her deeply, centring all her attention on him.

Then he moved his hand and stroked her breast through the flimsy fabric of her dress, and she shuddered, and felt the answering tremor of Jarrah's body, clamped so closely to hers.

When he lifted his mouth she reached for him

and brought it back, blindly seeking him.

He didn't disappoint her. Again he plunged them both willingly into the maelstrom, his hands roving freely, discovering the rise of her ribs, the swell of her hips, slipping under her skirt to caress her thighs. He lifted his head a fraction and looked at her, his gaze glittery through half-closed lids.

She moved her hands down and found them impeded by his tie. One finger hooked into the black bow and loosened it, and impatiently she plucked at the knot, half undoing it, encountered the white silk of his shirt, and pulled at the other half of the tie and opened a button.

'*Yes*!' He hissed the word, and his eyes closed, his head thrown back. She felt the involuntary reaction of his body, and paused.

'Go on,' he said hoarsely. 'Touch me, Skye.'

She undid two more buttons and tentatively touched him with her fingers, a tactile exploration of warm, faintly moist skin.

'Oh, yes,' he murmured deep in his throat, like a big cat purring. His own hands went to her hips, and he shifted his feet so that she stood between his thighs. 'Yes.'

She adored what she was doing to him, the sheer pleasure that he didn't attempt to hide. It made what he was doing to her even more thrilling, the tiniest movements setting off sparks of reaction all along her skin.

She wore nothing beneath the flimsy dress but a scrap of lace and satin, and he'd just discovered that and was running his thumbs along the shape of the bone under the inch-wide satin-cased elastic on her hips.

Frustrated by the still-closed buttons on his shirt, Skye tugged open another one, and another, running her palms over his hard rib cage under the loosened fabric.

'Take if off,' he urged, and kissed her again, easing his hold on her to fumble with something behind her, unfastening his gold cufflinks, she guessed.

As she hesitated again, he hauled the shirt out of his pants and discarded both it and his jacket, throwing them onto the floor, then seized her hands and flattened them against his chest, moving them sensually over his skin. He smiled tightly and took her shoulders in his hands again and closed his mouth over hers.

Her arms circled his body, finding the groove of his spine, the flat planes of his shoulder-blades. Her head was pressed into the curve of his shoulder, her loosened hair flowing over his arm.

'Bedroom,' he muttered when at last they surfaced again for air.

Distantly her mind said, *Are you sure?* But her

body was clamouring, *Yes, yes*! And then Jarrah kissed her again and swung her up into his arms and even the rush of cooler air as he carried her through the flat in the darkness failed to penetrate the white heat of desire.

She dropped one shoe in the bedroom doorway, and when he put her down beside the bed she stumbled and stepped out of the other.

'Sorry,' he murmured, steadying her with his arms about her waist. He kissed her temple, then his lips grazed her cheek and briefly explored the tiny, pulsating hollow of her throat. She felt the surprising silky tickle of his hair against her chin as he lifted his head and said softly, 'Turn around.'

His hands compelled her gently to do so, before they settled on her breasts, teasing the aching peaks; then he was finding the hook that closed the high, deceptively modest collar of her dress, and peeling the dress from her body.

Skye held her breath as the garment pooled about her bare feet. For a moment she stood alone, but there was a small sound behind her, the rasp of a zip, the quiet putter of fabric falling to the floor, and then Jarrah was touching her again, his arm warm about her waist, his hand raising her chin, tipping her head back to meet his mouth, and as he moved his hand down, cupping the throbbing centre of her desperate longing for him, and bringing her back against the hardness of his wanting her, she realized he was naked.

She thought she would die from the pleasure his hands were giving her, and when he lowered her to the bed she felt almost faint with desire. He dealt swiftly with the last barrier and she stirred anxiously, but before she had time to speak he whispered, 'Wait a minute,' and within seconds he was kissing her again, lifting himself over her.

At the first thrust she stiffened a little, and when he took his mouth from hers she drew in a long, unsteady breath.

'Skye?' he said, his voice gravelly and tense. 'You want me, don't you?'

'I want you,' she whispered, her teeth clenched. 'Yes. Yes.'

'Skye,' he said, her name a sigh on his lips. He moved, thrust deeper, and made an odd sound, like a groan. 'You are beautiful . . . beautiful.'

She was suddenly alight with happiness. She felt beautiful to him, she knew it. As he did to her – powerful, almost frighteningly so, and possessive and strange. But beautiful. Yes.

She moved against him, tentatively, experimenting, and revelled in his response, in his filling her with love and warmth and delicious sensation. She wanted to stay like this forever, so close, so intimate, so at one with this man who both terrified and delighted her.

Yet at the same time she wanted something more immediate, that she sensed was very close if only she knew how to reach it. She clung to Jarrah, searched for his mouth again, found it, took the thrust of his tongue into her mouth and knew how close she was – they both were – and then the world was shattering into tiny, brilliant pieces of light and flame tumbling over each other, spinning in a void of pulsing, marvellous sensation, coalescing in a white nucleus of fire.

She came back to earth and reality minutes later, panting against Jarrah's shoulder.

He still held her tightly, and when he carefully rolled off her, she didn't want to let him go.

But he left her while he went into the bathroom, returning with some tissues from the box she kept on the counter, and a facecloth moistened with warm water, handing them to her before he switched on the bedside light.

He bent and pulled on his underpants, and then sat on the bed beside her. 'Was that what I think it was?' he enquired quietly.

She looked into his eyes and saw a mixture of shock and doubt. Shrugging, she turned away, balling up the used tissues in her hand.

'Skye?' He reached out his hand and brought her round to face him. 'I can't believe that you

. . . You haven't done this before?'

She tried to sound insouciant. 'Lots of people prefer celibacy to taking unnecessary risks for a bit of fun.'

'People in your industry?' He looked sceptical.

'I wouldn't know the proportion,' she said coolly. 'But we've probably all seen friends die.'

Jarrah frowned. 'Did I pressure you?'

'No!' She shook her head. 'If you're feeling guilty, there's no need. I made the decision to . . . sleep with you. I know you'd have stopped if I'd wanted you to.' She hadn't wanted him to. She'd wanted him to keep making love to her forever.

'You don't regret it?' he asked searchingly.

Maybe she would later. She'd cherished a romantic notion that she would give her virginity to a man when they had mutually committed their lives to each other. Dimly she recognized the faint ache about her heart for the relinquishing of that dream. Jarrah had made no commitment and she had no reason to believe that he intended to. She hadn't asked for or received any promises. A flutter of compunction stirred inside her, and she deliberately doused it.

Jarrah said slowly, 'You didn't think of warning me? You realize I might have hurt you.'

'It didn't hurt.' A slight discomfort, perhaps caused by her natural fear of the as yet unknown more than any physical barrier. 'I . . . enjoyed it.'

'I did notice that.' He raked a hand through his hair.

'What's the matter?' Skye asked him. 'You didn't?'

'Enjoy it?' He appeared almost embarrassed. 'Yes – more than I had any right to, I'm afraid. When I . . . realized . . . I found it quite extraordinarily erotic . . .' He gave her a twisted smile. 'A very primitive male reaction.'

Her own reactions were pretty primitive too. She felt a sort of pride in having given him an experience he admitted had been special, *erotic*. 'I'm glad. But I can't give you quite the same experience again, can I?'

Jarrah looked rueful, then laughed. 'No, but the memory will always be there, every time we make love.'

Every time we make love. Then he anticipated there would be more. Skye lay back against the pillow and smiled at him with deliberate provocation. 'And when is the next time likely to be?'

'Are you sore?'

'A bit,' she admitted, although she'd scarcely noticed until he mentioned it.

'Then not yet.' He lifted the cover and slid in beside her. 'But is it okay if I hold you for a while?'

'Oh, yes.' It was what she had been wanting for the last ten minutes, ever since he'd left her side. 'I'd like that very much.'

He opened his arms and she snuggled into them. He felt warm and smelt faintly musky. She nuzzled her cheek against his chest and realized she was sleepy, and stifled a yawn.

Jarrah reached out and switched off the light, then put both arms about her. And slowly, utterly content, she drifted into sleep.

He made love to her again at dawn, with an exquisite care and thoroughness that made her want to weep for sheer grateful joy. She had never imagined that lovemaking could be like this, at the same time tender and fierce. Everything he did for her, everything he encouraged her to do for him, was new and exciting. He brought her to the peak again, and then to that delicious, sweet lethargy such as she had never experienced before.

Afterwards she slept again, and this time when she woke it was to the sound of the shower running in the bathroom.

Minutes later Jarrah emerged, dressed in his trousers but no shirt. 'Sorry if I woke you. I'm not used to this city life.'

'You didn't wake me.' Holding a sheet over her bare breasts, Skye squinted at the electronic clock by the bed. Just after seven. 'What time do you usually get up?'

'About five in winter. A bit later in the Wet.' He came and sat on the bed, leaning over to press a lingering kiss on her lips. 'You look delicious. Are you hungry?'

'What do you have in mind?' Skye fluttered her eyelashes at him.

Jarrah laughed, his eyes devouring her. 'What I have in mind would keep you in bed all day. But I need a change of clothes. I thought we could go to my hotel, and breakfast there before going shopping.'

'Shopping?'

'Markets, remember?'

'Oh, yes.'

'Unless you'd *rather* stay in bed all day?' He gave an exaggerated leer.

Laughing at him, Skye resisted the temptation, getting out of bed and going through an abbreviated version of her usual exercise routine while Jarrah watched in delighted fascination, telling her he found it sexy.

'You're making me self-conscious,' she complained.

He grinned at her. 'You must be used to being looked at.'

He'd said the same thing the night they met. She made a face at him and threw a pillow from the bed, and they ended up in a juvenile mock-fight that he easily won, throwing her down on the bed and kissing her until, flushed and breathless, she said, 'All right – I give in!'

They spent the morning bargain hunting. Skye bought a tall, urn-shaped scent bottle with a silver stopper, insisting it was a steal, and a green glass bowl, and soon Jarrah was swinging a plastic carrier bag of 'pre-loved' books from his hand.

He found an unframed Japanese woodcut, charming in its elegant simplicity, depicting a pair of lovers, their fingers just touching as they gazed shyly at each other. Jarrah bought it, not even trying to beat down the price.

'A present,' he said, pressing it into Skye's hands, 'to remember me by.'

CHAPTER 5

A tremor of foreboding stilled Skye's smile. She looked down at the print, hoping he hadn't seen the dismay in her eyes, and steadied her voice. 'It's lovely, thank you. I'll have to get it framed.'

'There must be frames around here,' Jarrah suggested, and took her hand to stroll again among the stalls.

They examined dozens of picture frames, some holding prints or photographs, and Jarrah rejected them all. In the end they returned to the city and in a photographic shop at The Rocks found a wide frame of natural polished wood that he said would be perfect.

Back at the flat Skye stood with her hand on his shoulder as he sat at her small dining table and fitted the print into the frame.

'There,' he said, holding it up for her inspection. 'What do you think?'

'You were right,' she told him. 'It's perfect.

Not that I don't think that green plastic one with the pink nylon flowers and gilt edging that we saw at the market would have done as well – '

The stall-holder had mistaken their fascinated horror for genuine interest and tried very hard to sell it to them. 'We'd have had to remove the picture of puppies and kittens that was in it,' Jarrah said.

'Yes, that would have been a pity,' Skye agreed. 'I'm not sure if I could bear it.'

'Of course,' he offered, 'I could go back and buy it for you now that we've framed this one.' He put it down on the table and stood up. 'You could have them both.'

'Would you do that for me?' She gazed at him wide-eyed.

Jarrah laughed, pulling her close. 'Anything,' he promised. 'Right after . . .' his mouth grazed hers '. . . we do this . . .'

An hour later Skye raised her head from its resting place on his bare shoulder, adjusted the tumbled sheet over them, and touched a fingertip to his collarbone. She could feel the lithe length of his body all along hers, and she still tingled with pleasure. 'Is it always better every time?'

He caught her hand in his and brought her finger to his lips, laughing softly. 'Different,' he told her.

'I suppose you've . . .'

Certainly she wasn't his first lover. For a moment she was piercingly, illogically jealous of the unknown women who had lain in his arms before.

'It's never been quite like this before,' he assured her. His hand skeined her hair, and he brought her down to him. 'You are . . . very special.'

She gave herself up to his kiss, killing the thought that maybe he was lying, that he knew exactly what to say to a woman who was foolish enough to question a man's feelings when they had just made love.

Later they hung up the picture, moving one of her posters to give it the right position on the wall.

In the following week she took him to a couple of fashion industry functions, warning him that his appearance at her side would lead to gossip in those circles.

He laughed. 'I'll be the guy with the most beautiful woman in the room on my arm. Why should I care what they say? Will you?'

'No. I'll be the girl with the handsomest man, so why should I?'

He laughed and kissed her. Skye put her arms about his neck and kissed him back.

She liked having him at her side, and when he was there she was spared the propositions and crass compliments that she'd become inured to. She had learned early to fend off unwanted attention, but it was a novel pleasure to have it taken care of with so little fuss.

He caused some interest, especially among the women. Skye found herself bridling at the way some of them made an obvious play for his attention. But he met their sly smiles and covert glances with bland courtesy, before returning his attention to Skye. He made her feel she was the only woman in the room.

When photographers approached he had a way of silently standing aside as the flashlights caught her, and coming back to take her hand or lay a light hand on her arm seconds afterwards.

'Are you camera shy?' she asked him. Though it was refreshing to be with a man who wasn't dead keen to pose at her side.

'It's you they're after,' he said. 'No one's interested in me.'

They were, she could have told him, not only because he was escorting her and the gossips were intrigued by a man quite outside their experience and their usual narrow circle of celebrities and hangers-on, but because he was obviously a man in command of himself and those around him, someone to be reckoned with in his own right.

Skye had an invitation to a gala premiere of a new Australian film, and asked Jarrah to attend it with her.

He dressed at her flat, and lounged on the bed while she finished putting on make-up and pinned her hair into a knot, and finally slipped into a deep violet satin dress that had one fitting wrist-length sleeve and left the other arm bare, the armhole cut into a deep, daring V. It was a designer model that she'd bought at a special price after showing it on the catwalk. The luxurious material skimmed her body to her hips and flared into graceful folds about her legs.

Jarrah rose from the bed as she reached behind her for the zip. 'Let me do that.'

He slid the fastener up slowly and bent to press a kiss at her nape before stepping away, taking her bare arm to turn her. 'You look fabulous,' he told her. 'I suppose we do have to go this thing? I want to take you to bed right here and now.'

Skye smiled back at him. 'That would be a waste of all the trouble I've just gone to.'

He sat through the film with his hand firmly holding hers against the muscular warmth of his thigh. Afterwards as they joined the crowd leaving the auditorium she felt his eyes caressing her in anticipation.

The celebratory party after the film was noisy and glittery, and flashbulbs added to the harsh lighting. Skye was hailed in turn by several people who knew her, and introduced Jarrah to them. While they were talking to a group of people involved in the film he ran a finger surreptitiously down the skin of her bare inner arm and she had to make a real effort not to turn and fling herself into his arms. Totally losing the thread of conversation, she smiled mindlessly at the film producer who was talking about his latest project, and hoped that her noncommittal comments were appropriate.

As a photographer approached, Jarrah steered her away. 'Do you mind?' he asked her.

'It's all right.'

'I suppose this kind of publicity is helpful for your career?'

'I'm not worried,' she assured him. 'There'll be plenty of other chances.'

'Other parties like this one?' He looked about them.

'You don't enjoy them, do you?'

Returning his gaze to her, he said, 'I'm finding it . . . quite interesting. How about you? You attend this sort of bash quite often, don't you?'

'Fairly often. As you said, it's part of the business.'

A slight, pale, middle-aged man in a silver and white checked jacket with a red bow tie and cummerbund bounced up to them, and enfolded Skye in an enthusiastic embrace. 'Darling! Where have you *been* lately! I've missed you, sweet!'

One of Jarrah's eyebrows twitched as Skye extricated herself. 'Hello, Perry. I've been right here in Sydney – '

'Ah! And you have a new man, I see.' Perry's inquisitive blue eyes inspected Jarrah with frank interest. 'Is the hunk the reason you've been hiding out? Do introduce me!'

'Jarrah Kaine, this is Perry Dexter. He's a wonderful art director.'

'Well, thanks for the testimonial, dear heart.' Perry twinkled at her and held out his hand, wincing theatrically as Jarrah's closed about it. 'Where did you *find* him?' he asked. 'I'm jealous.'

Skye cast a look of slight trepidation at Jarrah, to see him quickly kill a smile as he released Perry's hand. 'You're in the fashion business?' he asked pleasantly.

'What else *is* there?' Perry queried rhetorically. 'And this girl is one of my very *favourite* models. Love her, love her!'

'Thanks for the advice,' Jarrah murmured.

Skye flushed and cast him a fiery look. Perry

giggled and lightly slapped Jarrah's arm. 'Naughty,' he reproved. 'You've made her blush! Goodness me, have you actually broached the Snow Queen's defences? Well, well! And not before time, may I say?' He twinkled fondly at Skye.

'Snow Queen?' Jarrah looked from him to Skye.

'They call her that, but I always knew that there was fire under the ice,' Perry said smugly. 'I mean, look at her *photos* – it's all there, smouldering underneath.'

'Oh, do shut up, Perry,' Skye interrupted. 'I know you enjoy being a walking cliché, but do you have to lay it on so thick?'

Perry laughed delightedly. 'She's one of the few who can see through me,' he confided to Jarrah. 'Look after her, my boy. Or you'll have me to answer to. I'm very fond of Skye.' He eyed Jarrah's solid frame as though possibly thinking better of the threat, then staunchly added, 'And I have my ways, you know.'

'I'm sure you do,' Jarrah returned quite gravely. 'But I promise you'll have no need to resort to them.'

Perry's guileless blue eyes widened, then he turned a flashing smile on Skye. 'I like him!'

'So do I,' Skye said, hooking her hand into Jarrah's arm. 'Excuse us, Perry. There's someone over there I want to talk to.'

As she steered him away, she muttered to Jarrah, 'Sorry about that. He's harmless, really.'

'And genuinely fond of you, I think,' Jarrah said, 'in his way.'

'I'm quite fond of him too. At least he doesn't paw at me and the other girls under the excuse of showing us our poses or adjusting the clothes.'

Jarrah's brows drew together. 'Some of them do that?'

She felt his arm tense. 'A few. We deal with it.'

'You shouldn't have to!'

'In an ideal world, of course not. It's all right, Jarrah – as I said, we deal with it.' She smiled. 'A well placed stiletto heel can do a surprising amount of damage.'

She introduced him to more people, but although he talked and listened politely, she felt his restless tension, that matched her own. Looking around the room she recalled that in the early stages of her career she had enjoyed mingling with people who had creative energy and were not afraid to display it, sometimes not only in their work but also in their dress and their often flamboyant personalities.

Not having inherited her mother's artistic talent, she admired it in others and found it stimulating to be around those who had been gifted with it. Those whose passionate commitment to art of one form or another had brought them success and riches, and even the others who were still striving for recognition in their chosen field had an incandescent, inner sense of purpose that created a confident serenity in some, and a sort of frenetic, edgy quality in others. She found them stimulating, often obsessive, frequently maddening and occasionally stunningly self-centred, but always interesting.

Tonight, though, the rising tide of chatter, the shrieks of recognition or laughter, the patently phoney affection of some talentless but determined fringe-dwellers, made her head spin and engendered a faint depression – an unaccustomed ennui with a party that was suddenly too like hundreds of others she'd attended during her modelling career. The place was hot and stuffy and gaudy, the people a moving sea of screeching, overdressed humanity.

'How long do you want to stay?' Jarrah asked her, taking an empty wine glass from her fingers and looking about for a waiter.

'We can go now if you like.' If Skye wasn't enjoying this particularly, she guessed that he was bored out of his skull.

'I don't mean to rush you.'

Then a female voice said, 'Jarrah! What are you doing here?'

His hand on Skye's waist, Jarrah turned his head. Skye saw a flicker of something that might have been annoyance cross his hard features.

'Lisa,' he said.

Skye recognized the young woman who'd been his partner at the charity ball.

'How are you?' he was asking politely.

'I'm just fine.' Lisa's smile was a little too wide, Skye thought, her pale blue eyes too bright. Her gaze slithered sideways to Skye for an instant. Then she turned and drew forward a man who was at her elbow. He had a bland, handsome face and light brown hair slicked back from his forehead. 'This is my fiancé, Roger Meddowes,' she said. 'Roger is a company lawyer with Meddowevale Wines, his family business. His father is Sir Arthur Meddowes. Roger, this is Jarrah Kaine – he's a farmer from Queensland – and . . . ?' Lisa queried Skye, giving her a look so consciously blank that Skye was instantly sure the other woman knew very well who she was.

Smoothly Jarrah introduced her. Skye held out her hand to Roger Meddowes, noticing how closely Lisa watched them.

Skye kept her smile restrained. 'Congratulations on your engagement.'

Jarrah was saying to the man's fiancée, 'I wish you every happiness, Lisa.'

Her eyes flashed. 'Thank you, Jarrah. And what about you and . . . ?' She looked archly at Skye.

'Not as yet.' Jarrah's voice was low and quite unperturbed. 'When is your wedding day?

Something in Lisa's eyes changed, softened perhaps, before they left Skye's face and returned to Jarrah. 'We haven't decided on a date, but soon. I'll send you an invitation,' she offered brightly.

'Thanks, I'll . . . look forward to it. Now, if you'll excuse us, we were just leaving. Nice seeing you again, Lisa. And I'm very glad about your news.' He bent and kissed her cheek, nodded to her fiancé, and took Skye's arm.

In the taxi on the way to her flat he reached for her hand, and she let her fingers lie inert in his. But as he bent towards her she turned her head away, staring blindly out of the window.

When he followed her into her sitting room and pulled her into his arms she knew her body was stiff and taut, like a stretched wire, although she tried to respond to his kiss.

He drew away, his hands holding her waist, but Skye pulled out of his hold. 'I want a shower.' She turned to walk towards the bathroom, pulling pins from her hair. 'It was hot and stuffy there.'

She stood under the warm water and tried to

banish her feelings of anger and unease. She'd always known that she wasn't the first woman in Jarrah's life – the night they'd met, Lisa had been hanging on his arm. 'She needn't concern you,' he'd told her. And certainly they were no longer seeing each other – the woman was engaged to someone else.

And carrying a torch for Jarrah. Skye wondered if Lisa's fiancé had noticed.

It wasn't Jarrah's fault that Lisa had been hurt, she supposed. She was an adult, and of course he'd have made no promises of lasting love.

As he'd made none to Skye.

'Not as yet,' he'd said, easily deflecting Lisa's probe about his intentions.

Not ever. That was what Lisa's silent glance had told Skye – that she couldn't expect any more from Jarrah Kaine than what Lisa had got. Lisa didn't like Skye – had no reason to, and probably couldn't help it. But despite her patent jealousy, that single look had been a woman-to-woman female warning. *He'll do to you what he did to me. Watch yourself, girl. You're going to get hurt.*

Lisa had been sorry for her.

Skye came out of the shower wrapped in a thin robe firmly fastened at the waist. Jarrah was in the bedroom, dimly lit by the bedside lamp, and had taken off his jacket and tie and undone the top two buttons of his shirt. He stood by the window, looking out at the streetlights. A car went past on the road and the headlights flashed, briefly illuminating his face, bleaching the colour from it and making the angles of his nose and cheekbone and jaw more prominent.

'Are you all right?' he asked her.

'Yes.' She contemplated inventing a headache, but he'd get her aspirin, probably offer to make her a hot drink and tuck her into bed, and she couldn't bear the thought of his solicitude tonight. She paused halfway across the room, not wanting to get into bed, a tacit invitation to him to join her.

He gave a sharp sigh and came to stand before her, his hands on her shoulders. 'You knew about Lisa,' he reminded her. 'It was nothing.'

'You hurt her.'

'Perhaps,' he acknowledged after a moment. 'I didn't mean to, and she soon recovered. She seems happy with her lawyer.'

'The heir to Meddowevale Wines.'

'Yes.' He gave a ghost of a laugh. 'Obviously a better proposition than a Queensland farmer.'

The clumsy jibe had badly missed its mark. Jarrah thought it was funny.

Skye pulled away from his hold, but he only dropped his hands to slide his arms about her waist and bring her close to him. 'Forget it,' he said. 'It's all water under the bridge now. Nothing to do with us.'

Nothing to do with her was what he meant. He didn't want to talk about it.

She froze in his arms as he kissed her, not resisting but quite unable to respond. She had a mental picture of him kissing Lisa like this, in another flat or house somewhere in Sydney. Had he always found himself a conveniently willing woman for his occasional excursions south? How long had Lisa fulfilled the role? And who had been before her?

'Damn it, Skye,' he muttered, scowling as he raised his head. 'I've seen Lisa *once* since I met you. This stupid jealousy is pointless!'

'I'm not jealous.'

'The hell you're not!' He took her shoulders again in his hard hands. 'Do you want me to go?' he demanded.

Fear, unreasoning and swift, rose in her throat. She shook her head, wanting him to hold her close, stay with her, reassure her that he would never leave her, tell her that he loved her . . .

It was too much to ask.

'No,' she said. 'I don't want you to go.'

'Thank God.' His eyes softened, a familiar fire leaping in their depths. 'Come to bed.'

He picked her up and took her there, and within minutes he'd tugged the belt of her robe undone and discarded it on the floor along with his own clothing.

She was acquiescent rather than responsive, but she put her arms about him and made herself relax against him. His mouth parted hers compellingly, and his big, taut body brazenly conveyed his hunger for her. A residue of anger lent a ruthless edge to his lovemaking, and Skye discovered in herself a latent fierceness, a need to claim him for her own, that made her own eventual response shockingly wild.

He touched her and kissed her and brought her again and again to the most exquisite pitch of pleasure, so that everything in her became concentrated on him, with room for nothing else in her mind. He made himself the centre of her universe, the one thing in life she needed, wanted, must have. And it wasn't until she had floated down from the peak, still held in his strong, enveloping arms, that the tiny pain in her heart made itself felt.

Two days later Jarrah said, 'My aunt's been given a clean bill of health, although they'll be keeping an eye on her.'

Skye said, 'That's . . . good news!' It must be a huge relief for his mother as well as his aunt. She was ashamed that her first instinctive reaction to the news had been dismay that now Jarrah would be leaving her.

'My mother will be coming up to Sydney and we're to fly home together.'

'Yes,' she said, going still. 'Well . . .' she forced a bright smile to her lips '. . . it's been nice, Jarrah.'

'I'll try to get back here just as soon as I can manage it.'

Would he? Or would he forget about her, chalk up a pleasant interlude in his life and leave it at that? He hadn't suggested introducing her to his mother.

'I know you're busy, booked weeks ahead,' he said, and then paused. When she didn't fill the small gap, afraid that if she spoke her voice would betray her, he added, 'But try to miss me a little?'

She would miss him unbearably. Determined not to break down in humiliating tears, she battled for a calm demeanour.

Jarrah placed his palms against her cheeks, tipping her head. 'I'll phone you.'

'I may not be here.' To her great relief her tone was crisp, defensive. 'I have photo calls, and . . .'

'I know. But I'll keep trying. You do want me to be in touch, don't you?'

'Of course I do!' Perhaps he meant it after all.

'Good.' He kissed her more deeply, gathering her fully into his arms.

The morning he left he kissed her for the last time, leaving her breathless and speechless and starry-eyed.

'I've got to go,' he finally muttered against her mouth, his lips tasting, nibbling, savouring hers. 'Remind me.'

'You have to go,' Skye said with an effort as she removed her mouth from his.

He sighed, and laid his cheek briefly against hers. 'This has been fantastic, Skye. I don't want to leave.'

She resisted the temptation to cling and wheedle. Instead she gave him an unsteady smile. 'We both have our lives to lead.'

Jarrah nodded rather curtly. Then he stepped back, finding the door handle without taking his eyes from her. 'I'll see you – before too long I hope.'

He sent flowers again, an extravagant, scented bouquet of mixed roses. She put them in a vase on one of the end tables by the sofa, and their fragrance filled the small room. Every time she walked into it she was reminded of Jarrah, the heat of his body sliding against hers, the surprisingly fine texture of his hair beneath her fingertips, the warm possessiveness of his mouth . . .

She went about in a state of knife-edged tension, and when he phoned the sound of his voice sent a shudder of delicious heat through her entire body, a faint echo of the cataclysmic consummation of their lovemaking.

'What have you been doing?' she asked him.

'Fixing machinery, making gates. Working. It helps.'

'Helps?'

'To stop me thinking about you –' his voice was deep, intimate '– about being with you in your bed, making love to you. I hardly sleep at night for remembering what it was like.'

'Good,' Skye said softly, glad she wasn't the only one suffering.

'Good?' He gave a low laugh. 'Little sadist.'

'I'm not,' she protested.

'Not a sadist?'

'Not little. I'm five feet ten in my stockings.' Not really tall for a model, but *little* wasn't a term she'd often heard applied.

'Mm,' he teased quietly. 'Stockings. Do you wear them?'

'Are you a fetishist?'

Jarrah laughed again. 'Try me some time and see.'

She smiled, knowing he couldn't see. 'Your flowers are beautiful.'

'I'm glad you like them. I've seen the TV ad you mentioned. It doesn't do you justice.'

'Justice?'

'You're even lovelier in the flesh. Especially in the flesh.'

'Thank you.'

'Still . . . watching you on TV is better than nothing, I guess.'

Listening to him, she could picture his dark, waved hair, his firm, wonderfully sexy mouth, the deep glint in his eyes when he looked at her, letting her know that he wanted her.

She sat there with a foolish, wistful smile on her face for ages after he'd hung up.

Resolutely she promised herself not to sit at home every night hoping Jarrah would call. Besides a demanding career, she had friends whom she'd been neglecting lately, and a full social life. Self-preservation demanded that she continue to enjoy it. Because nothing that Jarrah had said or done indicated that he expected to be a permanent fixture in her life.

That week she made herself attend a party, arriving and leaving alone, and told herself she'd had a good time. Another evening she spent in a pub, 'celebrating' a friend's divorce with a group of women.

It was very much a bittersweet occasion, and the new divorcee kept up a brittle flow of laughing remarks, helped along by a string of misanthropic jokes from others in the group. But eventually the guest of honour's laughter turned to tears, and the other women hurried her out to a taxi and sent her home with one of their number to hold her hand and offer a sympathetic shoulder.

Skye went home depressed. She'd been at the woman's wedding only five years before, heard the vows exchanged of love everlasting, and now it was all over.

Making a relationship work was difficult. Perhaps her own ideals were impossibly unrealistic. Perhaps she'd taken a step that could only lead to heartbreak and tears.

But when Jarrah told her that he had a board meeting in Sydney and planned to stay on for the week, she said without even thinking about it, 'You can stay here.'

For part of the time she was working, but when she was free they strolled along the waterfront, visited art galleries or bookshops, had dinner or supper together, or just talked over glasses of wine in a café bar. And when they had done teasing themselves, going through the motions of 'dating' while the pauses in conversation became longer and the tension between them neared breaking point, they went back to her flat and tumbled into bed. Or onto the sofa, or a pile of her cushions, or just the Persian rug in the living room.

She'd bought a white, lacy suspender belt and sheer stockings, French satin knickers and a bra to match. The works. She put them on for Jarrah, and he first laughed while she did a sexy, flirtatious, deliberately exaggerated catwalk parade around the bedroom, and then he grabbed her, flung her on the bed and kissed her senseless before removing the silly, provocative garments and claiming her naked body with his own.

'Well, it seems to be true what they say about men and suspender belts,' she murmured afterwards, caressing his hair as he still lay across her, one hand on her hip, the other pinned beneath her shoulder. 'It certainly had an effect on you.'

'*You* have that effect on me,' he argued. 'No matter what you're wearing – or not wearing.' He raised himself and looked down at her, a comprehensive glance that made his eyes kindle with fire again. He moved his hand from her hip, stroking up over her ribs to her breasts, lingering briefly, then down across her flat stomach. 'I can't get enough of you,' he said with a kind of quiet despair.

She felt exactly the same.

'Didn't your mother and sister want to tag along when you came to Sydney?'

He shrugged. 'Neither of them likes it much. Too fast-paced. A couple of times a year they spend a day or two shopping at Mt. Isa, and they fly to Brisbane now and then and stay with Beth for a while.'

'Beth's the designer?'

'Mm. Fabrics and furniture. She's very successful. Different from the rest of the family.'

'In what way?' Skye lifted her head momentarily to look at him.

'Well . . . none of us has any artistic bent, or want to live in the city.'

'You like and understand art, though. Beth's been brought up in a family that appreciates form and colour.'

'Mm. I guess. She was always ambitious, too. And couldn't wait to get out in the big wide world and make her mark on it.'

Skye snuggled back to his shoulder. 'She sounds an interesting person.'

'Interesting . . . yes. You'd probably like her.'

'Don't you?'

'Of course! She's my sister – did I sound critical? I'm very proud of Beth, we all are.

But I'm sort of sorry for her too, because I think she always felt as though she didn't really fit in at Opal Reach. I'm glad for her, now she's found a man she loves and the job she's always wanted, and worked so hard to get.'

'Then you don't need to be sorry for her now, do you?'

'I guess not.' He stroked her hair, lifted a strand and let it fall through his fingers. 'You're right. But sometimes I get the feeling that she's afraid it's all going to be snatched away from her. She never seems very relaxed, to me.'

'You worry about your family, don't you?' She traced a series of tiny circles on his chest.

'No, not worry. I'm concerned for them. Don't you feel that way about your brother?'

'Yes, of course. But I don't see him much. We keep in touch by phone mostly. He seems pretty happy.'

'That's good. If you keep doing that you're going to make me *very* happy.'

Skye smiled, and turned her lips to his shoulder, moving her hand a little further down and continuing to make invisible patterns on his skin. 'So long as you make me happy too,' she murmured.

'I promise you I will . . .' He caught her hand in his and began kissing her fingers, then the inside of her wrist, and only dropped it to bring her head up and find her mouth, while his other hand swept down the long, curving line of her back and hip and closed over her behind. 'God, but you're gorgeous,' he muttered against her mouth, and lifted her over him, closing his eyes in a sigh of content as she settled into the contours of his body. 'Just stay there for a minute and let me feel you.'

She watched his face, fascinated by the taut, changing lines of it, the way his eyes darkened and glistened as his hard hands gently explored her thighs, the rise of her behind and the gentle curve of her waist, then slipped under her arms, and she lifted herself so he could cup her breasts in his palms.

Her hair fell about her face, brushing his shoulders, and she saw him swallow, his mouth tight with restrained passion. 'You beautiful thing,' he whispered. 'Kiss me.'

Skye smiled, slow and mysterious, and lowered her mouth with infinite slowness until it touched his, sliding her arms about his neck, and then he groaned and kissed her with something like desperation, parting her lips with his tongue, his body rocking under her, an insistent, explicit friction that told her what he wanted and set a slow fire building inside her.

She began moving too, gliding against him gently, rhythmically, while she took his tongue into her mouth, moved hers in an echoing rhythm against it, and felt the slight pull on her breasts still cradled in his big hands.

He groaned again, and she heard his breathing change, felt the surge of his body against her, and shifted her legs, enclosing his thighs in hers.

He wrenched his mouth aside. 'No. Wait. Damn, I –' He made to move his hands from her and she said, 'Don't. I'll get it.'

She fumbled for the packet on the bedside table, lifted away from him. 'Don't take away your hands,' she whispered, and he tightened them slightly, making her close her eyes momentarily and let out a tiny breath of pleasure.

'Skye.' His voice was deep and hoarse. 'Can you – ?'

'Yes.' She opened her eyes, looked down and carefully rolled on the gossamer sheath for him.

When she looked up at him again his eyes were slitted, his mouth clamped with an effort at control. He shifted his hands a little, clasping the dark, budding centres of her breasts between thumbs and forefingers, watching her reaction. 'Come here,' he said roughly, and she surged forward, cradling his dark head as he closed his lips about one throbbing, sensitive pink crest and then the other.

She made an inarticulate little sound, then

moved her hands to his shoulders and said his name.

Jarrah lifted his head, his teeth bared in a smile that looked like a snarl, then brought his hands to her head and pulled her to him.

He let a sigh into her mouth, and she lifted slightly, adjusted her body, found the hard tip of his erection and slid her own sleek, tight, welcoming heat over it, settling back down onto his thighs as she enveloped him, feeling him inside her, the whole satisfying, forceful length of him going deep, deeper, so that he felt truly a part of her, and she thought she would never let him go again, that she wanted him here like this, hers and hers alone, for the rest of their lives.

As if he knew, as if their thoughts too, were one, he stopped moving and lay still, only their mouths still tasting each other, their breath mingling, their tongues wrestling in erotic, teasing games.

She could feel the rise and fall of his chest, and knew that like her he was trying to breathe shallowly, to prolong the exquisite agony of anticipation, the moment of greatest intimacy. They floated together, tingling with the delicious ache of shared excitement, the sensation of skin on skin, mouth on mouth, tongue playing with tongue, male flesh enfolded by female.

Then she felt his hardness swell into her slick,

hot softness, and she lifted her head and moved, bearing down on him, moving around him, over him, onto him, wanting him deeper, harder, more, wanting everything she could have of him, until he cried out and she shattered about him, her voice mingling with his, her flushed cheek against his rough one, all of her convulsing in a long, dizzying, unbelievable climax, until at last she lay exhausted, with ripples of ecstasy still coursing through her while Jarrah held her and murmured to her and stroked her, his lips caressing her temple, her cheek, her shoulder.

At the end of the five days she said goodbye to him with her lips firmly pinned into a smile. She didn't know when she was going to see him again.

A few weeks later she had a photo shoot on Queensland's Gold Coast and Jarrah flew down and they spent one night together in a hotel before she had to return to Sydney. In the morning he suggested ordering a room service breakfast and having it in bed, but Skye laughingly overruled him, saying she wanted a jog along the beach first.

He didn't jog, but strolled on the beach waiting for her, and on their way back to the hotel she felt Jarrah's hand tighten on her arm, and heard the quick, muffled curse he uttered as he was hailed by a small woman with a cascade of glorious red hair. 'We'll have to say hello,' he muttered, as the woman plucked at the arm of the big man standing beside her and dragged him over.

'You're Skye Taylor!' The woman looked awed. 'I've got a magazine in my room with your picture in it.'

'She is,' Jarrah confirmed, and introduced the couple as Steve and Megan Poynter, who managed a property not far from Opal Reach.

'It's not nearly as big as Opal Reach,' Megan told Skye, almost successfully hiding the curiosity in her sherry-brown eyes. 'And the homestead's about half the size of the Kaines' place.'

'You're neighbours?' Skye assumed.

Megan smiled. 'If you call a hundred-mile drive being neighbours.'

'You must be very isolated.'

'It's not so bad in winter. But sometimes in the Wet the roads are closed with floods and the ground's too boggy to get a plane out. Actually I love the life, but now and then it's nice to come down here and live it up,' Megan told Skye. 'Beaches are the one thing I miss.'

'You're not originally from the outback, then?'

'No, from Sydney, actually. I applied for a job as a jillaroo on the station where Steve was foreman at the time. Did it for a dare, but I wouldn't want to go back to shifting files in an insurance office. Though Steve's handed over the office work to me on the station.' She laughed. 'I reckon that's why he married me. He hates bookkeeping.'

Her husband, a solid-looking man with a square jaw and crooked nose grinned. 'Yeah, and she's decorative too,' he said proudly, his eyes softening as they rested on his wife. 'Thought I'd better not let her get away. She might not have been the best jillaroo I ever hired – '

'I was too!' Megan asserted indignantly. 'I might have taken a bit of time to learn, but I did a pretty damn good job – *boss*!'

Steve winked at Jarrah. 'Gets her going every time. Fact is, she's the only jillaroo I ever hired. Didn't want to make her jealous, did I, love?' He grinned again.

Jarrah said, 'I've seen Meg in action on the station. She looked pretty clever to me.'

'Thank you, Jarrah.' Megan cast her husband a triumphant glance.

'Yeah,' Steve conceded. 'She had a good foreman. Taught her everything she knows.' He waggled bushy eyebrows at her. 'Didn't I?'

The look that passed between them hinted at things unsaid, and Skye exchanged an amused look with Jarrah.

'Have you two known each other for a while?' Megan glanced from Jarrah to Skye.

'A couple of months,' Skye answered cautiously as Steve claimed Jarrah's attention with some remark about beef prices.

'Trust Jarrah to take up with a famous model!' Megan chuckled. 'He wouldn't be satisfied with anything less than top shelf.' Lowering her voice, she added, 'With his looks and his . . . advantages, I guess he can afford to be choosy.'

'Advantages?'

'The Kaines have never been short of a bob or two, and specially since Jarrah took over the finances, updated Opal Reach and started investing. Steve reckons money sticks to him.'

Skye didn't know what to say to that. But Jarrah saved her from having to reply by saying they had planes to catch and they'd better get going.

Back in their room he said curtly, 'Sorry about that.'

'I don't mind.' The fact that she and Jarrah were having an affair wasn't something she expected to keep a secret.

Obviously he minded, though. A faint chill entered her heart.

He wasn't married. She'd taken his word for that, and the Poynters would surely have shown some sign of embarrassment if he was. But he was reluctant to admit her part in his life to anyone he knew.

She pulled her hand from the light clasp he'd had on it and said, 'I need a shower.'

'Shall I order breakfast?'

'For yourself, if you like,' she said, already on her way to the bathroom. 'And you can get me an orange juice.'

When she came out the waiter was just leaving. There was a basket of rolls and croissants, and coffee as well as orange juice. Skye drank the juice standing and began to pack, with the quick efficiency of practice.

Jarrah said, 'What's the matter?'

She answered crisply. 'I'm not hungry, that's all.'

'You should have something. Shall I put some marmalade on a croissant for you?'

'I haven't time.'

He glanced at his watch. 'There's plenty of time. You don't have to leave until after I've gone.' Coming over to her, he put his arms about her and pulled her back against him, his lips nuzzling her nape. 'Wanna go back to bed?'

'Jarrah . . .' The warmth of his body, and his breath on her skin stirred instant desire.

'Mm? I wish we didn't have to leave,' he murmured, and turned her and began to kiss her properly.

In the end he hung the 'Do Not Disturb' sign on the door, and made love to her one last time.

When he got up to have a quick shower she found her robe and put it on before raking a brush through her hair. Jarrah had kissed all the lipstick from her mouth, and it looked colourless. She smoothed a trace of pink gloss over it. There were faint blue shadows under her eyes. She'd have to disguise them with make-up if they didn't disappear before her photo shoot tomorrow. And after that . . .

She leaned closer to the mirror, looking for flaws.

'Don't worry,' Jarrah's amused voice said. He'd emerged from the bathroom so quietly she hadn't heard him, and was watching her. 'You're beautiful.' He came over and touched her hair, lifting a strand and then letting it fall, his gaze meeting hers in the mirror. 'Midnight hair and midsummer eyes,' he said softly. 'No man could resist you.'

She put up her hand and caught his fingers. The only man she wanted to be irresistible to was him.

He dropped a kiss on her hair and straightened, releasing her hand. 'I won't be able to get away again for a while.' He seemed to hesitate. 'And I know you're going to be pretty well tied up too – '

'Yes,' she said quickly. Was he trying to reassure himself that she wouldn't feel neglected?

'It's our busiest time on the station,' he explained, 'the winter mustering season, but if you were able to find a space in your diary – '

And if he were able to do the same, presumably he hoped that they could snatch another single night, or a couple of days.

She'd known from the start what kind of relationship this was, Skye reminded herself. But she realized with a pang of distaste that her role in it was that archaic, demeaning one of mistress – a convenient woman to be toyed with when he had some leisure time, and put aside when he was too busy to be bothered.

'I won't be available for a while anyway,' she said, making her voice light and brittle, as if it didn't matter greatly. She stood up and turned to face him. 'I'm leaving for America in a couple of days.' She wasn't dependent on him, she told herself hardily. Certainly not financially, and she didn't want to be emotionally.

Jarrah stepped back, frowning. 'America?'

Skye nodded. She'd put off her departure date as long as she could, but the season was at its peak on the west coast and her booker had arrangements made.

Jarrah bent his gaze momentarily to the carpet, and thrust his hands into his pockets before looking up, his eyes unreadable. 'So how long will you be away?'

Skye swallowed, gave a tiny shrug, and turned aside with an appearance of nonchalance. 'Eight weeks.'

CHAPTER 6

Jarrah's jaw suddenly seemed more prominent. 'You didn't think to tell me this before?'

'I was going to mention it last night – '

'Mention it – as in, "By the way, I won't be around for the next couple of months"?'

His sarcasm fired her temper. 'I'm sorry if it's inconvenient for you, not having me at your beck and call in case you have a couple of days to spare.'

'*What*?'

Skye put it into words, hoping he might refute it. 'I mean, that's the sort of relationship we have, isn't it?'

'I have a business to run!' he snapped. 'You know that, and I thought you – '

'And I have a career!' Skye reminded him tartly, silently swallowing her disappointment that he hadn't even tried to deny the casual nature of their affair. 'I told you I travel for the shows.'

'Yes, but I wasn't expecting – '

'You don't expect anything of me, you said.'

'I meant – '

'And I don't expect anything of you either, Jarrah,' she hastened to add, afraid that a shade of bitterness might have been discernible in her voice.

'What do you mean by that?' His eyes had gone opaque, his voice quiet and even.

'What I said. We have an arrangement that suits us both – and doesn't tie us down in any way.' Surely that was what he wanted? And if he'd found he wasn't satisfied with it then here was his chance to say so.

He didn't. Instead he said in clipped tones, 'You're right, of course. I'm sorry if I've been taking things for granted.'

So he wasn't disputing her assessment of the situation. Skye said huskily, 'I should have told you sooner. It just didn't seem to . . . come up.'

'Where will you be?' he asked abruptly. 'I mean, can I get in touch with you? What's the time difference between there and Queensland?'

Not remembering offhand, Skye said, 'I can give you an agency number in LA and the name of my hotel, but I won't be there much.' Offering an olive branch, she promised, 'I'll phone you after I get there.' She was more accustomed to calculating times in various parts of the world than he was.

His grim look lightened. 'You may find me camped on your doorstep with my bedroll when you come home.'

Skye smiled with relief. 'You can camp on my doorstep any time you like.'

'I may hold you to that.' He reached for her and drew her back into his arms, then paused, looking very serious. 'After you get back we have to talk.'

'Talk?' Hope and curiosity and fear mingled inside her. 'About what? Why not now?'

He hesitated, then decisively shook his head. 'This isn't the right time. I have a plane to catch and . . . you're not ready for it.'

How did he know what she was ready for? But before she could protest he was kissing her with a peculiar, almost desperate ferocity, and then muttering against her lips, 'I've got to go, dammit.'

He kissed her again, then tore himself away and picked up his bag. 'Call me,' he said. 'You've promised.'

She did call from her hotel in Los Angeles, and when a young female voice answered she asked to speak to Jarrah.

'Was that your sister?' she asked him after he

came on the line.

'That was Kelly, yes. She'll be dying to know what we're saying to each other, but I've shut myself in my office now.'

'Sorry.' She was sure he would rather his family didn't know anything about her. 'Have I given you away?'

'Don't worry,' he said drily. 'The cat's been well out of the bag since we met the Poynters in Brisbane. How was your flight?'

'Uneventful. I slept.'

'Are you phoning from your hotel? Give me the number,' he said. 'I've got a pen.'

She gave it to him, but warned him again, 'I may be hard to get hold of. I have a heavy schedule.'

She asked him about the station, and he told her they'd started mustering. 'I may be hard to get hold of too,' he said, making her wonder if he was playing tit for tat.

'Tell me about Los Angeles,' he said. 'I've never been there.'

'It's big and it's busy. If I have time I'll take some photographs,' she promised. She always carried a camera, and had taken note of the techniques used by the photographers in the fashion business. Her photography was only a hobby, not a profession, but she got a lot of pleasure out of it.

Her schedule was demanding, and she seemed to lack the energy to endure it, although usually she quite enjoyed these hectic trips overseas, the change of pace from her normal routine. Some of the other models were old friends, girls who were savvy and funny and nice, and there were the usual gossip sessions over coffee between assignments, but somehow they didn't seem as interesting as they used to.

She still enjoyed the company of her friends, and it was good to be with people who had shared the same triumphs and pitfalls as she had on their way to success in their chosen career. But even as she laughed and chattered and shared experiments with hair and make-up and swapped fashion magazines and exchanged news of mutual acquaintances, she was conscious of a sad little core of loneliness deep down inside that she had never experienced before.

She phoned her mother and talked for ages about nothing much, and then she phoned Jarrah and told him about the designer who had practically remade his creation while she was waiting her turn to go out on the runway, and the girl who had somehow left the dressing room with her zip undone, so that one of their male colleagues had to make an unscheduled appearance on the runway and do it up for her, and other minor disasters. When he laughed, she felt a warm, treacly sensation seep through her, and when he said he was missing her, she cupped her hand about the receiver and confessed, 'I miss you too.'

'Good,' he said. 'My turn for a bit of sadism.' But his voice was deep and slow, and she imagined him caressing her naked back as he said it, and her blood heated at the thought so that she could hardly muster a normal voice to say goodbye to him.

She slept badly and her dreams were either erotic or frightening. She had never felt like this in her life. If it was love, she thought, it wasn't all it was cracked up to be. Rather than sweet and ecstatic, it was scary and unsettling. She wasn't sure she wanted to be this dependent on anyone. Particularly on a man who hadn't given her any indication that he viewed their relationship as anything other than a pleasant, temporary one.

The weeks dragged by. Her telephone conversations with Jarrah became less frequent. Often they missed each other, leaving brief, uninformative messages. She wrote him letters, enclosing photographs of Los Angeles and San Francisco, and received in return a couple of hurried one-page scrawls. Jarrah was obviously not a man who expressed himself well on paper.

Or maybe he was a man for whom absence made the heart grow cooler.

Skye began counting the days, marking them off on the calender in the back of her diary. Three weeks . . . then four since that last night of lovemaking, of sleeping in each other's arms.

She became tense and irritable. The adrenalin flow that usually saw her through a shoot or a show had deserted her. The fashion business, that she'd always thought of as a dynamic, creative endeavour of talented people bringing glamour, entertainment and fun into a too-often drab world, suddenly seemed a trivial, frivolous round of essentially meaningless activity.

She'd been in it for nearly ten years. Maybe she was growing stale, needed to move on to other things. A favoured few top 'girls' had matured and still hung onto their sought-after status, but most were out of the business by the time they hit thirty.

And maybe Skye didn't have a choice.

There were things she wanted – needed – to say to Jarrah, but she shrank from trying to form the words using the impersonal medium of the telephone.

'Can you be in Sydney when I arrive?' she asked him, almost dreading the answer.

She wasn't sure if the slight pause before he replied was due to the vagaries of the international phone system. 'Let me know your flight number and time of arrival. I'll pick you up at the airport.'

In the arrival hall Jarrah came towards her and took over the baggage cart she was pushing. He paused, lifted her face with one hand and kissed her, first briefly and then again, with passion. She put a hand on his shoulder and kissed him back.

When he released her mouth he studied her face and said, 'You look exhausted. Let's get you home.'

Gratefully she let him carry the heavier bags and sat beside him in silence in a taxi. He took her hand in his and lifted it to his face, rubbing her fingers against his cheek.

When she let them into the flat it seemed dark and stuffy, and the first thing she did after they entered the bedroom was open the windows.

'What do you want to do first?' he asked her. 'Can I make you a cup of coffee, or something stronger?'

'Not alcohol.' Skye shuddered, and sat on the bed as he parked her bags in a corner near the wardrobe. She kicked off her shoes and lifted a foot to massage it.

'Let me do that,' Jarrah suggested. 'Lie back.'

It was a blessed relief to do so, and she let her

head rest on the pillow as he sat on the bed and laid her nylon-clad feet across his knees, his thumbs moving firmly against her insteps.

'Where did you learn to do that?' she asked him.

He laughed softly. 'Never mind. Is it good?'

'Blissful.' He'd probably done it for one of his previous girlfriends, she thought with a pang. An image of Lisa floated into her mind. She dismissed it.

He smiled at her and she smiled back almost dreamily. His hands were hard but gentle, his thighs warm and muscled. 'Are you wearing stockings?' he asked her.

'Panty-hose,' she said. 'Sorry to disappoint you.'

'I'm not disappointed.' His hands moved to her ankles, and one ran up her calf. 'Want to take them off?' The hand settled behind her knee, his eyes questioning her, teasing.

She felt a hot shiver of response, and knew he'd seen it in her eyes. 'Why would I want to do that?' she murmured.

Jarrah's smile deepened. 'You'd be more comfortable?' he suggested hopefully.

'Would I?'

The questing hand moved further up, sliding beneath her thigh, waking delicious sensations that she'd been afraid she might never experience again. He leaned towards her, his eyes laughing. 'Why don't we try it and see?'

His lips closed over hers as his hands intruded beneath her skirt and removed the panty-hose. And her mouth blossomed for him. She flung her arms about him and gave herself up to him, in a floodtide of relief and gladness that he still wanted her, that he'd come all this way to be there when she arrived home.

He lifted his mouth, but only to remove some more of her clothes, and she did the same for him, her fingers fumbling with buttons and zips, her lips feverishly finding his warm, hair-dusted skin as she peeled off his shirt.

He turned her over and kissed her back from the nape of her neck to her ankles, then lay down and pulled her against him, one hand on her breast, the other stroking her hip and thigh, moving to the smooth inner skin, and then between her legs, until she shifted and turned to face him, her arms about him while her mouth sought his kiss.

Their lovemaking was wild and sweet and raunchy, and when they lay panting and replete among the tumbled sheets afterwards she could hardly believe that less than half an hour had elapsed since they'd entered the flat.

'God, I've missed you!' Jarrah spoke against her hair, and leaned down to kiss her forehead, then her cheek, and settle his warm mouth in the throbbing hollow of her throat, his tongue making a tiny foray to explore the shallow concavity. 'You taste of honey and flowers.' His hand moved lazily from her shoulder to her hip, stopping briefly on the way for delicious little lingering caresses. 'Tell me you missed me.'

'I did.' More and more as the weeks passed, until the missing and the wanting him had been almost physically painful. 'I nearly flew home early.' For the last three weeks she'd had to grit her teeth and use all her willpower to get through the days.

Jarrah raised his head. 'Really? I've been tempted to hop on a plane and fly over there myself.'

'You never said – '

'Neither did you. For all I knew you were having a whale of a time. And I know you were pretty heavily committed. Sometimes I thought my phone calls were just an unwelcome interruption.'

'They weren't!' She couldn't have borne it if he had never phoned, although the calls had, she knew, grown progressively more strained – her responses stiff, his laconic. There had been awkward silences. Their worlds were so different, with no mutual point of reference, and the one thing that had been at the forefront of her mind she had deliberately refrained from mentioning. 'I'd have hated you not to phone,' she said.

'I'm glad to hear that.'

He sat up. 'And I'm a selfish brute. I offered you a cup of coffee, and all I've done is take you to bed.'

'I don't want coffee.' Skye pulled him down to her again. She needed to be close to him.

Because what she was going to say, what she had to say, might alter everything between them.

He didn't give her the chance. Turning his lips to hers again, he muttered, 'That's fine with me.' And as he kissed her and caressed her, sending all her nerve-endings into a singing, vibrating mass of ecstasy, she gave herself up again to mindless, endless pleasure

Afterwards she slipped into a depleted, luxurious sleep such as she had not had in weeks. When she woke it was almost dark, and distantly she heard sounds from the kitchen.

Feeling sticky and muzzy, she got up and did some exercises to combat the stiffness engendered by the long plane trip, and showered to wash away the effects of the journey and Jarrah's lovemaking. She put on a loose shirt and cotton trousers, straightened up the bed and unpacked, knowing that she was only delaying the moment of truth.

She laid a gift-wrapped parcel on the bed and went to the kitchen.

Jarrah looked up from shaking something about in one of her pans. 'I hope you like ham and tomatoes and oven chips.'

Skye forced a smile to her lips. 'Where did you get them?' She hadn't left much food in the place.

'I went shopping while you were dead to the world. Bought a bottle of red wine too. To celebrate your homecoming. How about you take the wine –' he indicated the uncorked bottle standing on the counter '– and find glasses for it?'

He was busy. Skye did as she was told, and poured the ruby liquid into two glasses. The table was already set for two.

Jarrah brought in the plates, the ham browned and topped with pineapple rings, the tomatoes halved, lightly cooked and sprinkled with freshly ground black pepper, the chunky oven chips crisp and golden.

'This looks . . . wonderful.' She tentatively tasted a chip and found that her stomach quite liked it. Encouraged, she took another.

She ate half of her ham, and left a few chips on her plate, but the meal had been good, and she felt better for it.

'You haven't touched your wine,' Jarrah said.

'You have it. I . . . don't really want wine tonight.'

'I bought some fruit,' he offered, taking her plate. 'I'm afraid my talents don't run to dessert.'

'I'd love some fresh fruit,' Skye assured him. 'You know I hardly ever eat dessert anyway.'

He brought in a bowl of peaches, nectarines and apples. 'Coffee's on.' He took an apple and cut it into quarters.

When he had poured the coffee he said, 'Shall we have this on the sofa?'

'I bought you a present,' she said, and went to fetch it, handing it over as she sank down beside him on the sofa.

He placed his cup on the side table and picked up the package, peeling open the tape that sealed it.

It was a man's kimono, white with a navy pattern.

'I bought it in San Francisco,' she told him.

He held it up. 'I'll keep it here, if that's okay,' he said. 'Thank you. It's very handsome.'

As he leaned across to kiss her cheek she wondered if he preferred to leave the robe in her flat because he didn't want to wear her gift around his family.

But perhaps she was being oversensitive. At

least he apparently expected to be around her place some more.

On the basis that her role in his life was an intermittent, casual one, and her flat a handy base for his trips away from home?

She stared into the depths of her coffee cup as he folded the kimono and laid it over the arm of the sofa and picked up his cup. 'You sent some great photographs,' he said. 'They look like professional standard.'

'I have a good camera.'

'And a good eye. The family's very impressed.'

'You showed them to your family?'

'Shouldn't I have? I didn't think you'd mind.'

'I don't mind.' Lightly, because she didn't want him to realize how hurt she'd been, she said, 'I'm rather glad I'm not a shameful secret any longer.'

'Shameful?'

She gave a little laugh. 'You were rather put out when the Poynters sprung us, weren't you? I'd begun to wonder if you were married, after all.' She bit her lip then, because he seemed not just startled, but possibly angry, his eyes greener than usual and hard. 'Joke,' she offered feebly.

His coffee cup was poised in one big hand. 'You only have one brother,' he said.

'Yes.' She'd told him that some time ago,

described her peripatetic childhood.

'Then you don't know what it's like in a large family. My brothers and sisters take altogether too much interest in my private life,' he said. 'In fact the whole district does. I tried to keep our relationship quiet, but not because I'm ashamed of it. I've come in for a fair bit of teasing from Kelly and Erik since they found out.'

She felt a little lighter. 'Is that a problem for you?'

'Nothing I can't handle.' He drank some of his coffee, then lowered the cup and saw her gravely regarding him. Shrugging, he reluctantly amplified. 'A few years back I was seeing a local girl. We almost ended up at the altar just because everyone around us seemed to expect it. She was sensible enough to realize what was happening – she left the district, and later married a real estate agent in Perth. I believe she's very happy.'

'Did you mind?'

'I was relieved. I'd been trying to think of a way out that wouldn't make it look as though I'd left her in the lurch.' He raised his cup to his lips and finished the coffee. 'But I was fielding commiserations for months afterwards.'

He'd hate that, people pitying him. Maybe that was why he preferred to have his girlfriends in Sydney now, away from the well-meaning curiosity of people who'd known him all his life.

Skye drank the rest of her coffee and he held out his hand. 'Can I take that?' He took it from her and put both of their cups on the side table.

Then he reached for her, but she clasped her hands tightly in her lap and stiffened her shoulders, shaking her head vehemently, so that he let his hand fall to the back of the sofa and regarded her in frowning puzzlement. 'Skye? What's the problem?'

She couldn't – shouldn't – put this off any longer. She'd been a coward, taking every excuse to delay the moment of truth. But it wasn't fair, and it wasn't right. It wasn't even . . . practical.

'The problem,' she said, each word carefully weighted, 'the problem is that . . . I'm pregnant.'

CHAPTER 7

Long seconds ticked by. Skye could discern no emotion on Jarrah's face, make no guess at his reaction.

'Are you sure?'

'Yes.' She'd been sure even before she had taken the test that had left no room for doubt.

'I've been taking precautions,' he said. 'You know that.'

Skye stared at him defiantly. 'It wasn't enough, obviously. There is no one else, Jarrah. This is your baby.'

'I'm not denying it! Damn! I should have made sure you were on the pill or – '

'You're not responsible for me, Jarrah. I knew the risks.'

He looked at her with an odd, searching expression. Then he got up and went to the window, fiddling with the blind cord in an uncharacteristically aimless way. Finally he turned to her, his face showing strain, and a determined control. She thought he had paled under his tan. 'So . . . what do you want to do?'

Skye, a sinking depression in her midriff, swallowed hard. 'What do you want me to do?' She had a horrible, queasy feeling that she knew.

His eyes held hers in an intent, brooding stare. 'I want you to marry me.'

She couldn't believe he'd said it, and wondered if she'd conjured the words from her own confused and occasionally wildly hopeful imagination.

Her astonished silence went on so long that he stepped towards her, the line between his brows deepening, his voice harsh. 'If you didn't want to go ahead with it, you wouldn't have asked me how I felt about it.'

'But marriage –' Taking his share of the responsibility was what she would have expected of Jarrah, but marriage was a huge commitment, and he'd given her no cause or excuse to imagine that he meant to marry her. 'That . . . isn't necessary.'

'Maybe it isn't . . . *necessary*. I suppose I'm ludicrously out of date, but I never pictured fathering a child outside of wedlock. How far on are you?'

'It must have happened the night we spent on the Gold Coast.'

He seemed to need to pause to absorb that. 'Eight weeks. You won't be able to work for much longer, will you?'

A shiver passed over her skin. 'No.' Already the gentle rounding of her stomach was discernible to herself if not others. She'd half-dreaded, half-hoped that he might have noticed when they made love earlier. 'But I'll manage somehow. Lots of women do.'

'Alone?' His mouth tightened. 'No. We're in this together, Skye, for better or worse.' He bent down and took her hands, drawing her up to stand before him. 'Marry me, Skye. Let me take you home to Opal Reach and look after you and our baby.'

It sounded blissful, but if she hadn't been pregnant he would not have proposed to her.

'Skye?' he urged, and tilted her face, kissing her almost roughly. 'Say yes to me, Skye.'

His kiss, his arms about her, quieted her misgivings. The familiar glitter of desire in his eyes gave her a measure of hope for the future. He wanted her – and he wanted their child. Why should she deny him? And herself? Or . . . most important, the child they had made, who was surely entitled to a father.

That was when Jarrah took over her life. Dizzy with relief that he hadn't repudiated her or suggested she get rid of the baby, and suffering a lethargy that her doctor told her was common in early pregnancy, Skye left everything to him.

Within a week they were married, flying to New Zealand for the ceremony after Jarrah discovered to his chagrin that Australian law wouldn't allow them to tie the knot in under a month.

All she had to do was tell her parents and wrap up the threads of her life in Sydney – which were surprisingly few. She'd been a transient since childhood, putting down only tentative roots even in the place she had decided to call home.

She had no trouble renting her apartment to another model from the agency. Her booker threw up her hands when Skye explained why she would be unable to fulfil her engagements, and the agent called her a silly girl but reluctantly agreed to tear up her contract. After a tense little argument with Jarrah, Skye paid the cancellation fees for the bookings already made, asserting a measure of financial independence but making a hole in her bank account.

Her mother had offered other solutions. When Skye said she'd made her mind up, Genelle asked bluntly, 'Do you love him?'

'Yes,' Skye admitted. 'I do.' She was relieved that her mother didn't ask whether Jarrah loved her. No doubt if Skye asked him point blank he would say yes. What else could a man say to the woman he was about to marry, who was carrying his child? Even if he gave her the words, she wouldn't have dared believe them.

'You're not going to be married in a registry office,' her mother decided. 'We'll have the ceremony here, at home.'

Home? Skye had never lived in the house her parents had bought in Auckland, but she was grateful for the offer. Her mother found a celebrant and approved the pale blue lace skirt and top that Skye had chosen to be married in. Her brother Mark phoned from London with his best wishes and promised to post a gift as he couldn't take time off from his job at such short notice to attend the wedding.

Her father had a quiet talk with Jarrah, and later asked Skye if she was sure this was what she wanted to do. 'You know your mother and I will stand by you, whatever you decide,' he promised. 'There's no reason to rush into a marriage you might regret.'

'Do you think I'll regret it?' Her father was a wise man and she respected his opinion.

He didn't answer immediately. Finally he said, 'Jarrah seems a fine young man with a strong sense of responsibility. Apparently he took over at Opal Reach when his father died and he's held it and the family together ever since. And financially he's pretty secure.'

'Financially *I'm* secure.' She'd been careful of the money she earned, and had invested a good proportion of it. 'And I don't suppose there's much to spend money on where we'll be living.'

'Life in the outback will be very different from what you've been used to. Do you think you can handle it?'

'I handled being moved from country to country when I was a child, adapting to different customs and languages.'

'You were cushioned to some extent by being part of the diplomatic community.'

'I've travelled a lot on my own since then. I'm pretty resourceful, Dad.'

He smiled. 'And determined.' He had been worried at the prospect of her taking up a career in modelling at sixteen, but at the time they had been living in New York and the agency she'd started with was well-known and respected. She had persuaded him and Genelle to let her seize the chance. 'If this is what you really want,' he said now, 'then you and Jarrah have my blessing.'

Jarrah's sister Beth flew over with her husband from Brisbane for the wedding, which was as memorable an occasion as Genelle was able to make it. Beth had her brother's dark hair, but her eyes were a deeper green, flecked with brown. She met Skye with a cool kiss on her cheek and a veiled look of speculation, and there was a dry note in her voice when she congratulated Jarrah. She was the only representative of his family who had made it to the wedding.

The following day Skye and Jarrah flew to Brisbane and spent the night at a hotel in the city, but had dinner with Beth and her husband, who had also invited his brother Dale.

Dale was as tall as his elder brother but with the lankiness of youth. He greeted Skye with a shyly admiring smile, and teased Jarrah about the sensation their marriage was likely to cause in the district round Opal Reach, but had little to say to Skye herself. Possibly he was overwhelmed by her looks; it was a reaction she had met before in young men.

'You could have stayed with us,' Beth told Jarrah. 'But I suppose as you're just married . . .' Turning to Skye, she added, 'Maybe he'll give you a proper honeymoon when the rains arrive. You'll discover that everything at Opal Reach has to wait for the muster or the rainy season.' Her smile had an ironic twist.

'I already gathered that,' Skye said as Beth's husband handed her the glass of soda she'd asked for. 'I expect I'll get used to it.'

'I'm afraid you'll have to, being married to my brother,' Beth said with a hint of sympathy. 'It isn't easy to drag him away from Opal Reach.'

'Do you miss it?' Skye asked her, curiously.

Beth shook her head. 'I miss the family sometimes. But I like city living. It's stimulating and exciting – I'd never go back now. Maybe Jarrah told you – I was always a misfit there. Couldn't wait to get out in the big wide world and spread my wings. And never regretted it for a minute.'

Later Jarrah suggested Beth might show Skye some of her fabric designs, and they all went to the studio that had been built onto the back of the house.

The men went off after a few minutes to switch on the television and watch a replay of a cricket match between Australia and England, and the two women were left alone.

'You're very talented,' Skye said warmly, admiring a swatch of fabric in blended colours of vivid ochre, amber and smudgy green and charcoal. 'This would be great on a suite or as curtains.'

'Mm. Actually, that's a design that was inspired by the colours of Opal Reach. I do have a sort of nostalgia for the place, even though I wouldn't want to live there again.' Beth leaned back on the long workbench and surveyed her guest. 'You haven't been there at all, have you?'

'Not yet.' Skye noticed to her own annoyance a slight tremor in her voice.

Beth looked at Skye doubtfully. 'I hope you know what you're in for.'

'I'm looking forward to it,' Skye said. It wasn't exactly a lie, but her anticipation was inevitably mingled with trepidation. She really knew very little about life at Opal Reach, had no idea what to expect.

Beth's lips tightened. 'I don't suppose you really have a clue,' she said. 'What on earth is Jarrah thinking of?'

As Skye's head went up defensively, Beth flushed. 'Sorry, I don't mean that – well, dearly though I love him, my brother can be a bit one-eyed at times. And very determined.' Her eyes dropped for a split second to Skye's still slim-looking figure. 'Usually it's not for himself – he'd do anything for any of us, so long as he's sure it's the right thing. And for Opal Reach. It's just that . . . well, I don't suppose any of us imagined he'd fall for someone who – who might not share his passion for the land.'

'I hope I will,' Skye said quietly. 'I know how important it is to him. And I'm very adaptable.'

'You'll need to be.' Beth sighed, and turned to put away the samples they'd been looking at. 'I don't mean to offend you, Skye. I'd like us to be friends.'

'I'm sure we will be, and I'm not at all offended. I understand your concern for your brother,' Skye assured her.

'And for you, actually. Still, you're both adults.'

'Yes, we are.' And soon they would have a child to care for. As adults, they had an obligation to the new life they had made. And Jarrah had, as his sister said, done what he thought was right.

As Skye and Jarrah were leaving, Beth told her, 'If you need a break any time, come and stay with us for a while. A couple of weeks of city life might keep you from going stir crazy.'

'Thank you.' It was a generous offer considering they'd only met tonight.

'You're family,' Beth assured her, perhaps noting her surprise. 'You're welcome.'

The following day they took a local flight to Mt. Isa, where Jarrah's own four-seater Cessna airplane was waiting.

'Do many people fly their own planes up here?' Skye asked him.

'Quite a few. It's the fastest way to cover the long distances.'

'Do you ever fly yourself to Brisbane?' she asked him.

Jarrah shook his head. 'The Cessna doesn't hold enough fuel to get to Brisbane. I'd have to refuel twice along the way.'

She'd always known Sydney was thousands of miles from his home, but hadn't fully understood how complicated and time-consuming a journey he'd had to make each time he visited her. 'I didn't realize how far you had to travel to come to Sydney. Changing planes and . . .'

'It takes a while,' he agreed. 'And in the Wet our airstrip at the homestead can be six inches under water, so we have a four- or five-hour drive just to get to Mt. Isa – if the roads aren't flooded.'

They flew over miles and miles of almost empty ochre plains and undulating country threaded with narrow, random rivers. The scale of it was awe- inspiring, and Skye gazed from the plane's windscreen almost hypnotized.

'We're flying over Opal Reach now,' Jarrah said after a while. 'There's the boundary fence.'

'Where's the other boundary?'

'You can't see the whole place from here.'

You couldn't? Skye blinked at the size of the station. 'Is it all fenced?'

'A couple of bits are so rough the stock wouldn't bother anyway. We finished fencing the rest a few years back.'

Skye couldn't imagine such an undertaking. It must have taken years of work.

Narrow borders of green marked meandering ribbons of creeks, and the rest of the land was uneven red earth sparsely covered with pale, dry-looking grass and studded with low, scraggly trees.

Scattered herds of cattle and sheep grazed here and there, and a bunch of horses streamed across an open plain and disappeared into a stand of bush pocketed deep in a gully. Skye leaned forward to follow their progress. 'You have wild horses?'

'Brumbies, yes. We round them up now and then.'

'Is that a windmill down there?' Skye pointed.

'Mm-hmm. There are ten of them around the station, pumping water out of artesian bores for the stock.'

'And those are cattle yards?' She peered down at a complex of railed enclosures.

'Drafting yards. Saves us driving a whole mob to the homestead yards when we're working a remote paddock.'

'How big is a paddock?' She could discern few fences.

'A small one's a few hundred square k's. Some are in thousands.' Lifting a hand from the plane's controls, Jarrah pointed to an irregular oval of water far below them, fed by a twisting stream and bordered by a ring of thick, dark trees. 'That's the waterhole the station's named for.' The plane began to lose height. 'And there's the homestead on the jump-up overlooking it.'

The sun gave the waterhole a mysterious, dark-rainbow sheen. At first Skye didn't realize how large the house was that overlooked it. Set on the flat top of a stony rise in a square of green lawn fringed with shrubs and taller trees, it was red-roofed and two-storeyed, a long rectangle with a veranda enclosing three sides of the lower floor and a covered balcony along the front of the upper one. Blue water glittered in the sun at one side of the house. 'You have a swimming pool?'

'Put it in a few years ago when the cattle prices were good. It's great to come home to when we've been out on the station and get back covered in bulldust.'

'I thought bulldust was a euphemism for a pack of lies.'

Jarrah grinned. 'Out here it's a reality.'

She glimpsed another windmill, and a black metal tower and the circular dish of a microwave receiver tilted skyward. 'Our link to the outside world,' Jarrah confirmed. 'The communication tower.'

He circled the buildings once, and a figure appeared below, running from the house and waving. Outside another building, where a couple of vehicles were parked, several more people appeared, gazing skyward.

'The welcoming committee,' Jarrah said.

Skye was too nervous to smile back. She was very conscious that Beth had been the sole representative of his family at the wedding, and she wasn't sure if it was only the lack of adequate notice and the difficulty of distance that had kept the others away.

He brought the little plane round and the ground came up to meet them. Skye fought nausea, closing her eyes as the wheels caught at the ground and they taxied to a halt.

The silence when Jarrah switched off the engine was startling. His fingers brushed her cheek and she opened her eyes. 'Are you all right?' he asked.

Skye nodded.

He pressed his lips briefly on hers. 'You're pale. We'll get you into the house and you can lie down.'

'I don't need to lie down, honestly.' She'd be all right, she hoped, when her feet were back on the ground.

The sound of an approaching vehicle made Jarrah turn his head. 'Here we are. Kelly's bringing the Nissan over.'

The few clouds overhead didn't mask the yellow sun moving down the sky. When he opened the door heat rose to envelop her. And this was winter?

Jarrah got out and swung Skye down, keeping an arm about her as he introduced his sister.

Kelly, a bouncy girl with short brown hair, wearing a plaid shirt and jeans, gave her an exuberant hug. 'Nice to meet Jarrah's best-kept secret at last! You're even more gorgeous than your photographs!'

Skye was embarrassed but grateful. 'Thank you – '

'Take Skye to the truck, Kelly,' Jarrah interrupted, 'while I get the bags.'

'Sure.' Her slightly surprised look indicated that Kelly might have wondered why Skye couldn't make it on her own the few yards to the vehicle, but she led the way and opened the door for her new sister-in-law to climb into the cab. Obviously she was used to obeying her big brother's orders.

Jarrah stowed the bags in the back and slid in beside Skye, one arm about her shoulders. 'Let's go.'

Kelly drove over the unsealed track that led to the house, a fine red dust rising under the wheels and swirling into the cab.

'Bulldust?' Skye queried Jarrah.

' 'Fraid so. You all right?'

Skye nodded. 'Fine.'

The vehicle hit a rut and she let out a small, involuntary sound.

Jarrah snapped, 'Careful, Kel!'

'Sorry.' Kelly glanced at Skye apologetically.

They drew up in front of the house. A dark-haired older woman in a fawn linen dress stood in the shade of the veranda before a big open door, and as Jarrah helped Skye to the ground she came down the broad shallow steps to meet them. Jarrah turned, his hand firm on Skye's waist, and said, 'Hello, Mother.'

'Well . . . so this is your wife.' Grey-green eyes, uncannily like her son's, surveyed Skye with a shrewd and not unfriendly gaze. 'She's very lovely.' She hesitated for a moment, then held out a work-hardened hand. 'We've seen pictures of you, of course. Welcome to Opal Reach, my dear.' When Skye took the outstretched hand, Mrs Kaine reached forward and kissed her cheek. 'We've all been looking forward to meeting you. I hope you'll be happy here.'

'Thank you, I'm sure I will be.' Skye tried to ignore the note of doubt in the older woman's voice. 'It's a beautiful house.' Close up, the white-painted walls, the broad veranda and upper balcony had a simple elegance, the austere lines softened by plantings of shrubs and climbers, some of them twining up the veranda posts, and a purple bougainvillea had rampaged all the way to the curved corrugated iron roof of the balcony and spread along it.

'Come inside,' Jarrah's mother said. 'I've made tea, but if there's something else you'd like . . .'

'Tea sounds great,' Skye assured her.

The floor of the entrance hall was polished boards and, coming in from the harsh light outside, at first she could scarcely see the pale gold round rug, the half table holding a brass bowl filled with garden flowers, and the pictures hung on the walls.

'Skye may want to freshen up first,' Jarrah said. 'And I'll get the bags upstairs.'

'We've got the master bedroom ready,' Mrs Kaine said, 'and moved your things in there.'

'Mother, that wasn't necessary.' Jarrah frowned. 'It's always been your room.'

'Well, now it's yours – yours and your new wife's. Of course, it was a bit of a rush – '

Dismayed, Skye said, 'We can't turn you out of your bedroom – '

'I've always preferred the view from the green room, and it's quite big enough for one person. I'll be very comfortable in there. The master bedroom has its own bathroom, by the way.'

Skye turned to Jarrah, and he shrugged. 'This way, Skye.'

She followed him up the staircase and along a wide corridor, glancing with interest at the artworks that lined the walls. Jarrah had understated when he'd said they had 'a few pictures' at Opal Reach. This was a very discriminating collection of mostly Australian works. Ochre landscapes under harsh light, distant mountains, grey-green trees with peeling bark, and an occasional cityscape or abstract.

Jarrah shouldered open the door of one of the rooms, and as she entered Skye's first impression was of a view that encompassed the waterhole and beyond and seemed to go on forever, the low hills far away on the horizon barely impinging.

Jarrah deposited the cases at the foot of a large bed with a carved wooden headboard. In one corner stood a huge double wardrobe with mirrored doors and matching carving. A rich gold brocade spread with silk fringing covered the bed.

Skye touched the curved footboard, running her fingers over the smooth patina of varnish.

'The furniture used to belong to my great grandparents,' Jarrah said. 'But it does have a good modern mattress. My mother likes the old things that came from the original homestead. You can replace it with something more modern if you like.'

'I wouldn't dream of replacing things that have been in your family for generations.' Skye loved the feeling of permanence the old furniture exuded.

She looked about the room. Glass-paned folding doors led to the balcony where a canvas lounger and a low table stood invitingly just outside. The fine-meshed insect screens were almost invisible.

'We don't have to use this room if you prefer one of the others,' Jarrah said.

'This looks very comfortable. Are you sure your mother doesn't mind giving it up?'

'You heard her. The bathroom's over there.' He indicated a painted door.

She rinsed her face and freshened her minimal make-up from the pack in her handbag. When she emerged, Jarrah had taken off his shirt and was pulling a plaid one like his sister's, and a pair of well-worn jeans, from the wardrobe. 'I'll just have a quick wash,' he said. 'Do you want to change?'

'Should I?' Skye glanced nervously at her light trousers and silk blouse.

'Only if you want to. You look fine.' He smiled and came towards her. 'As always. Sure you wouldn't like to rest?'

'I'm not an invalid.' Part of the nausea she was feeling was nerves, she knew, rather than the result of pregnancy. 'I'll feel better when I've had a cup of tea and something to eat.'

'You *are* feeling rocky, then?' He peered at her face.

'No, really. A bit tired, that's all.'

He stood frowning down at her a moment, then said, 'I won't be long,' and disappeared into the bathroom.

When he came out she was standing on the balcony, so absorbed in the vista of low, undulating country stretching beyond the gums and acacias fringing the waterhole that she didn't know he was there until his arms slid about her waist, bringing her back against him. His lips touched her temple. 'What do you think of it?'

'Opal Reach? It's . . . very big,' she said inadequately.

'It'll take some getting used to.' He turned her in his arms. 'As I'll take some getting used to having you here.' His hands roved gently over her body as if to assure himself she was real. 'I want to kiss you, but I'm afraid I won't be able to stop. My mother and Kelly are waiting for us.'

'Yes.' Skye moved out of his arms. 'We'd better go down.'

The tea was served on the veranda overlooking the swimming pool. Skye was relieved to see sandwiches as well as buttered scones with jam and cream on the wrought-iron table. The china was pretty and delicate, and she wondered if it had been brought out of some cupboard in honour of her arrival.

She nibbled at a sandwich, and answered Kelly's questions about her life and career, and Mrs Kaine's occasional query about her family. Afterwards Kelly said she had to see to the dogs, and Mrs Kaine declined Skye's offer to help clear up, suggesting, 'Why don't you show Skye around, Jarrah?'

'If she feels up to it.' He looked at her inquiringly.

'Of course.

'Come on, then. The house first.'

The rooms on the ground floor were big and airy, nearly all with folding or sliding doors leading to the shady veranda. In the dining room an imposing Victorian glass-fronted dresser held a collection of antique china.

'How old is the house?' Skye asked.

'This was built in the sixties, when my father brought my mother here after their marriage. She had a lot to do with the final design. The homestead my great-grandparents built is over there, with the old workers' quarters.' He pointed out of a window, indicating a square wooden house some distance away, built high off the ground and with the roof lifted over what Skye guessed to be a cooling air space. A longer building with a veranda spanning its length, almost as wide as the building itself, stood still farther off.

'Nowadays we don't employ much permanent staff, only two men who live in the old homestead. But some others have come in for the muster. I'll introduce you later.'

The formal sitting room had an air of seldom being used, the furniture a mixture of periods and styles happily coexisting. 'Family stuff,' Jarrah said. 'Some from the Kaines, and a few things my mother inherited from her parents.'

Another room looked more casual and lived-in, with a TV set in one corner and several shelves full of books. 'This is the library?'

'That's over here.' He led her through a doorway to a long, narrow room furnished with a rosewood desk, a chaise and two comfortable armchairs. Three walls were filled with shelves of books and magazines, and on the other French doors opened to the side veranda. 'It's not very big, but it holds quite a lot of books.'

'It's wonderful!' She walked in and gazed about her.

'We'll have to make room for your books.'

'I sold most of them.'

'Why?'

Skye shrugged. 'In my family we're used to getting rid of surplus belongings when we move on. I kept a few.' Two boxes packed with things she couldn't bear to part with were somewhere in transit between Sydney and here. 'They won't need much space.'

CHAPTER 8

Upstairs Jarrah indicated the green room that his mother had taken, without opening the door, but as it was a corner room Skye guessed that it had windows on two sides, and perhaps that was what Mrs Kaine had meant when she said she preferred the view from there.

As far as Skye could see, except for the deep, opaque pool overlooked from the front of the house, the views in all directions were very much the same – endless vistas of red earth and sparse, dusty vegetation.

Jarrah pushed open the door to his own former bedroom, overlooking outbuildings behind the house. She peered at a photo on the wall and saw a younger, grinning Jarrah, a wide-brimmed hat pushed back on his head. He held a rope in his hand and a huge bull with vicious-looking horns lay at his feet, its legs tied together.

Skye turned to him and raised her brows.

His soft laugh seemed faintly embarrassed. 'In my younger days,' he confessed, 'I fancied myself as a bull-catcher.'

'You lassoed them?'

Jarrah laughed outright. 'No, the trick is to chase them through the brush on horseback until they get tired. Soon as they slow down a bit you come up alongside, jump off the horse, and hang onto the bull's tail until he turns to have a go at you. That's the precise moment to give the tail a twist and bring him down. Once he's on the ground you rope him and tie him.'

'It sounds horribly dangerous.'

'We don't do it that way any more. Even then –' he nodded to the picture '– most people had gone over to using motorized bull-catchers. But on Opal Reach it was a sort of rite of passage. We had some die-hard old ringers on the station – men who'd worked with cattle all their lives, and they reckoned that was the only way to do it. And my father . . . wasn't a man who took easily to new ideas. He took a fair amount of persuading before he came round to using motorized bull-catchers. When I first suggested it I think he figured I'd lost my nerve.'

'Were you ever hurt?'

'Frequently. Covered in bruises after every muster, and one big, mean scrub bull ripped my shirt open and grazed me from neck to navel. It was only a scratch but it bled like blazes and I think after that my mother put the hard word on Dad and he agreed to bring in contractors with vehicles to do the job.'

'You don't have a scar.'

'No, I told you it was a scratch.'

There were several unused bedrooms as well as a couple of bathrooms, one with a full bath and another with a shower. Everything was plain and functional, but there was plenty of space. Even the passageways were wide, the ceilings high and airy.

Downstairs the station office held a utilitarian desk, a laptop computer, a filing cabinet, and stacks of folders and papers on shelves. Skye was impressed. 'It looks very businesslike.'

'This is a business. If you don't run it like one, you're dead. Even some of our stock sales are made by computer these days.'

As they passed through the big kitchen dominated by stainless steel benches and a long, solid wooden table, Jarrah's mother turned from putting away something in one of two huge refrigerators and smiled at them abstractedly.

Off the kitchen Jarrah led Skye to a utility area with laundry facilities, a shower room and a walk-in freezer. By the outside door a row of pegs held broadbrimmed hats and rainproof jackets. Jarrah reached up to collect one of the hats, dropped it over Skye's hair and adjusted the angle.

He pulled on a pair of boots from a row of them by the door, glanced at the trainers she was wearing, and apparently decided they'd pass before he led her outside.

He guided her by a fenced vegetable patch shaded by nylon net. Beyond the garden a couple of dozen hens scratched about in a wire-netting run.

On the veranda of the old homestead several men lounged about with cans in their hands. 'Come over and meet the boys,' Jarrah said, 'before they die of curiosity.'

The men, their weatherbeaten complexions ranging from sunburned brown to black, shuffled to their booted feet at the approach of a woman, and regarded her with guarded interest.

'Hey, fellas, this is my wife, Skye,' Jarrah said.

A cigarette dropped from one man's hand and a creased and dusty boot ground it into the dust at the foot of the greyed wooden steps. 'Well, you're a dark horse, Jarrah!' He stepped forward. 'Gidday.' He snatched the stained stockman's hat from his grizzled head and held out a calloused hand to Skye. 'Jack Anderson. Pleased to meet ya, Skye. You gonna keep this bloke of yours in order, then?'

'I'll try,' she promised as Jarrah cocked an eyebrow at her, daring her.

'Jack's been mustering with us for fifteen years,' Jarrah told her. 'In his misspent youth he was a drover, before all the stations started trucking their cattle out in road trains instead of walking them to the railheads, and he likes to think he taught me all I know.'

'I did, young fella, and don't you forget it,' Jack said.

The others crowded round, tipping their hats to her or offering their hands as Jarrah introduced them. Skye realized that the group included a woman, wife of one of the men, and dressed like her companions in boots, jeans and an open-necked shirt.

While they talked, several dogs in a wired enclosure under a stand of trees some distance off started barking, and another vehicle roared into the yard. A battered four-wheel drive, it had a stout looking metal framework attached to the front, and several tyres fastened to that. 'Here's the bull-catching team,' Jarrah told her, and introduced the three men who tumbled out of the vehicle and ambled over to meet them.

They were young and cocky-looking, grinning at her with open appreciation. She was amused to see their expressions change abruptly to something like deference when Jarrah introduced her as his wife.

'You'll be a nine-days wonder,' he predicted as he led her away to show her the generator that supplied power to the house, and a shed where several vehicles were parked, including a tractor and a big yellow grader.

'We have to maintain our own roads on the property,' Jarrah explained, seeing her eying the grader with surprise. 'And we're putting in more all the time.'

A dozen sturdy horses corralled in a post-and-rail enclosure snorted and snuffled. 'Plant horses,' Jarrah said.

'Plant?'

'Our station horses, brought in for the muster.'

'So you still use horses?'

'A few. Most stations now just use helicopters and motorbikes, but Opal Reach has some heavily wooded country, and the smart old bulls head for the scrub the minute they hear the chopper. I prefer hunting them out of it on horseback, with help from the dogs.'

'And what about those?' Behind a wire fence more horses stood flicking their tails under a handsome, spearleaved coolibah.

'Our brood mares.' Jarrah walked in that

direction, his hand at Skye's waist.

'Thoroughbreds?'

He smiled and shook his head. 'Australian Stockhorses. They're a kind of hobby of mine.'

Leaning on the gate beside him, Skye studied the group grazing the sparse golden grass. 'They don't look very big.'

'The Stockhorse is a medium size, workman-like breed,' Jarrah told her. 'Good all-rounders. Some are top-class eventers and show jumpers, but they were meant for working cattle. I still like to use them in the muster. It's what they were bred for originally, and the horses that move well and keep their cool as well as having good lines are the ones we breed from.'

'They're a recognized breed?'

'That's right. We register them and try to keep the lines.'

One of the mares lifted its nose, whinnied, and ambled over to the fence, snuffling at Jarrah's shoulder. A light bay, it had a delicate, intelligent head and big, liquid dark eyes with long lashes.

'Can you ride?' Jarrah asked Skye as he rubbed the horse's nose.

'I had a pony once when I was eleven or twelve.' Then the department had moved her father on again, so the pony had to be sold. It had broken her heart, and she'd refused the offer of a new one, afraid of suffering the same pain all over again.

He patted the animal's gleaming neck. 'Say hello to Skye,' he said.

Tentatively Skye stretched out a hand. The horse danced restively, tossed its head and shook its mane at her.

Jarrah laughed. 'This is Stardust. She's in foal to Moonfleet. She wasn't supposed to be – at least, not yet, and not to him. He's a working horse, though I might put him to stud later. He broke down a fence one night and got to her so she's pregnant at the wrong time. But the foal should be a good one.'

Stardust lowered her head and blew gently through her nostrils, then craned forward to sniff at Skye's shirt. Skye tentatively stroked the warm sleek pelt of the horse's neck, and caressed her long, bony nose, down to the soft, furry end. 'She's beautiful.'

'She's got a good head and well-set shoulders, and she's quick and light on her hooves. That's what we hope she'll pass on to her foal. Without her temperament, though.'

'What's wrong with her?'

'She's not vicious, just a bit unpredictable. Highly strung and inclined to be wayward.' He cast Skye a deliberately provocative glance and said, tongue in cheek, 'Very female.'

Skye made a face at him and he laughed.

'Maybe I could learn to ride again.'

'Not while you're pregnant. And certainly not on Stardust.'

Very male, Skye thought, amused rather than indignant at his masterful pronouncement, and decided not to argue. The books of instruction to new mothers she'd read said moderate exercise was good for pregnant women but that it was unwise to take up any new strenuous activity. She supposed as it was so long since she'd been on a horse, riding would count as a new activity.

The house when they returned to it was quiet and still. 'I need to go out and check on a few things round the station,' Jarrah said. 'My mother should be about somewhere.' He looked around.

'Don't bother her. I'll unpack and maybe have a short rest.'

'Good idea.'

With an unreasonable dip in her spirits, she felt that he was relieved. Perhaps he had been chafing to get out and 'check on a few things' ever since they'd arrived, but hadn't known what to do with her.

Skye found empty drawers and hangers, and put away her things. Then she folded back the heavy brocade cover from the bed and lay down, but was too tense to doze off. As soon as she heard movement in the passageway outside she got up and rinsed her face, ran a comb through her hair, and made her way downstairs.

She found Mrs Kaine preparing what looked like a mountain of vegetables, while the rich smell of roasting meat pervaded the kitchen.

When Skye offered her services the older woman looked a little disconcerted, but hesitantly accepted. 'Erik will be in for tea,' she said. 'Then you'll have met the whole family.'

'I'll look forward to it.'

Kelly came in, and her cheerful chatter eased the strain between her mother and Skye. Mrs Kaine, Skye felt, was determined to make the best of things, but she must have been disappointed at the suddenness and near-secrecy of her eldest son's wedding. Maybe in his choice of bride too. Like her daughter, Mrs Kaine was probably as much at home on the back of a horse or behind the wheel of a four-wheel drive vehicle as she was in the kitchen. Already Skye was feeling her inadequacy as the wife of an outback man.

Skye helped Kelly set the polished oval table in the dining room.

'Five places,' Kelly said. 'The musterers will have theirs in the kitchen, but there isn't room for everyone.'

Skye went upstairs again to freshen herself before the meal. She didn't suppose the household 'dressed for dinner' but she'd been in the same clothes all day and it seemed courteous to make some small effort for her first dinner with Jarrah's family.

Wrapped in a towel after a cooling shower, she was riffling through the clothes she'd hung up earlier when Jarrah came in. He'd taken off the boots he'd donned before going out, and his jeans and shirt were smudged with red dust, his hair damp with sweat.

As she turned to face him he smiled, a slow fire in his eyes. 'You look deliciously fresh and sweet,' he said. 'I won't touch you – I'm filthy. Have you finished in the bathroom? I need a shower.'

'Yes. I'm just wondering what to put on for dinner.'

'We call it tea out here. Wear that swishy blue thing I like. I guarantee it'll have my little brother slavering.'

'Jarrah!'

He laughed at her, on his way to the bathroom. In the doorway he paused, looking back. 'Of course, if you're still wearing that towel when I come out he may never get to meet you after all. I might just throw you down on the bed and ravish you – for the rest of the night.'

That would certainly offend his family. Skye gave him a severe look. 'You'd better make that a *cold* shower.'

The 'swishy blue thing' was a bias-cut satin slip dress with ribbon straps and very little skirt that lightly skimmed her body but was loose enough to disguise the slight weight gain she'd made. She couldn't wear a bra with it, but it was, she assured herself doubtfully, perfectly modest, if rather dressy for a family dinner. Still, if she wore it without adornment it was surely simple enough to pass.

They had pre-dinner drinks on the veranda by the dining room. Mrs Kaine was still wearing the dress she'd had on earlier, and Kelly had changed into a cotton skirt and blouse.

'You look gorgeous,' Kelly commented, admiring the blue dress. 'But then you'd look gorgeous in anything.'

'Thank you.' Skye took the chair Jarrah guided her to, and stopped herself from returning the compliment, knowing it would sound patronizing. Kelly was a nice-looking girl, but this wasn't the right moment to say so.

Jarrah poured drinks for the women and was opening himself a short stubby bottle of beer when a four-wheel drive vehicle came racing along the track towards the house and skidded to a halt.

The young man who jumped out, dressed in boots, jeans and a crumpled shirt, had Kelly's colouring but resembled Jarrah in build.

'You must have smelled it,' Jarrah commented, lifting the stubby in his hand. 'I suppose you want one of these?'

'Thanks.' The young man grinned and vaulted the verandah rail, landing lightly on the boards. His gaze homed in on Skye. 'Wow! You must be my new sister-in-law. I'm Erik.'

'I guessed.' Skye smiled at him.

'What a knockout. I can see why old Jarrah here wanted to get a ring on your finger before he brought you home,' Erik told her. 'He'd have had all the bucks in the district sniffing around – '

His mother said, 'Erik!'

'Sorry,' he said, but cast an unrepentantly teasing look at his brother. 'Do I get to kiss the blushing bride?'

'Ask her,' Jarrah said. 'But keep it *brotherly*, brother. And maybe you should have a shower first.'

Erik's smile widened. 'How about it, sis?' he inquired of Skye, his blue eyes dancing.

She smiled back at him and presented her cheek, allowing him to brush his lips against it.

'Wow!' he said again, straightening. 'Trust

big brother to get himself the best-looking woman in Sydney! How did he persuade you to let him rope and tie you and haul you way out here?'

'I got her pregnant,' Jarrah said coolly, 'as you've probably guessed already. And I'd appreciate it if you don't talk about it to the whole district – it's strictly family business. The neighbours also don't need to know the exact date of the wedding.'

Skye flushed, and there was a tiny silence before Kelly said hurriedly, 'Nobody's bothered about that these days, anyway.' Glancing at Mrs Kaine, Skye found the older woman looked unsurprised, perhaps resigned.

'Here.' Jarrah handed Erik a bottle. 'Get this down you. Skye, can I pour you another bitter lemon?'

She held out her glass, and as he bent over her his eyes met hers, with some message in them. Perhaps apology, or a silent justification. *Best to get it out in the open, they might as well know now.*

He was probably right, Skye thought. Soon there would be no point in trying to hide the reason for their hasty marriage. She wondered if he'd even told his mother of her pregnancy when he'd sprung the news of his impending nuptials. She hoped so, but in Skye's admittedly limited experience, Jarrah wasn't prone to explaining things in detail.

Erik seemed to have taken it in his stride, lifting his squat beer bottle in a casual toast. 'Congratulations, bro'.'

He hitched himself onto the broad rail of the veranda, and Jarrah leaned against a nearby post, saying, 'We saw a fair mob of brumbies up in the Thirty Mile as we were coming in. When we've finished mustering the stock we'll look at doing a cull.'

Erik nodded. 'Yeah, there's been plenty of feed about the last couple of years, and I guess they're getting out of hand.'

Skye sipped at her lemon drink, noticing that with darkness falling the air was suddenly much chillier. The two men were discussing a bore that was in need of repair – something to do with casings and joints.

Mrs Kaine excused herself to check on the dinner, and soon afterwards Kelly followed. Erik finished his beer and went off to shower and change.

Jarrah turned to Skye. 'We're neglecting you.' He came away from where he was lounging against the veranda post. 'Want another drink?'

Skye shook her head. Her glass was still half full. She put it down on the wrought-iron table, and shivered.

'You're cold! We should have gone in earlier.'

Kelly called that dinner was ready, and Jarrah held out his hand, bringing Skye to her feet. He slipped an arm about her and rubbed his palm up and down her arm. 'Come inside and get warm.'

Skye ate little of the roast beef and vegetables and the baked pudding that followed. She would have liked a salad and some crusty bread. The conversation flowed around her, and every so often Jarrah or Kelly would turn to her and explain what they were talking about. She gathered that the start of the muster had been delayed pending Jarrah's return. Erik had left the station's two permanent workers at 'Top-hat Paddock' to finish repairing the yards there.

Kelly said, 'It's a shame you couldn't have taken the time for a honeymoon. Most people here have their weddings in the Wet, after the last muster.'

Skye smiled. 'There must be a lot of rainy wedding days.'

'You're right there. Getting married in New Zealand was probably a pretty smart move.'

In their room later Jarrah said, 'I'll be up early, but I'll try not to disturb you.' He was pulling off his shirt on his way to the bathroom.

'It's all right,' she said to his back. 'What time should I go down?'

'Whenever you like. If there's no one about

you can get yourself something to eat in the kitchen.'

'Your mother – '

'She'll be around, probably.' He disappeared into the bathroom.

When he came out again Skye was ready for bed, wearing a red satin nightgown. Since she'd been sleeping with Jarrah she had discarded her comfortable cotton nightshirts. At the flat they'd more often than not slept nude in her bed, but before the wedding she'd gone out and bought herself glamorous but generously cut sleep-wear as some sort of gesture to her status as a new bride.

Jarrah looked at her with a deep spark in his eyes. 'God, you're beautiful!'

Skye put a hand on her stomach. 'I'll soon be showing.'

'You'll still be beautiful,' he assured her, and came over to take her in his arms. 'Beautiful with my baby. How are you feeling?'

'I feel fine.' She'd had slight waves of nausea, but nothing serious. 'Just a little tired.'

'Too tired . . .' his voice was husky '. . . for this?' He kissed her gently, holding her close so that she could feel the stirring of his body.

Skye put her arms about him and kissed him back, needing the comfort of his arms, the closeness of his lovemaking. She felt disoriented and rather scared of the huge changes that were taking place in her life. 'No,' she said when he stopped kissing her, 'I'm not too tired.'

He took her to bed, and among the tumbled sheets he made her writhe and pant beneath him, and she heard her own voice crying out that she loved him, loved him . . .

'My lovely, lovely wife,' he whispered back to her, and then he filled her with himself and gave her the ultimate pleasure, leaving her exhausted and physically satisfied. But afterwards while he slept with an arm across her midriff, Skye lay for a long time with her eyes open, staring into the night.

It wasn't Jarrah's quietly leaving their bed that woke her in the morning, but the noise of a helicopter hovering overhead, the beating of its rotor blades intruding on her dreams.

She'd been walking by the sea, holding a child of about four by the hand, and she had been very happy in the dream.

The alien sound startled her, and she woke alone, the space beside her empty and cold.

The helicopter landed and she heard the whinny of a horse, men's voices, the whine of a motorbike.

Somewhere along the passageway a door slammed. The house was awake. She pushed back the covers and got up, going to the window. The night had been surprisingly cold, and the air was still chilly. She wrapped her arms about her, shivering in her satin nightgown.

Dawn was barely breaking. High, blood-red clouds streaked the vast sky but the land below was still swathed in the remains of the night, except for the waterhole that reflected the sky like a giant, fiery black opal.

Spellbound, she watched as the white trunks of the ghost gums on the other side of the water began to emerge from the darkness, and then the outlines of the lesser trees crammed at the edge, and the unruffled surface of the pool became a sheet of orange flame that faded in turn to green while the sun rose and the land emerged from sleep, stretching away for miles in all its stark, understated beauty.

Turning at last from the sunrise, she had a quick shower, fighting a bout of nausea, and pulled on jeans and a T-shirt and sneakers, then went down the stairs and headed for the kitchen.

There were plates stacked on the stainless steel bench, and a smattering of toast crumbs on the long table. A lingering aroma of fried onions hung in the air, and outside she could hear a hum of activity.

The door stood open, and when she stepped

out she saw the helicopter standing not far from the Cessna on the airstrip. Near the old homestead horses jittered and snorted, their riders adjusting cinches and fastening swags to the saddles, and three men straddled motorbikes. Vehicles of varying sizes were haphazardly parked, and on the back of one of them several yipping brindled dogs danced about.

Opening a gate in the fence and carefully closing it behind her, Skye saw Kelly among the riders, and picked out Jarrah's tall figure. As if he felt her eyes, he turned from shortening a stirrup strap on a handsome, dark brown horse, and gave her a surprised, glinting smile. He took the reins in his hand and led the horse over to meet her, pushing back the broad-brimmed hat he wore. 'Did we wake you?'

'It's okay, I don't mind.'

He leaned down and kissed her, his lips barely brushing hers.

'What time will you be home?' she asked.

He looked a little startled. 'It's a three-day muster,' he said.

'Three days?' She couldn't hide her dismay. 'I . . . didn't realize.'

'Don't worry, my mother will take good care of you.'

'I'm not worried.' It was foolish to feel he was deserting her. Jarrah had a job to do, he was in charge, and already the start of the muster was overdue. 'I'll be all right,' she promised.

'Good girl. See you when we get back.' He kissed her again, but almost absently, and turned away to go and speak to his mother, who had appeared from behind a small, shabby truck loaded with what Skye guessed to be food supplies.

Left standing while everyone bustled about, she felt distinctly redundant, and returned to the house, pausing in the doorway as nausea again struck her.

The thing to do, she thought, was eat something.

Averting her eyes from the remains of steak, onions and gravy lying in a big roasting dish on top of the stove, she found some bread and toasted a couple of slices in a toaster that was made for four. Waiting for it to brown, she tidied the random stacks of plates and ran hot water on some of them in the generous stainless steel sink, letting them soak.

She ate the toast with a thin coating of marmalade from one of two big jars sitting on the table, and felt a little better. There was a coffee-maker on the counter with a couple of inches of dark, thick brew in it, and she helped herself to that, diluting it with hot water.

Outside the engine noises swelled and roared,

and then died into the distance as the musterers moved out. Mrs Kaine came in while Skye was washing the dishes she'd piled into the sink.

'Oh, Skye, there's no need for you to do that. We have a dishwasher. Jarrah put it in years ago.' She put a basket full of eggs on the table.

Skye turned. 'I'm almost done now. Good morning, Mrs Kaine. I'm sorry I wasn't down in time to help with breakfast. I was watching the sunrise.'

'We didn't expect you. And you'd better call me Ella, I think. I don't suppose you want to call me Mum – you have a mother of your own, don't you?'

'Yes, I do. Thank you . . . Ella.'

'Have you had something to eat?'

'Yes, I made toast. Jarrah told me to help myself in the kitchen.'

'Of course.' Mrs Kaine found a tea-towel and began drying the plates. 'You're family, not a guest.'

'Then I hope you'll let me help around the place.' Skye let the water out of the sink and found a hand towel. 'Tell me what I can do.'

'You must be tired after your long trip, and today you should probably take it easy. When the musterers come back will be the busy time.'

'Do you have any paid help?'

'It's hard to get. We do pretty much everything for ourselves, except during the muster. Jarrah hires a camp cook then to go out with them, and to help me here when they bring the cattle back to the homestead yards. But it's not like the old days when we had no electricity and no telephone and had to bake our own bread.'

'It must have been hard living here then.'

'Yes, it was.' Mrs Kaine hung up the tea-towel and carefully straightened it. 'Even the butter came in tins, though Jarrah's grandmother used to keep a couple of house cows and churn her own. Now of course we buy butter in bulk and freeze it, and use powdered milk.'

'Did you always live around here?'

'My family had a property over Blackall way. My mother was from South Australia, one of the old families. She met my father at a cattle sale down there.'

'Where did you meet Jarrah's father?'

'At a picnic race meeting on one of the stations. I married him two years later.'

Two years, Skye thought. She had known Jarrah just over four months, and for over half of that time they had been apart.

CHAPTER 9

'I . . . did Jarrah tell you I was pregnant?' Skye asked.

'Not in so many words,' Ella admitted, 'but it wasn't difficult to guess. I take it the two of you hadn't planned it?'

'Heavens, no!'

'It must have been quite a shock for you. With your career . . .'

'It was a shock for both of us,' Skye said ruefully. 'And . . . it must have been for Jarrah's family too, I think?'

Ella nodded. 'You could say that. We'd never even have known he was seeing you, except for the Poynters – I believe you met them at Surfers.' She looked away.

'Yes.' Skye tried to control a flush rising to her cheeks. 'They seemed a nice couple.'

'Megan's settled well here. She was a city girl, you know.'

'Yes, she told me.'

'Mm.' Ella looked rather pensive, still doubtful, Skye thought. 'It's not the best start to a marriage,' she said frankly, 'but Jarrah's never been one to shirk his responsibilities, and he's had plenty of them. And he doesn't give up on anything easily.'

'Neither do I,' Skye assured her calmly. 'I understand that you're . . . concerned. But Jarrah and I both want to make this work.' She wanted to say that they loved each other, but the words wouldn't come. She wasn't sure enough of exactly what Jarrah felt for her. Desire, certainly. Affection, even. But once-in-a-lifetime, till death us do part love? Despite the promise he'd made on their hurriedly arranged wedding day, she wasn't sure.

'Well,' Ella said, 'that's all anyone can ask, I suppose.'

In the afternoon Ella said she was going to fetch the mail from the gate, and it wasn't until she returned much later in the utility vehicle that Skye realized the mailbox on the public road was forty kilometres away. She wondered if she would ever get used to the scale of things here.

Skye offered her services each day, but Ella assured that there was little to do until the musterers arrived back. She spent most of her time familiarizing herself with the house and its surroundings, swam in the pool to cool down in the afternoons, and indulged her unusual feeling of lethargy by loafing with a book on the lounger on the screened balcony outside her and Jarrah's bedroom.

At dusk three days later the musterers drove several hundred head of cattle into the home yards, and they had time for only a quick dip in the pool, a shower and a change of clothing before Ella, with Skye's probably unnecessary help, had their 'tea' on the kitchen table and they were tucking into what looked to her like an enormous meal of steak and vegetables with a hearty pudding to follow.

The helicopter pilot, Lee McGinnis, was invited to eat with the family in the dining room. Lee was a pretty young woman with a frank, friendly manner, who greeted Skye with a smile and a firm handshake. 'So you're the woman who's finally hogtied Jarrah Kaine,' she said. 'All the boys have been talking about you. They didn't exaggerate. Kaine's got the pick of the bunch again.'

Skye smiled and deflected the subject. 'Is your job unusual for a woman?'

'Fairly.' Lee grinned. 'I learned from my dad. He flew choppers in Vietnam, and came back to the family cattle station after he married my mum.'

Erik said, 'She's better than most of the men.'

Skye wondered if he was biased. Jarrah had idly commented earlier on his brother's extra well scrubbed appearance, and she'd noted Erik's covert, sparkling glances at the pilot. But Jarrah agreed. 'Lee's more patient and careful than most male pilots, and she understands cattle. Some of the men go in too close and too fast and get the stock racing about every which way, so the riders on the ground can't get them under control. The first time my father used a chopper he swore it would be the last.'

'It was years before we could persuade him to try it again,' Erik recalled. 'And he always grumbled about using machines for mustering.'

'He had a point,' Jarrah conceded. 'Helicopters and bikes are faster, but if you push the cattle too hard they get stressed and lose condition.'

Lee went off to bed early in one of the spare rooms. Jarrah watched a news report on the television, and soon afterwards he yawned, smiled lazily at Skye and asked if she'd like a swim before going to bed.

'Yes, all right,' she agreed.

'Anyone else?' Jarrah asked.

His mother went on reading the magazine she

had on her lap, Erik said, 'Not for me,' and Kelly shook her head. 'Too cold, now.'

It didn't feel too cold to Skye. She went upstairs with him and changed into a stretchy swimsuit, wrapping a towel about herself. Jarrah pulled on shorts and flung a towel about his neck, then took her hand.

The air outside was considerably cooler, but the pool water, once the first shock was over, was warm and satiny.

Skye did a leisurely breast stroke up and down while Jarrah covered several lengths at a fast crawl. Then he swam to the side and waited for her, standing on the bottom with his arms resting along the pool rim. Light from the house gilded ripples on the water, but she couldn't see his face properly.

When she reached him he lifted his hands and pulled her to him, the water sleeking her arms as his hands closed on them.

She put her hands on his shoulders. Her legs tangled with his. Her arms slid about his shoulders, and she felt his lips, at first cold, then warmer, trail across her bare shoulder, her throat, and finally reach her mouth.

She leaned into him, felt him slip.

The coolness of the water about them contrasted with the heat generated between their bodies. Jarrah moved his hands to her waist, then her thighs, and lifted her to him, the water making her almost weightless in his arms. Instinctively she wrapped her legs about him, and felt his immediate physical response.

She made a soft little sound, and Jarrah's hand slid up her spine, tugged at the bow that held the swimsuit around her neck, and peeled the wet fabric away from her breasts.

'Jarrah!' She whispered an alarmed protest.

'Shh. I want to feel you against me.' He folded his arms about her and kissed her again.

The water lapped softly around them, and he held her easily, his arousal pressing against her through their thin swimsuits.

He shifted his grip, one hand under her, the other going to her breast, and tiny waves rippled between them, cooling her skin. She shivered, half with cold, half with desire, and as he touched her, her head went back, her mouth parting.

He lifted her more, his mouth closing over her breast, and she gasped, her legs tightening about his waist to keep her balance as she arched over his arm.

His mouth left her breast and trailed to her throat. He lowered her and his hands went to her waist, her hips, pushing at the stretch fabric of her swimsuit. 'Get this off. I want you now!'

'Jarrah – we can't!' She looked at the lighted

windows of the house. 'Not here!'

'No one will disturb us,' he said with quiet confidence. 'And it's dark, they can't see a thing.'

'But –' He silenced her with another kiss, and when he'd finished she let him complete taking off her suit without a murmur. He tossed the wet little bundle onto the tiles and quickly shed his own briefs.

'Now, come back here,' he muttered, 'right where you were before.'

She gave a slightly shocked little breath of a laugh, and then he had has hands underneath her again and was lifting her to him, fitting himself inside with a long, guttural sigh.

It was like nothing she had experienced before. The encompassing, silken caress of the water, the silence of the night, the cool, wet kisses they shared, the whispered words they exchanged, the sensation of weightlessness and the delicious feelings that coursed through her added up to a magical experience, rather dream-like and yet undoubtedly physical.

When the rush of sweet sensation finally overwhelmed her, she buried her mouth against his shoulder to muffle her cry of fulfilment, and as he followed half a minute later, he caught her mouth under his and groaned as he surged into her.

She stayed as she was, panting, for minutes afterwards, and he slowly lowered her and climbed out of the pool, turning to haul her after him.

She was shivering, and he picked up her towel and wrapped it about her, fixed the other about his waist and picked up their swimsuits, rolling them into a tight wad that he held in one hand, putting the other arm about her shoulder. 'Come on, we'll get you inside.'

She realized the lights in the house had gone out, but when they went in a dim glow lit the stairway.

Quietly they trod up the stairs and Jarrah let them into the bedroom.

'A hot shower, I think,' he decreed, and bundled her into the bathroom, turning on the water and testing the temperature.

He stepped in with her and when she stopped shivering he turned the warm stream off and grabbed a clean towel, rubbed her down and then rough-dried her hair. 'Into bed,' he ordered. 'I shouldn't have kept you out in the pool so long.'

'I'm all right, really.' She was, but she loved being pampered by him. She felt wonderfully warm and full of wellbeing, now.

She went into the bedroom, dropped the towel and donned a clean, fresh nightgown.

When he climbed into bed beside her he reached for her and settled her comfortably into his arms.

'You must be tired,' she said.

'Not too tired,' he answered with a silent laugh. 'As you probably noticed. What about you?'

'I've done practically nothing,' she confessed, 'except feed the hens and collect eggs and clean them. And a bit of dusting. That took a while.' The pervasive dust invaded the house and coated everything. 'Your mother's a frighteningly efficient lady – I feel I'm just getting in the way.'

'She's been doing it for a long time. There's no hurry to take over.'

'I have no intention of taking over!' She didn't want to usurp his mother's position in the house. 'I just wanted to do something. I'm not going to spend my days sitting around waiting for you to come home.'

'You'll have the baby to think about in a few months' time. You won't be doing much sitting around then. Why not just enjoy doing nothing for while?' He found her mouth with his and kissed her lingeringly, his hands roving over her newly burgeoning body, and despite their recent lovemaking, a faint echo of the familiar liquid fire raced through her.

Then he kissed her cheek, her forehead, and tucked her head against his shoulder, and went almost instantly to sleep.

Skye's attempt to help with breakfast for the musterers the next morning was notably unsuccessful. The smell of the sizzling steak and onions sent her retching to the utility room, and after that she kept out of the way until the cooking odours had dispersed.

Before ten o'clock Ella made an enormous batch of scones and a bowl of pikelet mixture. Skye turned the pikelets on the skillet that her mother-in-law had used, she said, since the early days of her marriage when all the cooking was done on a wood range in the old homestead.

'I'll get these into the Nissan and take them down to the men for smoko,' Ella said as they finished buttering a pile of scones and placed them in baskets lined with clean tea-towels. 'You'll be all right for a while, Skye?'

'Couldn't I come along?' The yards were not far from the house; she could hear the distant bellowing of the cattle, and even an occasional male yell.

The older woman looked doubtful. 'It's dirty and smelly down there.'

'I'd still like to come.' The sickness of the morning had passed off and she felt quite normal. 'Can I help you carry some of these?' She picked up a basket of still-warm scones wrapped in a checked tea-towel.

The cattle milling about in the yards raised a red haze over the area. The rich, pungent reek of manure filled the air, and when the workers gathered round to grab their share of Ella's baking the smell of sweat was almost as strong. Over an open fire nearby a large soot-blackened billy had been boiled, and most of the men had a tin cup of steaming milkless tea along with their buttered scones and pikelets.

As Skye uncovered a basket of scones and held it out for the eager men, waving away the flies that threatened to beat them to it, a hand fell on her shoulder. 'What do you think you're doing?' Jarrah's voice said in her ear.

'Helping your mother.' She turned to him, meeting the grey-green eyes under the shade of his bushman's hat. His face and throat were streaked with sweat and red dust, and his shirt was damp. 'And having a look at what's going on.'

Kelly came up, briefly removing her own hat to push back wayward strands of hair and grinning at her. 'Good on you, Skye.'

'You haven't even got a hat,' Jarrah grumbled. He removed his own and dropped it on her head.

'You should know better than to go out without one, with your skin.'

She tipped the hat back a little and smiled at him. 'Next time I'll remember.'

'See that you do.' He wasn't smiling. 'Are you feeling okay?'

'Absolutely.'

The men finished their tea and returned to work, and Jarrah walked away and picked up a clipboard he'd left lying on the ground by the metal-barred fence.

Skye and Ella shook crumbs from the tea-towels and stacked the empty baskets. Ella climbed into the driver's seat and waited for Skye.

Skye put her hand on the door frame and paused. 'Would you mind if I stayed for a while and watched?' she asked. 'I can walk back when I've had enough.' It couldn't be more than a mile or so to the homestead.

Ella hesitated. 'I'm not sure what Jarrah will say about it.'

'I'll deal with Jarrah,' Skye told her confidently. 'See you later.'

She stepped back and waved, but it was a second or two before Ella turned the key and the Nissan started moving away, and Skye made her way back to the yards.

Hundreds of beasts were milling about in a holding paddock. Stockmen herded them to the yards, and others operated gates into narrow races leading to a series of pens and a central ring.

Jarrah stood outside the ring, with one foot resting on a fence rail, making notes on a clip-board and pointing or calling an instruction to the men who swung the gates to deftly send their charges in the right direction.

Cows were temporarily separated from their young calves, and Skye felt a pang of sympathy as the mothers were shunted off to a grassed paddock while their imprisoned offspring blatted pathetically. Some of the cows gathered anxiously about the fence-line, while others grazed indifferently, now and then raising their heads to give a reassuring moo to their babies trapped in the pens.

A big brown bull charged into the enclosure, snorting and tossing his horned head, and rushed straight for one of the stockmen standing by a gate. The man hastily nipped round the gate and shut it.

The bull's sharp, curved horns rang against the metal, then it backed off to race around the ring, kicking up a dust storm.

'He missed dehorning,' Skye commented.

Jarrah glanced at her. 'That's a scrubber – a bull that's dodged the muster for a couple of years.'

The bull lowered its head and started across the confined space towards them. Jarrah's hand closed on Skye's arm, hauling her back as the short but deadly horns raked the fence.

'Truck the brute!' Jarrah called to the stockmen at the gates.

'Are you getting rid of him because of his temper?' Skye asked.

'It doesn't help his chances, that's for sure. We can do without his genes in the herd.'

One of the men, a patterned kerchief tied over his nose against the choking dust, stepped into the enclosure. 'Come on, you stupid bastard, this way!' He waved his arms.

The bull, accepting the invitation, snorted and trotted menacingly towards him.

The man leapt for the bars of the fence near the open gate and perched on top.

The bull stopped at the gate, suspicious, then backed off.

The stockman leaned down with a cattle prod in his hand and gingerly touched the animal's flank. The bull jumped indignantly and shot forward, only to fall over its own feet and come crashing down between the metal sides of the narrow race.

Jarrah swore quietly and the man at the gate did so much more loudly and a good deal more colourfully.

The bull roared and struggled, jammed in the confined space, its legs through the bars and its short neck twisted.

'Here, hold this.' Jarrah handed the clipboard to Skye, and her heart leapt into her throat as he vaulted the fence into the ring.

Two men were already gingerly trying to help the downed animal. Of course it didn't appreciate their efforts, waving its lethal horns and kicking its deadly hooves at anyone who came near.

It took five men and a rope, and when in the end the bull was hauled upright and sent off down the race with a slap on its rump Skye's hands were damp on the clipboard she was clutching to her chest.

'Go easy with the prod,' Jarrah tersely advised the stockman on the gate. 'You know it stirs them up.'

Wiping dust and sweat from his face with a crumpled kerchief, he crossed the ring again and rejoined Skye, taking the clipboard from her. 'Where's my mother?' he asked her. 'Isn't it time you two were getting back?'

'I'm walking back. Your mother's gone.'

'She left you here alone?' He scowled.

'I asked her to, and I'm not alone. I'm with my husband.'

'I don't have time to look after you, dammit!'

Skye counted to five. 'I don't need looking after. I'm a grown woman with two perfectly good legs, and when I'm ready I'll walk back to the house.'

'It's too far.'

Skye laughed at him. 'I'm used to jogging further than that. And I can do with the exercise." '

Another group of cattle were trotted towards the ring, and one of the men called, 'Hey, Jarrah! You ready?'

'Hang on!' he called back, his eyes still on Skye. 'Then you'd better start walking,' he suggested.

He was dismissing her like a naughty child. He didn't want her here.

'Your hat.' She raised her hand to take it off.

'Keep it on,' he said curtly. 'I don't need it.' He turned away and nodded to the men.

Skye swung on her heel and stalked off.

Skirting a corner of the yards, she saw Kelly with a bunch of men near the pen where the younger calves were, and detoured to have a look.

The calves were pretty creatures, with big dark eyes and soft ears. One frightened little animal was let out of the pen, and two men grabbed it and locked it expertly into a metal cradle so that it was firmly confined and lying on its side. Kelly took an iron rod from a cylindrical apparatus on a tripod with a gas bottle underneath. Skye guessed, seconds before the glowing end was applied to the calf's rump, that the rod was a branding iron. A man closed an instrument that looked like a pair of pliers on one of the calf's ears, and another man wielded a knife that glittered in the sun – Skye closed her eyes.

When she opened them again the calf was released and scrambled to its feet, castrated, earmarked and branded, and was allowed to run off to its anxious mother who came galloping to its side and sniffed it all over before allowing it a comforting drink while the next calf suffered the same fate.

The smell of blood and singed hair and flesh was strong, and Skye abruptly turned to walk blindly in another direction.

Her vision swam, and she had to swallow down a sudden sickness. She stepped on a stone buried in the dry red earth, and stumbled.

Then a hard hand closed on her arm and Jarrah's voice said, 'I told you to go home.'

Skye didn't dare look up at him. 'I'm going.' She tried to pull away. 'I got a bit lost.'

'Already?' His voice was harsh, maybe sarcastic.

Skye turned her head away so he couldn't see her expression. She had a nasty feeling that she'd gone white under the gritty film of red dust.

'Skye?' Jarrah whipped his hat away from her face and looked at her closely. 'You're ill!'

'I'm all right,' she said. 'I'll just . . . sit down for a minute.' Her temples were cold and black spots had started dancing before her eyes. She was horribly afraid she was going throw up at Jarrah's feet.

She sank down by the nearest fence, and he squatted beside her, letting go a stream of soft curses as she lowered her head onto her raised knees, fighting the waves of nausea.

'You shouldn't have tried to watch,' Jarrah said.

'I didn't realize – I haven't seen it before.'

'It looks cruel, I know. I can't say it doesn't hurt them,' he admitted, 'only that we use the most humane methods we know of, and it's all over in a matter of seconds.'

Skye lifted her head carefully and nodded. 'I'm all right now.' To her relief the surroundings had steadied and she could look Jarrah in the face. 'I'm sorry. Go back to work.' She started to get up.

'The hell I will.' He helped her to her feet. 'Erik!' he yelled. 'I'm taking Skye to the house. Five minutes, okay?'

He bundled her into a vehicle, and in a couple of minutes was skidding to a halt outside the kitchen doorway. Before she could protest he was helping her down and marching her into the kitchen where Ella and a little bow-legged man were preparing a mountain of substantial sandwiches.

'Skye's feeling seedy,' Jarrah told his mother. 'Look after her, will you? I have to get back to the yards.'

He grabbed his hat from Skye's head, kissed her cheek, and then he was gone.

'I'm all right,' she insisted to Ella. 'Jarrah's fussing. It was just a bit of nausea, but it's over now.'

She'd reacted badly to the unexpectedly gory scene, and no doubt she'd been a thorough nuisance to Jarrah, he'd made that all too obvious.

Refusing to lie down and rest, she weighed in to help instead – buttering, filling, piling sandwiches onto plates, and cutting slabs of fruit cake to follow, while she quietly fumed.

She wasn't alone with Jarrah until the end of the day, when she was standing at the open doors to the balcony in her nightgown, gazing at the immense black arch of the sky blazing with stars all the way to the horizon.

Then he came and took her in his arms and let out a long sigh, nuzzling his cheek against her hair and said, 'I've been waiting for this for hours! You scared me today. Are you sure you're feeling okay now?'

And she didn't have the heart to start a quarrel.

The next phase of the muster was farther afield, and Jarrah was away for five days.

Skye's boxes arrived on the rural delivery run, and she arranged her books and a few treasured curios on a set of shelves in the master bedroom. The woodcut that Jarrah had given her she hung on the wall near the bed, replacing a rather faded tapestry picture of an English-style thatched cottage.

Unpacking her Pentax, she remembered there was some film in it. She must see about getting some more. The next morning she crept down the stairs at dawn and took some photographs of the opal waterhole, the stark outlines of the ghost gums against the morning sky, and a solitary ibis that stalked along the edge of the water before flapping its wings and soaring off into the sunrise.

When she asked about having the film developed Ella said, 'Send it away in the mailbag, and it'll probably be back with next week's run. You can order some more film at the same time.'

Ella was considerate and sympathetic to her bouts of sickness, but Skye suspected the other woman preferred to carry on with her established routine without having to make room in her schedule for a willing but inexperienced daughter-in-law.

The carefully tended shrubs and trees around the homestead were a triumph of will – and water – over the harsh outback conditions. Surprisingly, there were a number of rose beds planted with mature, healthy bushes. 'They do well here,' Ella told Skye. 'They like the dryness.' She had even established a small orchard with the aid of water pumped from the creek that fed the waterhole.

When her rolls of film arrived Skye photographed the garden and the house from all angles, and used a whole roll at the opal pool, capturing the changing colours of the water, the reflections of the trees, the big long-billed and spindle-legged brolgas that sometimes danced with outspread wings at its reedy edge, and the flocks of red-winged parrots that settled in the branches and exploded without warning against the limitless outback sky.

When the musterers at last took a break Jarrah gave them a week to rest before the next phase. Most of the men promptly disappeared in their four-wheel drives, a dusty convoy roaring away down the road, raising clouds of bulldust that hung in the air long after the engine noises had died. 'Heading for the pub at Coolya,' Kelly guessed knowledgeably.

'Well, I'm heading for the pool,' Jarrah said. 'Skye? How about a swim?'

'Me too,' Kelly joined in. 'You coming, Erik?'

Skye wrapped a loose robe over her swimsuit, and didn't slip it off until she was ready to go into the water. Although she told herself this was only family, she was conscious of the now perceptible changes in her figure.

Kelly and Erik splashed about and horse-played, but Jarrah wasn't allowing any of that near Skye. He stayed at her side, and when she got out he climbed out too, and after she'd partially dried off with a towel, he picked up the robe to drape it round her shoulders, keeping his arm about her as she made to go inside.

'You don't need to come with me if you'd rather swim some more,' she told him.

Jarrah shook his head. 'I've cooled off. That's all I needed.'

In their room he closed the door and she went into the bathroom to wriggle out of her wet swimsuit and hang it over the bath. She was wrapping a towel about her when Jarrah tapped on the door and walked in, naked and with his swimbriefs in his hand.

He slung them from the shower rail and

turned, catching her from behind as she fastened the towel under her arms. 'How's Junior?' he murmured, his lips on her shoulder, his hands resting on the slight mound that hid their baby.

Something moved under his palm, and she said, 'Does that answer your question?'

His soft laughter warmed her skin. One hand began stroking her, moving to her towelling-covered breast. 'And how are you?' He breathed in. 'You smell wonderful.'

'I probably smell of chlorine.'

'No, you smell of woman. My woman.'

'Caveman.' But her voice was uneven, breathless. She could already feel his arousal.

'Mm.' Jarrah's hand found her hair and gently tugged, turning her to face him. He was smiling tautly, his eyes almost pure green, lazy-lidded. 'Me Tarzan,' he grunted, and caught her laughter with his parted lips on hers.

His hands slid under the towel behind her, and he lifted her against him, their mouths still clinging, and walked into the bedroom, laying her down gently on the cover and turned so they were face to face on their sides.

The towel was soon discarded, and a finger circled her breast. 'They're different,' he said.

'Do you mind?'

'Of course I don't mind! He shaped the new

fullness with his palm. 'I did this to you. I find that very . . . exciting. Do *you* mind that?'

Her heartbeat had just increased. 'No.'

'Are they tender?'

'A bit.' But she placed her hand over his to keep it there.

'I'll be very careful,' Jarrah promised, and lowered his mouth to kiss her there.

Skye lay back with a sigh of bliss. 'I've missed you,' she confessed quietly.

He lifted his head, while his hand made a foray across her breasts, down to the soft rise of her belly. 'I've been crazy with wanting you. I hardly slept.'

She lifted a knee, and he ran his hand up her thigh and back again. 'I had fantasies of racing back to you at midnight, throwing you over my saddle and riding off with you.'

Skye laughed. 'On Moonfleet? He'd hate that.' The stallion had disdained her effort at friendship, lifting his head suspiciously and looking down his long nose as he snorted at her.

Jarrah's roving hand closed about her ankle, his thumb moving over her skin. He lifted her foot and kissed the curve of her instep. 'Even your feet are gorgeous.'

'Soon I won't be able to see them.'

He smiled at her, running his hand up her calf

and back to her thigh and hip. 'Does it bother you?'

'Losing my figure? Only if it bothers you.'

Shaking his head, he said, 'How could it? That's my baby – and you're not losing anything, you're gaining.'

'Weight, yes!' Skye grimaced.

'Loveliness,' he argued, his palm skimming her breasts again, her throat, settling on her cheek. 'Don't you know you're more beautiful than ever? My mother said some women glow when they're pregnant. You're one of them.'

If the look in his eyes was anything to go by, it was true. And his physical state certainly affirmed his words. She killed the sneaky thought that any woman might have looked wonderful to him after days on end of battling ever-present dust and mobs of recalcitrant, smelly cattle, and hooked her arms about his neck. Instead of one snatched night when he would make love to her with the greatest care and consideration, but fall instantly asleep afterwards and be up before dawn to ride out with the other musterers, they had a whole week. She parted her lips to his deeply satisfying kiss.

'Tell me what you want,' he murmured against her throat. 'Don't let me hurt you.'

'You never hurt me.' He was so cautious with her she sometimes became almost impatient.

'I'm pregnant, not breakable!'

'You look breakable.' He stroked her shoulder, her arm, picked up her slender fingers and took them to his mouth. 'You're so . . .. fine-boned.'

'Illusion,' she told him. 'For God's sake, Jarrah, make love to me properly!'

She heard his breath catch in his chest, and moved her legs so that he couldn't mistake the invitation. Then he gathered her to him and did as she'd asked.

'We should have a party,' Kelly suggested at breakfast, 'to introduce Skye to the district.'

Her mother looked from her to Skye. 'If you feel up to it, would you like that?'

'Of course she would!' Kelly answered for her. 'She's hardly seen anyone except stockmen and contractors, and the women are *dying* to meet her.'

'Won't it be a lot of work for you?' Skye worried, turning to Ella.

'We're used to large-scale entertaining here. If you'd like it . . .'

'It's not a bad idea,' Jarrah decided. 'But everyone's mustering. Make a date for next month, give people time to work round it.'

'Great!' Kelly put down her coffee cup. 'So when would be a good day?' By the time breakfast was over she'd got Jarrah pinned down to a date and was ready to start phoning and faxing the 'neighbours'.

After she'd helped clear the table, Skye went to the office where Jarrah was working on the computer, and tentatively mentioned that she was overdue for a medical check.

'I'll fly you to Mt. Isa,' Jarrah promised. 'My mother and Kelly will probably come too. We can spare a couple of days.'

'Isn't there a doctor at Coolya?'

'The road's pretty rough. Flying to the Isa's quicker, and anyway, the doctor only has a clinic up here once a week.'

'You mean there's no permanent doctor?'

'The nearest one's five hours off by road.'

Carefully Skye said, 'Then what happens when I go into labour?'

'Don't worry,' Jarrah said easily. 'We'll make sure you're well away before then.'

CHAPTER 10

Away.

Skye went cold. 'Away?'

Jarrah looked blankly at her, then stood up and urged her into the chair he'd vacated. 'You can't have it here,' he said patiently, as if it was something she ought to have known. 'You'll have to leave at least six to eight weeks before the baby's due.'

'What about the flying doctor service?'

'That's for emergencies. They don't encourage pregnant women to wait until the last minute. Most women go to the nearest town with a hospital and a permanent doctor and stay at a motel or with relatives. You could fly down to Brisbane and stay with Beth.'

'You said you wanted to look after me and the baby!'

'I *am* looking after you. I'll get you the best medical care available. If you're worried that something's wrong we can phone the flying doctor service and get advice any time.'

'It's just that I assumed there'd be someone closer. And I didn't expect to have to leave weeks before the baby's due! If I need to do that I'd rather go and stay with my parents in New Zealand.'

Jarrah leaned back against the desk, and looked thoughtful. 'Probably not a bad idea. I'd know you were being looked after then.'

'You . . . you're not intending to come with me?' Skye felt hollow – winded.

He shook his head regretfully. 'I'll be there in time for the birth, but I can't see us finishing the cattle muster before we have to start sheep-shearing. The last of the cattle won't be trucked out until November. We had a late start this year.'

And that, of course, had been because of her.

After accompanying her to the medical centre in Mt. Isa and checking that the doctor had found nothing to cause concern, Jarrah suggested they visit the bank and have Skye's signature added to his bank account and credit card.

'I don't need your money,' she told him.

'Not yet, maybe. I'd just like to know you can use my accounts if you have to,' he said.

'I don't know what for. And then you should

have access to my accounts too,' she pointed out.

'It's not the same.'

Skye smiled. 'Why not?'

'You're not earning, for one thing.'

'I have interest from some investments, and the rent from my flat.' But she agreed to fill in the necessary forms, warning him that she probably would never use them. Then he went to inspect farm equipment while the women did their shopping.

Mt. Isa was a sprawling town surrounded by red hills, and smoke from the mines hung over its heart. They stayed in a motel and ate at a nearby restaurant. Next day Skye found a bookshop and bought a couple of photographic magazines as well as a how-to on developing for beginners. She had never had time to think about processing her own films, but she'd become frustrated with sending them off and waiting for them to be returned on the rural delivery van. She could at least investigate the feasibility of learning how to do it, find out what equipment and chemicals she'd need.

'I need a new dress for the party,' Kelly had decided. 'What about you, Skye? I know you've got plenty of lovely clothes, but will they fit you now?'

She was going to need maternity clothing. She was rapidly approaching the stage where leaving buttons and zips undone and wearing her shirts and blouses outside skirts and jeans wasn't going to be enough.

While Kelly tried on dresses, Skye found a pair of maternity slacks and some rather uninspiring dresses and skirts made for mothers-to-be, and asked for opinions.

'The pink dress was all right,' Ella said. 'The slacks are too short in the leg.'

Kelly wrinkled her nose. 'No, they all look yuck on you.'

'That's what I thought.' Skye sighed. 'Do they have pattern books here? If I could find some material maybe I could make some up.'

'Can you sew?' Kelly asked her.

'A bit.' She had learned basic sewing at school, and having watched designers and their staff at work, sometimes almost remaking a dress on the model, she had picked up some useful knowledge. 'I sewed some of the furnishings for my flat.' She had enjoyed that, creating pretty surroundings for herself. Now her sewing machine was sitting in the bottom of the wardrobe at Opal Reach. 'You don't sew?'

'I tried a couple of times in the Wet, but I kept sewing the wrong pieces together and having to unpick all the time, and I got fed up with it in the end. Not my thing. Anyway, let's see what we can hunt up.'

Skye bought patterns and several lengths of fabric, and all the thread, buttons, stiffening and zips that she needed, using her credit card.

Kelly had taken a fancy to one of the patterns herself, and Skye offered to make it for her. Delighted, Kelly selected a fabric with her mother's and Skye's help.

'I used to make clothes for the children,' Ella confided, 'but now I use the machine mainly for mending. I'd rather be in the garden.'

The week was soon over and the men came whooping back ready for another round of mustering. Jarrah had spent much of the time since returning from Mt. Isa catching up on paperwork, Kelly had involved Skye in plans for the party, and it seemed to Skye the time had gone far too fast.

At night she had Jarrah to herself. She had looked forward to having the chance to really talk together in private, but when it came to the point she realized with a faint sense of panic that she knew nothing about his day-to-day activities, and that whatever she did all day was not exactly a riveting topic of conversation.

Answering questions about Opal Reach and cattle management soon palled for Jarrah, and eventually he'd laugh and tell her to stop playing the dutiful wife asking her husband how his day had been, pull her into his arms and kiss her ruthlessly into silence.

After they'd made love he would hold her and press soft kisses on her temples and cheeks, and tell her to go to sleep.

Jarrah went off again with the muster, and Skye kept herself busy sewing. She thought Ella was probably relieved that her daughter-in-law had found something to occupy her besides getting in the way with unwanted offers of help. But she was allowed to take part in the preparation of quantities of food required for the party.

It was a noisy, rather boisterous affair. Whole families arrived from mid-afternoon onward, and the women invaded the kitchen. The old homestead and workers' quarters housed some of the guests, while others brought their own tents. Tables were set up on the veranda, and after dark Erik and some other men barbecued sausages and steaks over an open fire, though the night was distinctly cool, and even the children had forsaken the swimming pool and put on warm clothes.

After everyone had eaten, the men, with tinnies of beer in their hands, congregated in groups near the barbecue and the women gravitated inside.

Skye wore one of her newly made dresses, not

too obviously designed to disguise pregnancy, but she felt nevertheless the covert stares that came her way, and guessed that speculation was rife.

Jarrah was congratulated on all sides and came in for a good many teasing remarks about dark horses and disappointment for the local girls. A couple of the women appeared overawed, blurting out that they'd seen Skye's picture in magazines, or watched her TV ads.

She was glad to recognize the couple she and Jarrah had met at Surfers Paradise. Megan Poynter greeted her with mock commiseration on joining the ranks of 'outback wives'.

Megan was full of a new scheme that she and her husband had devised to supplement their income. 'We thought we'd try advertising for overseas guests who want to experience station life. We've already had a few visitors. It's fun. We get to meet people from all over the world, and we've been invited to visit some of them. Next Wet I intend to persuade Steve to take me to Japan. We had the dearest Japanese couple with us for a week, and they said they'd show us round, because we don't know a word of Japanese. I might enquire about lessons though. The Japanese tourist trade would be a good thing to get into.'

'I could help you if you like,' Skye suggested.

'I know the language.'

'You speak Japanese? That would be fantastic! Someone to practise on, even if we have to do it by phone.'

One of the neighbouring station owners made an impromptu speech welcoming Skye to the district and congratulating Jarrah on his good fortune, referring to his well-known penchant for 'the best of everything', citing stud bulls, stallions and machinery, and apparently comparing them with the 'world-renowned beauty' he had secured as his wife.

Exaggeration aside, Skye wasn't thrilled with the analogies, but appreciated the sentiment, she told Jarrah in whisper, answering his laughing, rueful glance at her before he replied to the toast and the enthusiastic applause that had followed.

Kelly put on a sentimental dance record, and Jarrah swung Skye into the space that had been cleared in the big front room.

Other couples joined them and he looked down at her, smiling. 'Enjoying yourself? Or is it all something of an ordeal?'

'A bit of both,' she confessed. 'Everyone seems nice, but I'll never remember all their names.'

'No one will expect you to. You'll get to know people in time.'

Skye wondered when she'd get the chance.

'Do you do this sort of thing very often?'

'Not often,' he admitted. 'We have a yearly campdrafting event, and when the muster's finished we hold a dance to celebrate.'

'Campdrafting?' Skye was bemused. 'What's that?'

'That's when our horses come into their own. People come from all over for it. And in between those shindigs, there's always the phone,' he added. 'Some outback wives are best friends with women they've never even met face to face.'

Having talked with the women, Skye was awed at the activities they managed to pack into their busy lives. Many of them worked the stock alongside their men, besides cooking for large numbers of seasonal workers and supervising their children's lessons. Several were taking correspondence lessons of their own, and one had qualified in computer science and set up a part-time business as an internet researcher.

'You look fantastic tonight,' Jarrah told her, sweeping her into a turn. 'I'm the envy of every man in the district.'

Skye grimaced down at the bulge which prevented him from holding her close and said, 'Even with this?'

'Even with this.' He dropped his hand and touched her. 'My son – or daughter.'

'Do you mind which it is?' They had never discussed if either of them had a preference.

Jarrah shook his head. 'As long as it's healthy and has the requisite number of fingers and toes, that's all I ask.'

He put both his arms about her and laid his chin against her temple, murmuring, 'I see young Erik's chatting up our helicopter girl.'

'Don't you approve?' She detected a note of reservation in his voice.

'He's young yet. Mind you, she'd be an asset to the family.'

'Your own tame muster pilot?'

'There is that.'

She'd be more useful than Skye, then. A girl who'd been reared in the outback, who knew cattle and modern machinery. One who wouldn't faint at the sight of a branding iron, and could work alongside her man.

The band finished the bracket with a flourish, and Jarrah tucked her close to his side. 'Come for a walk in the moonlight with me,' he said, his eyes glinting as he looked down at her. 'I thought I'd go check on Stardust. She looks due to drop her foal any time now, and as it's her first I want to keep an eye on her.'

The moon was full and bright tonight, and Skye waited by the fence as he unlocked the gate and went into the paddock.

The mare was down, and Skye saw Jarrah bend over her, heard her whicker at him as she raised her head.

He stayed there a few minutes, then came back to her. 'She's started, but I don't like the look of things. Do you remember Clem Williams?'

'The vet, yes.' She'd talked with him for a while earlier.

'See if you can find him and ask him to come and have a look, will you?'

'Of course.' She started to hurry away, and Jarrah said sharply, 'Don't run. Just get him here when you find him.'

It took a few minutes, and she followed the man back down to the paddock. While the two men worked over the mare she stood by, feeling helpless and in the way but reluctant to leave.

'Can I do anything?' she asked finally.

Jarrah said, 'No.'

'Go to her head and talk to her, stroke her if you like,' the vet instructed. 'Try to keep her calm.'

Jarrah looked up and she thought he might object, but he said nothing. She knelt by the animal's head, murmuring whatever words of comfort and encouragement she could think of.

After a while Kelly joined them. 'I heard you were looking for Clem,' she told Skye, 'and guessed why.'

'Glad you're here,' Clem said to her, and sent her to fetch something from his car. 'She's not doing too well,' he muttered. 'Come on, girl, you've got to work at it, you know.'

Skye wanted to snap, 'She is!' The mare's deep grunts and spasms of effort wrung her heart, and under Skye's stroking fingers the silky coat was damp with sweat.

Kelly came back and shone a torch on proceedings while the two men struggled to help the foal and its mother. Skye concentrated on her task of trying to keep the mare calm.

At last the vet said, 'Here we go! Yep, that's it.'

In the torchlight Skye saw a wet, shining, shapeless bundle, and put her arms about the horse's neck. 'You did it!' she said into the twitching ear. 'Good girl!'

Then she heard Jarrah's low curse and an exclamation from Kelly.

'What is it?' she said, straightening, and began to get to her feet. 'What's the matter?'

'Sorry,' Clem said regretfully.

Skye started towards them, her eyes on the foal that she couldn't see properly. Then Jarrah reached out and swung his sister's arm up, and the light danced wildly, dazzling Skye as it turned towards her. 'What is it?' she repeated. 'Is it dead?'

'No, but –' she heard Kelly say, even as Jarrah's harsh, 'Yes,' overrode his sister.

Confused, and blinking against the light, Skye said, 'Can't you do something?' Weren't there ways to get a newborn animal breathing?

Clem stood with his hands on his hips, looking down. 'It's up to you, Jarrah.'

Jarrah said, 'Go back to the house, Skye.'

'But – '

'Don't argue,' he said roughly. 'Kelly, take her away, will you.'

'Sure.' Kelly stepped forward and put an arm about Skye's waist.

'I just want to see – '

'No, you don't,' Kelly said firmly. 'Jarrah's right. Come on, Skye, let's go.'

Reluctantly, Skye let herself be led away. 'Couldn't Clem do anything?' she asked. 'What was wrong?'

'It's not exactly a perfect foal, that's all. Jarrah will be awfully disappointed.' Kelly grimaced wryly. 'Even he can't get it right every time.'

Skye's new dress was covered in dirt and horse sweat. In the bathroom she put the dress into the laundry basket, and had a shower. When Jarrah came in twenty minutes later she was in bed with the lamp on.

'Are you all right?' he asked her.

'Yes. I didn't think anyone would mind if I didn't go back to the party.'

He was dirty too and his clothes had blood on them. 'I'll just clean up.'

'You'll want to go back to your guests.'

He stopped in the door to the bathroom. 'Not necessarily. They won't miss me.'

When he returned she had switched off the lamp but was still awake. Outside the sounds of revelry were dying.

The mattress depressed as he slipped under the sheet beside her. He touched her shoulder, murmured her name.

'You killed it, didn't you?' She stared at the dim whiteness of the ceiling. 'The foal.'

'We put it down, yes.'

'Kelly said it wasn't perfect.'

'It had a deformation. Maybe there's a recessive gene involved. We can try mating Stardust properly with a different stallion.'

'What if she has another one like that?'

'It's unlikely, but if that happens I'll have to eliminate her from the breeding programme.' Jarrah put an arm about her. 'I should have sent you away sooner.'

'I'm not made of glass!'

'You didn't need to see that, though, in your condition.' He kissed her cheek. 'You were very helpful tonight.'

Her help hadn't saved Stardust's foal. And after sending her to find Clem, Jarrah hadn't thought she could be of any more use.

Jarrah's mouth wandered to her lips. Irritably she shrugged away from him. 'It's been a tiring day.'

'I guess it has,' he said after a moment. 'I'll let you go to sleep.'

Somehow the thought of the foal she had never clearly seen haunted Skye. She even dreamed about it sometimes, troubling dreams full of foreboding and tears.

When there was another pause in the mustering routine Jarrah told Skye to book an antenatal appointment and asked if afterwards she'd like to go to Brisbane or even Sydney for a few days. 'We haven't had a honeymoon, and I can spare a week or ten days.'

'You can?' She hadn't meant to sound sharp. She knew that he wasn't personally to blame for the unrelenting work schedule that kept him out on the property from dawn till dusk for eight or nine months of the year. And she wasn't normally an unreasonable person.

Perhaps it was her pregnancy that made her feel fretful and neglected. 'I'd like to stay near a beach,' she said, deliberately softening her voice. She had never been so far from the sea before and was surprised at how badly she missed it.

Jarrah booked them a room in a luxury hotel at Surfers Paradise. For a whole week they lazed, and walked on the beach, and swam, and dined in the hotel's elegant ambience, or for a change in one of the small ethnic restaurants nearby. And for eight nights they returned to their room on the tenth floor and, with the curtains opened to the black starry sky and the darkened sea outside, made love in the wide, luxurious bed.

Jarrah was careful to temper his passion with tenderness, and always ensured that she wanted him as much as he desired her.

She had worried that despite his repeated assurances in the early stages, he might be turned off by her ballooning shape, but he told her she had grown more beautiful than ever, and when he brought her to sobbing fulfilment in his arms, she cried out her love to him, over and over.

'You'll be a good father,' she told him one afternoon, lying in the tumbled sheets while the sun cast a filtered golden light through the curtains as it dipped low in the sky.

'I'll try to be,' he said, putting one hand over hers where it lay on his chest, and settling her more comfortably against his shoulder.

'What was your father like?' she asked. All she knew of him was a photograph on the seldom-used piano in the homestead's front room – a head and shoulders shot of a blue-eyed, square-jawed man with his brown hair sleeked ruthlessly back, staring at the camera with an air of discomfort.

'What was he like?' Jarrah repeated. 'He was . . . a big man. In every way. Not talkative, and not given to shows of affection. His praise was hard-earned, but when he gave it you knew you *had* earned it, so you valued it. He was fair-minded, but also bloodyminded on occasion. Once he'd made a decision he stuck with it come hell or high water. So he didn't make them lightly.'

'You said he wasn't very open to new ideas.'

'Right. But once he'd looked at a thing from all angles and finally made up his mind, there was no changing it.' Jarrah gave a small laugh. 'I believe my mother was practically engaged to someone else when Dad first sighted her.'

'She said they'd known each other for two years before they were married.'

'Well, he soon saw the other guy off, I'm told. But all the same, he wasn't going to rush into anything.'

'*Who* told you?' Skye asked curiously. 'Your mother?'

'Hell no! And certainly not my father. One of my uncles let it out when we were talking after my father's funeral. He'd had a few drinks, and . . . well, it was that sort of day. All sorts of reminiscences and confidences came out – family skeletons.'

'Skeletons?'

'Not really. But my uncle did tell me things I hadn't known about my parents. Dad was a good bit older than my mother, and she was a looker in her day. Uncle Pat thinks he worried for a while about the age difference. It was a long courtship, partly because of the distance he had to travel to see her, and partly, I should think, because he – or both of them – needed to be sure they weren't making a mistake.'

'But they had a lot in common.'

'Yes – and I think they were happy.'

'Your mother must miss your father a lot.'

'We all do. As I said, he was a big man, and he left a large hole in our lives.'

'And you were expected to fill his shoes, at only twenty?'

'It wasn't easy,' Jarrah admitted. 'I'd gone head to head with the old man several times over modernizing some of the ways the place was run, but when the responsibility suddenly devolved on me – that was scary.'

'Didn't your mother advise you? She must have known a lot about the station by then.'

'She'd never had to make the decisions about

how or when things were done. That was Dad's job. And when I took over, it was mine. One thing, she never criticised when I made mistakes.'

And, Skye guessed, Ella had carefully not criticised his choice of bride either. Even if she thought that too was a mistake.

Then they returned to Opal Reach and the everlasting demands of the muster, and over the next couple of months the closeness they had begun to forge seemed to evaporate.

The musterers were working one of the far paddocks and expected to take ten days or so to brand and castrate the cleanskins and walk the fats and weaners in for trucking.

A week after they'd left Kelly drove in to take some fresh drinking water and supplies to the muster camp, 'Because the water at that bore is too minerally for human consumption,' she explained to Skye.

The Nissan was loaded with a wire cage, 'To pick up calves,' Kelly said. 'New ones get exhausted if they have to walk too far to the yards. The camp where they'll be tonight is about a day from the yards they're headed for, so I'll take some calves up and drop them off for a bit of rest, and they'll be matched up with their mothers when the rest of the muster comes in.'

'I wish I could come with you,' Skye said.

'Why don't you?' Kelly suggested. 'You could stay overnight and I can bring you back tomorrow when I've dropped off the calves at the yards.'

Could she? 'You wouldn't mind?'

'Why should I? You're not getting sick any more, and you're not likely to go into labour or anything at this stage, are you?'

'I promise I won't. What do I need to bring?'

'I'll fix you up with a swag for sleeping. You might want a change of undies, and a clean shirt. And your toothbrush.'

Ella was doubtful about the plan, but Kelly and Skye were not to be deterred. 'You rode stock when you were pregnant, Mum,' Kelly reminded her. 'And Skye's only got to sit in a nice comfortable cab while I drive. It can't do her any harm.'

'I was used to roughing it,' Ella worried. 'It's different for Skye.'

Skye laughed. 'I'm no frail flower. The doctor says I'm very healthy, and believe me, I haven't been used to being coddled. Modelling demands stamina and a certain level of fitness.'

Ella shook her head, but made no more objections. Skye climbed into the cab beside Kelly and they took off.

The sun climbed over a gold and ochre landscape of grass, rocks and scarred earth. Kelly detoured around big termite mounds jutting randomly from the ground, and flocks of birds were startled from the scattered trees by the approaching vehicle.

A dozen kangaroos bounded along parallel with the Nissan, and Kelly drew to a brief halt while Skye got several photos before the animals disappeared over the brow of a jump-up.

'Do you have many of them on the property?'

'We keep the numbers down,' Kelly said pragmatically. 'They eat feed that we need for the cattle. But we don't want to wipe them out altogether. Jarrah doesn't have any time for people who weep over every dead kangaroo, but he's pretty hot about the ones who shoot them just because they're there. He won't even lay poison for dingoes.'

'Are there a lot of dingoes?'

'It's not a huge problem round here. Most people put down 1080 poison. But that'll kill our dogs too. We do shoot dingoes that we see near the stock, and sometimes we have to hunt one down that's taking the calves or lambs. They're more of a problem with sheep than cattle.'

Over parts of the journey Skye could discern a faint track across the scanty grass between the sparse and twisted trees, but often Kelly seemed to be driving blind. Skye asked what the trees were, and Kelly pointed out ironbark, sandalwood, wilga and gidgee. 'Keep away from gidgees after rain.' She drove through a thicker belt of trees, under branches that scraped the canopy. 'Their other name is stink-wattle, and water brings out the most awful smell from the bark.'

Then they were out the other side and the only vegetation was sparse, stunted bushes and the long, pale Mitchell grass.

A cloud of dust rose behind them. After a while they saw a larger cloud some distance away, and the helicopter darting about like a black mosquito above it.

Kelly said, 'There they are.' But when she drove the vehicle into the camp it was deserted except for the cook, who was pleased to see the fresh food they'd brought and glad of their offer to help prepare it.

A windmill fed long water troughs for cattle, and there were wire-fenced yards for holding the cattle overnight. A small building housed a gas-powered refrigerator where the cook stowed the perishable supplies the women had brought along, and at Kelly's suggestion she and Skye took advantage of the primitive showers before the mob was driven into the camp.

A distant thunder and the sound of constant mooing, accompanied by the growl of motorbikes and the rapid thunkety-thunk of the helicopter, heralded the arrival of the mob.

Led by a couple of musterers on horseback, the herd crested one of the low ridges, the leaders breaking away and down the slope, and bikers streaked after stragglers on the outer edges of the mob, guiding them into the fenced yards. Dust cast a red pall over everything. Skye, standing beneath a tall, shivering gum tree on a knoll, snapped several pictures of men and animals, capturing both the weariness and the excitement of a successful day's muster.

The cattle were driven into the outer fenced enclosure, the outriders on motorbikes keeping the mob intact, the helicopter zipping away now and then to herd back a breakaway faction.

The cattle settled, and the horses were relieved of their saddles and corralled. Then Skye saw Jarrah striding towards her, pulling a kerchief from about his neck and wiping his face with it as he approached, leaving streaks of red dirt.

Something about the purposeful way he walked made her heart flutter a little, but it wasn't until his hand closed on her arm with a painful grip to lead her away from the others, and she looked up and saw his eyes glittering under the brim of his hat that she realized he was in a towering temper.

CHAPTER 11

'What the hell are you doing here?' Jarrah demanded roughly. 'Did Kelly bring you?'

'Yes, I – '

'I'll skin her alive! I thought she had more sense.'

'What's wrong? I just came along to – '

'What on earth possessed her – whose idea was it, anyway?'

'I won't get in the way,' Skye promised. 'I said I'd like to come, and Kelly saw no reason – '

Jarrah swore. '*Kelly* saw no reason! Didn't *you*?'

He hadn't even said hello, or shown any pleasure in seeing her. 'No, I didn't. Why are you making such a fuss? I'm going back tomorrow.'

'You bet you are! A muster camp is no place for a pregnant woman. Didn't that occur to either of you?'

'No, actually,' Skye retorted coolly. 'Kelly said your mother *helped* with the mustering when she was pregnant. And the doctor hasn't – '

'Not once my father knew she was, she didn't. And my mother was used to the life. You're not. Why the hell didn't *she* stop you? Did the doctor give you permission to drive across country – '

'I don't need permission, Jarrah! Not even yours.'

'Yes, you damn well do,' he said between clenched teeth. 'I run this station, and no one – *no one* – uses station vehicles without my permission, or turns up at a muster camp without my say-so.'

Skye gaped at him. 'Do you expect to be consulted about my every move? You don't own me!'

'You're carrying my child!'

'That doesn't give you proprietary rights!'

'Oh, for God's sake! As if – '

'Skye!' Erik was hurrying up the rise, pulling off his hat and grinning at her. 'What are you doing here?'

At last Jarrah released her. 'Sightseeing,' he told his brother curtly. 'Kelly brought her up. And tomorrow,' he turned and directed a hard stare at Skye, 'she's taking her home. If it wasn't so late I'd make her turn around and head for the homestead right now.'

Erik's smile faded a little as he glanced at his brother's grim face. 'You don't approve.'

'What the hell is it with this family?' Jarrah exploded. 'Of course I don't damn well approve! How would you feel if your pregnant wife took it into her head to visit out here?'

'I don't have a pregnant wife,' Erik pointed out. 'But if I did, I reckon I'd be pretty pleased to see her.' He looked at Jarrah questioningly.

Jarrah made an exasperated sound. 'You look after Skye, then. I'm going to find that sister of ours.'

'And give her a piece of his mind, I guess,' Erik said as Jarrah strode away. Transferring his gaze to Skye, he added, 'He's not happy.'

'Not a bit,' she agreed, trying to smile.

'He'll get over it. He's just worried about you.'

About her or *his* baby? Skye wondered. 'He shouldn't blame Kelly. It's not fair.' Maybe she should follow him and try to intervene.

'Don't worry about Kelly. She can stick up for herself, and Jarrah's bark is worse than his bite.'

'Does he often go off the deep end like this?'

Erik pursed his lips. 'No, not often. When he does it's awesome, but he's usually pretty fair about things. He'll come round.'

Perhaps he did. Later when the men had cleaned up a bit and were seated around the open fire over which the cook had placed a grill plate on legs, Jarrah filled a plate for her with steak, vegetables and one of the fresh eggs that she and Kelly had delivered, and then he sat beside her to eat his own meal.

The air had grown cold, and she was glad of the warm jacket Kelly had made her bring. But the fire was warming and romantic, and the camaraderie among the musterers was infectious.

The men called her 'the missus' and joked with Jarrah about his bride not being able to stay away from him, and he returned the banter with a taut smile.

Once the meal was over bedrolls were spread on the ground and Kelly handed Skye a swag.

As she was about to spread it beside Kelly's Jarrah snagged her wrist in his fingers. 'Over there.' He indicated a tree a bit farther away from the fire.

Kelly gave him a cheeky, knowing sideways look, then grinned at Skye and raised her brows. Apparently whatever he'd said to her earlier hadn't intimidated her, anyway.

Skye smiled back, and followed Jarrah.

He spread his roll under a big multi-stemmed bloodwood with rusty, mottled bark, and did the same with hers, taking over the task as she tried to emulate him. She lay down at his side, and could see the stars beyond the pale, pointed leaves.

The cattle were still bellowing and grumbling, and restless hooves thumped the ground. A crescent moon gave no light as the landscape sank into impenetrable darkness.

'I'm sorry if you don't want me here,' Skye said quietly, 'but I'm glad I came.'

Jarrah turned his head. 'Glad?'

She tried to put her feelings into words. 'I wanted to see it for myself.' What she wanted to say was that she'd gained some dim understanding of what the land meant to men like Jarrah and women like Kelly. That she had felt the elemental power and attraction of what he'd called his demanding mistress. 'Opal Reach is . . . awesome,' she said. 'Beautiful in a . . . a stripped down sort of way.' The contours of the land were unadorned by forest or flowers, and even the tortured trees didn't hold enough leaves to disguise their twisted, angular branches. 'It's as if nature can't be bothered with prettiness here. Nothing's dressed up, but there's a sort of naked splendour about it.'

Jarrah laughed a little. 'That more or less sums it up.'

Tentatively, she stretched out her hand and touched him, encountering the hard warmth of his shoulder.

He grasped her fingers, carrying them to his mouth. 'I didn't mean to bawl you out,' he told her. 'It was a bit of a shock seeing you here.'

He moved her hand down and tucked it inside the bush shirt he still wore, holding her palm over his heart, and she recalled the first time they'd met and he'd held her hand like that while they danced. Only this time there was no clean linen shirting between her palm and his naked chest.

'I'll be much happier when you're back at the homestead,' he said. 'Try to get some sleep.'

'Try' was the operative word. The cattle weren't sleeping. They were accustomed to roving freely over the vast paddocks in search of feed and water, and none of them was particularly happy about their confinement. Subdued lowing and the deep bleat of the calves busied the night, accompanied by the muted shuffling of hooves, and occasionally punctuated by hoarse bellowing from the bulls.

Jarrah's eyes seemed closed, showing no light, but Skye didn't think he was really sleeping.

Then suddenly all sound ceased. The strange stillness was so abrupt and uncanny that Skye felt herself holding her breath, the fine hairs at the back of her neck prickling.

Her hand, still lying against Jarrah's chest, was flung off and he sat up. In the dying light of the fire she saw other huddled figures sit up too.

'What is it?' she whispered.

Jarrah's hand closed on her shoulder. Then she heard a faint 'ping' and he let out a low expletive. 'It's a rush.'

'*Rush*! A bloody rush!' someone shouted, and the mooing started again and the muffled sound of hooves, and she felt the ground under her tremble.

'Out of your swag!' Jarrah said. 'They're heading this way.'

She scrambled out and he bent swiftly, bundling up their bedding, and pushed her towards the nearby tree, just as she dimly saw the mob moving through the darkness towards them.

She stumbled on the rough ground and Jarrah's arms came around her, his body pressing her against the blessedly substantial main bole of the tree.

She gasped, automatically clinging onto him, her cheek pressed to his shirt, and then they were surrounded by thundering hooves and snorting breath and the thick, steamy smell of panicked animals as the herd charged past them. Shaking, Skye closed her hand on Jarrah's shirt, terrified that one of the horned bulls would turn aside long enough to take a lethal swipe at him. Dust got in her eyes and mouth, and she began to cough. Jarrah's hold tightened and he said in her ear, 'It'll be over soon.'

It seemed to go on for ever, and distantly she

heard men yelling above the bellowing and the hoofbeats and wondered if the others were all right. But they'd been nearer the fire and the building, and out of the direct path of the rush, she hoped.

At last the rumble of the escaping mob receded into the distance, and there was silence except for the blaring of a calf that had been left behind.

Jarrah eased his hold on Skye and brushed back her tumbled hair from her face. 'That's it. Are you okay?'

'Are you?' she said.

He kissed her swiftly. 'I'm fine.' Then he turned his head to answer an anxious shout from the direction of the camp fire. 'We're okay! Anyone hurt over there?'

No one was, and a couple of the men on motorbikes had set off after the herd, but they soon returned. 'Couldn't turn them,' they admitted. 'They were going like bloody bats out of hell.'

'No use trying to bring them back now,' Jarrah said. 'Too dangerous in the dark. We'll have to start again in the morning and hope they haven't gone too far.'

'What caused it?' Skye asked as they settled down again, this time closer to their companions.

'No idea. Sometimes they get spooked by a

strange noise, or one goes crazy and starts the rest off. Maybe a dingo was prowling round and they scented it.'

'Would that make them go quiet like that? You knew they were going to rush before they broke out, didn't you?'

'Usually a silence like that means a rush. It can last for up to five minutes – gives us time to get out of the way, and if we're lucky time to stop them. But not tonight.'

'This will hold up the end of the muster, won't it?'

'Not too much, I hope. Maybe a couple of extra days.'

The stray calf woke Skye in the morning, calling for its mother. She looked around and discovered the small sandy-brown creature standing with knobbly knees splayed, but when she approached it skittered away.

After several minutes of coaxing, eventually it came warily, with many fits and starts, to nuzzle at her outstretched fingers.

'It's hungry,' she told Jarrah as he came up beside her. The calf lolloped away a few steps and regarded him warily. 'What'll happen to him?'

'If he's lucky he'll find his mother when we get the mob in again.'

'Will you get them all back?'

'Most of them will have stuck pretty much together. We'll probably miss a few that get clean away.'

The calf wandered back and sniffed at Skye, and when she tried to stroke its head, a long tongue came out to lick her fingers. 'Can't we give him something in the meantime?'

'You can try mixing up some milk powder for him if you like, but I don't know if he'll take it.'

While the camp cook made breakfast, Skye and Kelly mixed milk powder and water in a bucket and coaxed the calf to it.

'It won't know how to drink,' Kelly explained. 'Dip your fingers in the milk and let it suck them, so it'll get the idea.'

Skye tried it, and the calf sucked strongly at her fingers, curling its rough, warm tongue around them. After a few minutes Kelly left them to it, and Skye dipped her fingers again and again, trying to guide the little creature's nose into the bucket of milk. But it couldn't seem to take to the idea. Patiently, she knelt on her haunches and went on dipping and encouraging.

'Breakfast's ready,' Jarrah said, coming to her side.

'He's hardly taken any,' she said despairingly. She cupped her hand, filled with milk. The calf sucked at her fingers again, snorting as the milk got up its nostrils, and lifting its head to shake it.

Jarrah said, 'He'll learn if he's hungry enough. Come and have breakfast.'

'Not until I get him to drink.'

'That could take all day.'

'I don't care.' Stubbornly she remained where she was, holding out her milky fingers to the calf until he came back and started sniffing at them and licking them again.

'All right,' Jarrah said in long-suffering tones. 'Here, give the bucket to me.'

Between them they managed to get the calf to dip its nose into the milk, and after a good deal of inexpert snuffling and indignant choking and coughing it was able to drink nearly all of it.

Skye sat back triumphantly. 'There! We did it.'

'Right.' Jarrah put down the bucket. 'Now will you come and have something to eat?'

She let him pull her to her feet, and laughed as the calf trotted after them. But when they neared the other musterers it shied off and went to curl up under the tree where Skye and Jarrah had sheltered during the rush.

'Can I do anything?' she asked him after breakfast as they were discussing rounding up the lost cattle.

'To help?' He glanced at the bulge that her loose shirt failed to hide. 'Definitely not.'

Kelly said, 'If I took one of the plant horses and helped round up the cattle, Skye could drive the Nissan and pick up calves . . . Can you drive?' she asked Skye.

'Yes,' Skye said eagerly. 'Why don't I?'

'It's a crazy idea,' Jarrah said shortly.

'But I'm sure – '

'I said no, Skye!' He turned to his sister. 'You can take her back now. We'll leave the calves until tomorrow.'

One of the men shouted something to him, and he turned and waved, then bent to kiss Skye quickly on the lips. 'Drive carefully,' he admonished Kelly. 'And when you come back you'd better be on your own.'

Kelly made a face at his retreating back, looked at Skye and shrugged.

A motorbike roared by the bloodwood tree, and the startled calf twitched its ears, staggered to its feet and blared. It spied Skye and trotted towards her, nuzzling at her jeans, catching the end of her loose shirt and trying to suck it.

'Don't, silly!' She went on her knees to gently remove the material. 'You've had breakfast.'

'He thinks you're his mum now,' Kelly told her.

Skye stroked the calf's silky coat. 'What'll happen to him if his mother doesn't turn up, or he can't find her in the herd? She ran off with the others and left him, so she's not a terribly good bet, is she?'

Kelly didn't answer, and Skye looked at her enquiringly. 'He'll die, won't he? He's too young to wean.'

'Yes, he is. We can't save every lost calf. It's not like a dairy herd of a few hundred beasts. Our cattle have to fend for themselves.'

'The survival of the fittest.'

'Something like that. But Jarrah won't just leave it to die like some men would. He'll make sure it doesn't suffer.'

'Couldn't we take this one home with us?'

Kelly looked dubious. 'We don't usually bother with poddies now.'

'Poddies?'

'Orphan calves. When I was a kid Dad used to bring them home sometimes and we had the job of feeding them milk until they were old enough to eat grass and fend for themselves.'

'I'll feed him. How often does he need milk?'

'A couple of times a day to start with.' Kelly stood chewing her lip. 'I don't know. Jarrah's already furious with me for bringing you out here.'

'I didn't mean to get you into trouble. Erik says Jarrah's bark is worse than his bite.' The calf butted at her leg and slobbered over her jeans.

Kelly grinned. 'Yeah, well. Okay, we'll take your baby home. You realize he'll have to go out with the others when he's big enough, though?'

'That's okay.' She just couldn't abandon him to an uncertain fate when he was so small and vulnerable.

The musterers left, and Kelly and Skye loaded the calf into the cage on the back of the Nissan, and followed.

Kelly drove slowly, avoiding the holes and small rocks that pockmarked the ground. The riders on their horses and motorbikes had fanned out across the wide plain, and the helicopter took off and soared over their heads, dipping and swinging when Lee spied a group of cattle lurking in the trees.

The bull-catching team roared past, and some time afterwards came racing back after a big, long-legged, sand-coloured bull that the horsemen and dogs had startled out of a thicket.

Kelly swung the wheel of the Nissan and came to a halt under a spreading tree nearby, at the edge of a patch of bush that dipped into a broad gully. 'Watch this.'

The bull, snorting and furious, galloped past them with the battered four-wheel drive in hot pursuit. Skye leaned from the window and snapped a couple of pictures as the tyre-padded front gently nudged the animal a couple of times.

She caught her breath and winced when the bull went down and the vehicle came to halt with the panting, struggling beast pinned under the bars on the front.

'He's not hurt,' Kelly assured her as the three men in the vehicle sprang out. 'That's the skill in bull-catching.'

The men were tying the bewildered bull's legs with practised speed, and Skye asked, 'What happens to the bull after this?'

'A truck will be along,' Kelly said, 'and winch him on board. Some of those big old scrubbers are too wild to walk with the herd. Lots of station owners just shoot them, but we make more than fifty thousand dollars a year on them, sometimes a hundred, so Jarrah reckons it's worth the effort and expense of catching them.'

'Is it okay to get out now? I'd love to get some closer shots.

Kelly hardly hesitated. 'Yeah, the boys'd love that.' She climbed out too and leaned on the cab as Skye approached the now firmly trussed bull and the three bull-catchers, who grinned and tipped their hats as she approached with her camera in her hands.

'Do you mind?' she asked.

'Fire ahead,' one of them answered. 'Whaddya reckon, boys?'

The others agreed enthusiastically, and arranged themselves about the bull, one leaning on the bonnet of the dusty vehicle, one placing his booted foot on the poor creature's flank like a Great White Hunter, and the third standing close with thumbs hooked in his belt and feet apart, his hat pushed to the back of his head.

Skye walked far enough away to get the bull, the men and the tyre-padded vehicle all into the frame, then said, 'I'd like to take a couple more.' She stepped backwards several more yards and adjusted the lens so that she got Kelly and the Nissan in the frame too, and a view of the red earth and a thicket of trees from which she could hear the barking of the dogs. She pressed the shutter just as the helicopter approached, and she lifted the camera to get that too, then moved backward still farther and shifted the frame away from the Nissan and the thick stand of trees behind it to get the bull-catchers and a wide view of the red plains to the other side and the pale sky above the sparse vegetation, giving a sense of the scale of men and manmade machines against the vastness of the outback.

The aircraft buzzed deafeningly overhead as she quickly took two more shots while the men clowned, clambering onto the bull bars and holding them with one hand while they posed for her. She was still peering through the view-finder when something blurred across it, and she lowered the camera, to see the three men leaping to the ground and piling into their vehicle, and noticed that Kelly had moved forward but was now running back towards the Nissan – and an enormous horned bull with saliva streaming from its panting mouth was heading straight for Skye, with two dogs in hot pursuit.

Then a horseman burst from the thicket in the wake of the dogs – Jarrah, lifting the reins, kicking at Moonfleet's flanks and bending low over the horse's neck as he galloped towards her behind the bull.

A tree, Skye thought, looking wildly round her. The nearest tree looked awfully inadequate, spindly and low. Involuntarily she stepped back, ready to turn and run, and stumbled on a protruding stone, not falling but slowed by trying to keep her balance. Vaguely she was aware of the bull-catcher reversing away from the trussed bull, of the Nissan gunning forward, but the bull filled her vision, lowering its head, and as she stepped hurriedly aside, trying to give it a clear path, it swerved towards her. Frightened and angry, the animal had her in its sights and knew she was human – the enemy.

Too late to run, the bull was much faster. Her only hope was to wait until the last moment and, like a bullfighter, try to avoid the deadly horns as the creature raced past – unless Jarrah, fast gaining on the bull but still lagging by several yards, could get to it first.

Hoping to divert it, she held the only thing she had, her camera, out to one side at arms' length, swinging it by the strap, and braced herself to jump and roll, her mouth drying in anticipation. She knew Jarrah was shouting at her, but the helicopter's engine drowned all sound, making everything else soundless by comparison.

She could see the beast's hot, dark eyes when Jarrah leaned down, coming level with the bull, kicked the stirrups from his feet on the fast-moving horse and leapt, and in a blur of dust and speed the bull was suddenly brought to the ground, sliding with its own momentum, dragging the man behind it who held grimly to its tail.

The two vehicles converged at almost the same time, skidding to a stop on either side. The bull-catcher slid to within a foot from the downed bull as it struggled to get up, and inched forward until the bars were over its heaving flanks, trapping it while the men leapt out with ropes and trussed the flailing legs.

'Skye!' A white-faced Kelly jumped from the Nissan and flung an arm about Skye's shoulders. 'Are you all right?'

'Yes.' She was shaking, though. 'Jarrah – '

'He'll *kill* me!' Kelly moaned. She dropped

her arm and took a step back as Jarrah, having relinquished his catch to the bull-catching team, got to his feet and picked up his hat from where it had fallen, using it to beat some of the dust from his shirt and moleskin trousers, wiped a sleeve across his forehead, and then came purposefully towards them.

Skye stood her ground, but swallowed nervously as she saw the sweat and red dirt that streaked his cheeks, the ragged new tear in his sleeve and the bloodied skin it revealed, and not least the ominous set of his jaw and the glitter in his eyes.

CHAPTER 12

The helicopter swung away and the roar of the blades receded. Skye held out her free hand to touch Jarrah's arm. 'You're hurt – '

Then her hand was jammed between them as he gripped her shoulders and jerked her forward, his mouth crashing down on hers in a kiss so forceful it was practically an assault, her head going back, her breasts crushed against his hard, heaving chest.

It was brief but devastating, and his eyes still glowed half-savagely as he lifted his head without loosening his bruising hold. 'Don't you *ever* do anything like that again!' he growled deep in his throat.

'I'm sorry,' Skye whispered.

But he was looking over her shoulder at his sister. 'And as for you – I'll deal with you when I get home.'

'It wasn't Kelly's fault,' Skye said.

'Yes, it was,' Kelly argued miserably. 'I shouldn't have let you get out of the Nissan.'

Skye turned to her, pushing away from Jarrah's hands. 'You weren't to know – '

'She knows bloody well,' Jarrah contradicted grimly, 'that it isn't safe to be on foot when the bulls are being mustered.'

'I did try to call her back when she walked so far from the vehicles,' Kelly said, 'but the helicopter – '

'I'm sorry,' Skye apologized to her too. 'I didn't hear a thing.'

'Of course not,' Kelly agreed. 'I suppose Lee was having fits up there too – she'd have had a view of everything that was going on. I guess she was trying to head him off but it didn't work. I didn't know a thing either until the damned scrubber shot out of the trees and past me and headed straight for you. The boys were busy posing and they wouldn't have seen it until it passed them.' She squared her shoulders. 'Jarrah's right, though. It was my fault. I should have made you stay in the Nissan.' Looking at him, Kelly added, 'She did ask, and I thought it would be okay. She only wanted to photograph the bull-catchers. I figured it was safe enough with them around.'

'Surely,' Skye said, 'it was a million to one chance – I just happened to be in the wrong place at the wrong time. You can't blame Kelly for thinking I couldn't come to any harm when the bull-catching team was right here.'

'All right,' Jarrah snapped, sounding scarcely mollified. 'But for God's sake do as you're told this time, Kelly, and take my wife *home*!'

'Your arm –' Skye tried again to catch his sleeve and look at it, but Jarrah shook her off impatiently.

'It's a scrape, that's all. I'm more worried about you.' A firm hand at her waist urged her towards the Nissan as Kelly climbed into the driver's seat. 'Are you sure you're okay?'

'I wasn't touched,' she protested. 'Thanks to you. I just had a nasty fright and I'm sorry I caused so much trouble.'

'Just stay out of the way in future.' He laid a hand on the door handle and paused. 'You weren't the only one who got a fright,' he said, and lifted his hand away from the door to touch her lips with his thumb. 'Did I hurt you?'

Her shoulders were probably bruised, but she gave him a slightly trembly smile and shook her head. 'It can't have been as bad as being gored by a bull.'

He tipped her chin and bent to touch her lips lightly with his, a silent apology. Then he opened the door and helped her in, slamming it decisively behind her. 'Drive carefully,' he admonished Kelly through the open window, and stepped back.

The bull-catcher got out of their way and roared off again, the men waving cheerfully and whistling. Kelly started the engine.

She pressed down on the accelerator and the truck lurched off over the uneven ground. 'We'd better get you back, pronto. And no more detours.' She gave Skye a half-hearted grin.

'Because Jarrah said so?'

'He's the boss.' Kelly waved to one of the men on the motorbikes as they passed. 'Thanks for sticking up for me. He did have a point though. I should have stuck to the rules.'

'Is it difficult, having your older brother for your boss?'

'Not usually. I think he's careful to try and separate family things from work, when there are other people about.' Kelly steered around a rock sticking up from the red earth, and straightened out again. She glanced at Skye. 'Jarrah's all right, but if you let him he'll make all your decisions for you. He wanted to send me off to university, and we had some almighty rows before I persuaded him I wasn't cut out for an academic career, that I'd be much happier staying on Opal Reach and learning how to run a cattle station.'

'You stood up to him.'

'You have to, you know.' Kelly looked at her sideways again. 'I suppose it's because he feels responsible for all of us.'

'Your mother's a pretty efficient lady.'

'Yeah, and she's in charge around the homestead and of course she's the head of the family. But Jarrah's the boss out here. Mum helped out a lot when she was younger, but she always left decisions about the running of the station to Dad, and he'd been training up Jarrah to take his place. Though no one expected it to be quite so soon. You know he died when Jarrah was only twenty?'

'Yes . . . how?'

'Jarrah didn't tell you? He turned over a tractor and got pinned under it, building a dam out on the station. It crushed him.'

'How awful. I'm sorry.'

'Yeah, it was, at the time. We've got used to not having him around now. But Mum still . . . I think she misses him. I s'pose when you love someone for years you never get over their death. And poor old Jarrah had to grow up in a hurry. I didn't realize at the time – I was just a kid and he seemed like a grown-up, but it must have been hard for him. He's done a good job.'

'So what about you? Is your ambition to run a station of your own?' Skye looked at her curiously.

'I guess. It won't be Opal Reach, because Jarrah's wedded to this place. But some day maybe I'll apply for a manager's job on another station.'

Skye said thoughtfully, 'It seems to me the outback is still very much a man's world.'

'Yeah, but there are some stations owned and run by women. I reckon I can persuade someone to give me a job. One thing about Jarrah, once he came round to the idea he never stood in my way again.'

When the animals for trucking out were driven into the yards, Skye drove down there in the utility vehicle with her mother-in-law.

She saw Jarrah in position outside the central ring, and squared her shoulders as she went towards him. He had one foot on a lower rail, the clipboard on his knee as he kept the tally.

He couldn't have heard her approach on the dusty ground, but he turned his head when she was still yards away, and straightened, his brows snapping into a frown over narrowed eyes. Then he looked behind her and said, 'Get back in the truck, Skye.'

'I promise not to be in the way. I'd like to take some photos – '

'You can take as many as you like – from the truck.'

She looked at him and knew it was no use arguing. If she didn't move he'd probably pick her up and deposit her on the seat himself. 'It's hot,' she muttered.

A ghost of a smile crossed his mouth. 'It's cooler in the cab – at least there's shade there.' He took one step forward and kissed her quickly. The brim of her hat touched his and the hat she'd taken from the utility room fell back onto her shoulders, anchored by the thin strap at her throat.

Someone whistled, and Skye stepped back just as Jarrah's hand skimmed down her back and landed on her waist. His eyes gleamed. 'Now be a good girl and do as you're told.'

Skye's eyes flashed, but she set her lips and stalked off to the cab of the utility truck, reflecting that even she knew the yards were no place to indulge in a marital spat.

She stayed though, until the cattle were all yarded for the night. And then Jarrah handed the reins of his horse to Kelly and swung into the driver's seat to drive her and his mother back to the house.

Ella went straight to the kitchen. Jarrah, an arm about Skye's shoulders, opened the door of the utility room and she went in with him and picked up a bucket from the floor.

'What are you doing?' Jarrah asked as she

opened up a container of powdered milk.

'I have to feed the calf.'

'Calf?'

'Didn't you notice?' she asked him half guiltily. 'We – Kelly and I brought it home, the one that was left behind when the cattle rushed. It was in the cage when . . . when we had the – um – incident with the bull.'

'I was busy making sure you weren't going to be carried home on a stretcher.'

If the calf had been curled up on the hay at the bottom of the Nissan's tray she supposed he'd have missed it. Or perhaps he'd been too preoccupied with the drama to notice. 'I didn't think its mother was very reliable. And if you didn't find her, or she didn't find him . . . well, I couldn't just leave him.'

'And you've been feeding it?' He looked down at her.

'Every night and morning. He's thriving,' she said proudly.

Jarrah watched her mix up the milk powder, and when she picked up the bucket he took it from her and carried it outside to the enclosure that she and Kelly had rigged between two of the station outbuildings.

He regarded the calf with a jaundiced eye, but didn't overtly object to Skye looking after it. 'Don't make a pet of the thing,' he warned. 'It won't always be a cute little baby, and we don't want a big, half-tame steer making a nuisance of itself around the house.'

Skye didn't ask to be taken out to a muster again, and Jarrah made it clear he didn't want to see her at the home yards either. He said so when they were getting ready for bed the night he arrived home. She was drawing the curtains against the dark, already in her nightgown, when he came out of the bathroom, naked and with his freshly washed hair slicked to his skull. 'Just stay away,' he told her, as she turned with a protest on her lips. 'It's no place for you.'

'I'd like to take some photos,' Skye argued, angling her chin defiantly. 'I won't get in the way, I promise. Or faint. I've been feeling much better lately. The sickness seems to have gone – '

'No.'

No? Indignant, she said, 'Look, I know you're lord and master here, but – '

'Yes, I am,' he said calmly, making her gape. 'And I say you're not to go near the yards. I don't want any more accidents.'

'But surely that was a million to one chance. There aren't too many scrub bulls among the cattle you bring down here, are there?'

'That's not the point. If the boys hadn't been fooling about for the camera they'd have seen the bastard when he came out of the bush and went for you. You start pointing that thing at the men down at the yards, the next thing you know they're busy posing instead of keeping their minds on the work, and showing off so you'll take their picture. I can't afford the distraction.'

'I'm sure they wouldn't – '

He made a derisive sound. 'You don't know them. Just having a woman around is likely to set some of them off halfcocked and get them pulling silly stunts to impress you and your camera. It's a natural male instinct.'

'*You* don't seem to have it,' Skye retorted.

Jarrah grinned. 'What do you think I was doing when I jumped that scrubber out there? And I tell you what – I *never* want to experience anything like that two minutes again.'

He hadn't been showing off, he'd been quite possibly saving her life. The reminder made her determination to defy him seem petty.

'You can snap around the house and garden as much as you like,' Jarrah said, as if awarding a consolation prize. 'But keep away from the yards.' And then he drew her into his arms, murmuring, 'I died a thousand deaths when I saw you standing there, just waiting for the bull to mow you down. I don't want *anything* to happen to you, or to Junior, here.' He ran his hands down her body, and rested one of them on her belly, then leaned forward and kissed her, tender concern turning to desire within seconds. And in minutes he was whispering against her hair, 'Let's go to bed.'

Skye snapped the huge road trains as they passed the house, big rigs towing two, three or even four double-decked trailers, that came rumbling in to take away the sale cattle. The drivers waved and one slowed to a halt, grinning at her as she took his photo because he so obviously expected it.

And she photographed the men sitting around on the porch of the old quarters, smoking and playing two-up and cards, and got up early to take pictures of the musterers getting the dogs and horses and vehicles ready to go out at dawn for another phase of the never-ending task.

Some of the men grinned and posed for her in exaggerated macho attitudes until Jarrah reminded them they had a job to do and they could stop making like film stars. Maybe he'd been right about their probable reactions if she turned up while they were trying to accomplish the risky and skilled tasks of drafting and loading cattle on the trucks.

She handed out pictures to the human subjects when they were developed, and on Jarrah's birthday gave him a framed enlargement of the water-hole with an ibis taking off into the sunrise.

He seemed delighted with it, and hung it in the dining room.

The calf grew fat, and then leggy and solid, and within two months was surviving solely on grass, sharing the brood mares' paddock. In time it was branded and castrated and turned out into the huge open 'bush paddock' with a mob that had been brought into the home yards. Skye watched it trot away among the other weaners with a mixture of triumph and sadness. Remembering Jarrah's instructions, she hadn't even given it a name.

In August a horde of visitors arrived and were accommodated in the old workers' quarters, and the homestead was a hive of activity. Horse trailers were parked all around as campdrafters from as far away as New South Wales and Western Australia turned up with their mounts.

By now Skye had a fair idea of what campdrafting was, and she was looking forward to seeing the sport for herself.

Jarrah told her to 'wear something nice', and she put on a soft cotton dress she'd made herself, with a floral pattern in subtle, earthy colours shading into shadowy purples and blues. She'd found a wide, plain straw hat in Mt. Isa on her last visit to the doctor, and had trimmed it with dried flowers and a floppy ribbon bow fashioned from the same material as her dress.

Some of the visiting women had dressed up, while others wore jeans or moleskin trousers. A few were people she'd met at the party, and Megan Poynter had brought along her latest paying guests, a group of French-speaking New Caledonians. They reacted with pleasure and surprise at Skye's command of their language, and the men showered her with Gallic flattery.

Jarrah cocked an eyebrow and asked her as he moved her away to talk to another group, 'What were they saying?'

'Nothing much,' she answered demurely. 'Compliments, mostly.'

'Is that so? Well, I hope you told them to keep their compliments strictly verbal if they don't want to be punched in the nose.'

'Don't be so neanderthal,' she admonished. 'They were just being polite.'

'They were just practically eating you up with their eyes,' he observed drily.

'French men appreciate women.'

'Let them go and appreciate someone else's, then.'

Skye laughed. His jealousy was tempered with pride. He liked showing her off; it was obvious in the way he insisted on introducing her to everyone. 'In my condition, it's rather nice to be looked at and spoken to as though I'm still . . . attractive.'

'Do you doubt it?' Jarrah asked her. 'Of course you're still attractive – gorgeous. Don't I tell you that often enough?'

'But you're my husband.'

His eyes glinted, a half smile on his mouth. 'So don't I count?'

'The thing is,' she explained patiently, her hands shaping the mound under her dress, 'this is your doing – so you're bound to try and persuade me that it hasn't diminished my looks.'

His hands came over hers, warm and strong. 'I'm glad it's my doing. And if those French guys help to persuade you that I'm not the only one who thinks you're more beautiful than ever, then I guess I'll put up with them ogling you.'

'They weren't ogling! They're much too sophisticated to ogle!'

'Huh.' He lifted her hands away with his, and kissed them each in turn, giving the gesture an exaggerated flourish. 'See? They're not the only ones who know how to charm a woman.'

'I know that,' Skye said drily, placing one hand back on her stomach. 'How else did this happen to me?'

* * *

One visitor was a freelance journalist toting a camera, and when he saw Skye's Pentax he began swapping photographic lore, then moved to talking of magazines he'd worked on. They soon discovered mutual acquaintances among the art directors and photographers they'd worked with, and for a time were deep in conversation. 'I knew you as soon as I saw you, of course,' he told her. 'Heard someone talking about you the other day, as a matter of fact, saying you'd just dropped out of sight. I never expected to find you here.'

The day's programme began with events for children riding ponies of various sizes. The adults cheered them on, and commiserated with the losers and the few who lost contact with their mounts, and then the serious business of the day began.

Jarrah had put folding chairs under a sun umbrella for his mother and Skye, and he leaned on the rail nearby.

There were events for women and for men, and open events. Campdrafting was a sport that had developed from the normal work of mustering cattle, and was designed as a formal arena to show off the skills of the stockhorse and its rider as they cut animals from the herd and worked them in prescribed patterns.

'It's a sort of rodeo, I suppose?' Skye queried Kelly.

'Well, it uses horses and cattle, but the events are quite different, and it's less dangerous, as long as the riders know what they're doing. The ringers used to run their own rodeos in the old days, in their time off, but Jarrah put a stop to that. The flying doctors object to coming out to treat broken bones and concussions because a bunch of bored jackeroos decided to play cowboys, and it left us shorthanded when they got hurt.'

A pen full of cattle provided a pool of stock for the competitors to demonstrate their cattle handling ability and horsemanship, and how quickly and cleanly they could cut out a selected beast from the herd and drive it in the prescribed pattern around the competition arena.

Erik took a third placing, and Kelly triumphed in first place in the women's open event. Then the veteran ringer who was announcer for the day called for entrants for the Opal Reach Challenge Cup, and Jarrah left Skye's side and reappeared, last in the lineup of competitors, on Moonfleet, his favourite mount.

As he walked the horse to the 'camp' outside the arena where the herd milled about in the dust, Kelly came to lean on the rail in his place. 'Looks good, doesn't he?' she said cheerfully.

'I didn't know he was going to ride,' Skye confessed. She got up from the chair and stood beside Kelly, lifting a hand to shade her eyes against the glare.

Kelly glanced at her. 'Jarrah always rides. He's the district champion – didn't he tell you? He's won the cup four times in a row.'

He hadn't told her, only that the cup sitting on the dining room shelf had been donated by his father for the yearly event. And that was after she'd asked about it.

Like the other competitors, he was dressed in a long-sleeved button-down shirt with a tie, moleskin trousers and leather boots, and a stockman's hat.

'There he goes,' Kelly said as the signal was given and Jarrah went into action.

Horse and man seemed one entity as they skilfully cut the chosen animal from the nervous herd in the holding yard and galloped alongside, heading the bullock off when it tried to make a break in the wrong direction. Hooves pounded on the hardpacked earth, raising puffs of dust. Under Jarrah's firm hands the horse headed off the bullock, bringing it back on track and heading for the gate. Jarrah called for the gate to be opened, and herded the animal into the arena.

'Okay!' Kelly said softly. 'Way to go, bro'.'

Skye's hands were gripping the top rail of the fence.

The course inside the arena was a figure of

eight. The horse's muscles flexed under its gleaming coat, and the man's body leaned into its movement, his hands and thighs keeping his mount at the bullock's side. The horse's body seemed to curve impossibly, only inches from the bullock, forcing it to change direction, guiding it tightly into the required double circle, executed with breathtaking power and grace, the man on its back almost a part of it, they moved in such perfect harmony.

The horse, the man, the fleet-footed bullock, made an almost flawless pattern, before the bullock was allowed back through the gate. As the animal trotted away to rejoin its companions with an irritated kick of its hind hooves, Jarrah brought the horse to a disciplined halt, leaned forward to pat Moonfleet's glistening neck, and left the competition area at a steady walk.

Skye realized she was gripping the rail in front of her and had completely forgotten to take pictures. 'He was good, wasn't he?' she asked.

Kelly chuckled. 'Just about damn near perfect.'

In the next phase the competitors had to take their mounts through their paces in a complicated reining pattern, showing off the horse's athleticism and its ability to respond to the rider's commands. Jarrah and Moonfleet worked beautifully together, every flowing movement performed with precision and panache. 'He's got it again!' Kelly said, and turned to hug Skye. 'Opal Reach keeps the cup.'

'A good result for Opal Reach,' Jarrah said, waving off the last of the visitors after a substantial brunch the morning after the contest. He stretched and rubbed the back of his neck.

Skye looked at him, thinking how handsome he was, and remembering the speed and fluid beauty of his performance in the ring. 'You didn't tell me you were going to ride.'

'I always have. It's nice to keep it in the family.' He looked at Kelly and Erik. 'We all held our end up pretty well.'

'Congratulations are due to all of you,' Skye concurred. 'You did Opal Reach proud.'

'So did you,' Kelly told her. 'Those Frenchmen were blown away.'

'Her New Caledonian friends,' Jarrah said. 'I noticed.'

Skye shook her head deprecatingly. 'I only said a few words to them in French.'

'You're a woman of many talents,' Kelly told her solemnly. 'And you, brother, are a lucky swine.'

'I know,' Jarrah assured her, his lazy gaze caressing Skye.

'Megan said you've been a wonderful help

with her Japanese lessons,' Kelly told her. 'I heard the two of you yabbering away.'

'She's very keen,' Skye said. Megan phoned once a week to try out her pronunciation on Skye, and the camp drafting had given her an extra opportunity to brush up on it. 'It's a good chance for me to keep up my language skills too.'

'Had you met that journalist guy before?' Erik asked her. 'I saw you showing him your pictures.'

Kelly cut in. 'He told Skye she should try selling photos to magazines.'

'What magazines?' Jarrah asked.

Skye answered, 'He mentioned a couple that he thought might publish photos of outback life.'

Jarrah looked at her questioningly. 'Are you interested?'

'But . . . I'm not sure I'm good enough for that.'

'If he thought you are –' Kelly said, 'why not give it a go. He seemed dead keen for you to have a try, and didn't he say you'd be in with a chance?'

'He said that an art director I used to work with is on the staff of a travel magazine now.'

'So it's a contact,' Kelly said. 'Go for it.'

'Yes,' Jarrah encouraged her. 'Why not?'

In bed later Jarrah held her against his chest. 'Did you know the journo before?' he asked her.

'No, we'd never met, but he's in the business and he's seen photographs of me. We know some of the same people.'

'Do you miss it?' he asked her.

'Miss what?'

'Your job. The glamour, the admiration, the . . . excitement?'

'No!' she assured him. 'What would be the point, anyway? Look at me!' She touched her palm to her rounded stomach.

'I never tire of looking at you. Only I feel guilty about doing this to you.' His hand laid over hers, and his voice was troubled.

'Don't,' she begged. Lots of men would have left her to fend for herself, washed their hands of any responsibility. Jarrah hadn't done that. 'You have nothing to feel guilty about. I'm . . . happy.'

His hand moved and he twisted his body, looming over her, and kissed her, coaxing her mouth to open for him, and she put her arms about him and sank back against the pillow as the sweet flood of desire overwhelmed her.

CHAPTER 13

The muster was interrupted by unseasonal rain, and for a few days Jarrah, Erik and Kelly were confined to the house. Jarrah spent much of the time in the office, but at least every night Skye had him to herself. And one day when she was in the library he came in and found her going through some of the books on the shelves.

'Looking for something special?' he asked her.

'No, I'm just fascinated by the old books, and some of the inscriptions. This one must have belonged to your grandfather.'

He glanced at the copperplate writing on the flyleaf. 'Yes, a present from my grandmother.'

'You take them for granted, all these beautifully preserved old books.'

'I suppose so. They've always been here, as far back as I can recall. I don't think they're of any particular value to anyone but the family. Do you spend much time in here?'

'No. But it's a lovely room.'

Jarrah looked about. 'I've always liked it.' He pushed the door half closed behind him and came over to her, taking the book from her hands and replacing it on the shelf. His arms looped about her and he looked down at her. 'Feeling okay?'

'I feel fine now. Your mother says this is the best part of pregnancy, the middle months, when you stop being sick and haven't got too heavy yet.'

He kissed her, long and slowly, then lifted his head as someone came into the other room next door. 'Damn,' he said softly. 'Do you think they'll believe we've been sitting here reading?'

Skye shook her head. 'Probably not.' Kelly and Erik were inclined to raised eyebrows, side-long glances, amused smiles and the occasional teasing remark about the lovebirds in their midst. Skye had begun to sympathise with Jarrah's former wish to keep his love life a secret from his siblings.

'Here.' Jarrah grinned, thrusting a book into her hand and lowering her to a chair. Then he grabbed one for himself and sat down in another, yards away from her, and opened it.

Then Kelly opened the door, saying, 'Skye – do know where Jarrah's – '

Jarrah looked up with an absent expression, as

if he'd been deep in his reading. Skye tried to look equally innocent and relaxed, her finger in the volume Jarrah had handed her as she turned to Kelly too.

'You wanted me, Kel?' Jarrah enquired.

His sister looked from one to the other of them suspiciously. 'Yeah – one of the boys reckoned you promised to help him with a job application for when the muster's finished, and he thought you might have time . . .'

'Oh, yeah.' Jarrah closed the book with a show of reluctance. 'Tommy. Tell him to wait for me in the office, I'll be there in a minute.'

'Right.' Kelly lingered for a moment, evidently puzzled, and then retreated.

Jarrah put his book on the shelf and ambled over to Skye, picked up the one in her hand and laughed. It was a book about stock raising and seemed at least thirty years out of date. He replaced it, and leaned over her chair from behind, a hand under chin, pressing his lips to hers and bringing them tingling to life.

'Have to go,' he said, regretfully. 'See you later.'

When the rain stopped the musterers prepared to go out again, and Ella said, 'At least it's laid the dust for a while. I thought I might take Skye to Coolya for a day while you're out. Would you like that, Skye?'

Jarrah said, 'It's too rough.'

'It's not that bad,' Kelly argued. 'She's never even seen Coolya, Jarrah.'

'There's nothing to see,' he growled.

'I'd like to go,' Skye volunteered.

'It's not a good idea. Not while you're pregnant.'

He seemed to think that settled the matter, but as he turned away Skye said stubbornly, 'Your mother wouldn't have offered if she thought there was any risk. And I'm sure she's experienced enough to know.'

Jarrah scowled. 'If you really want to see the place,' he said, 'I'll take you when we get back from this phase of the muster.'

Kelly's mouth dropped momentarily. 'Don't you trust Mum to drive her?' she asked, then rather obviously bit her tongue as Jarrah cast her a piercing look.

'That has nothing to do with it,' he told her. 'I guess you'll want to come along too?'

'Sure,' she said, rather obviously swallowing her surprise. 'Thanks.'

Jarrah was as good as his word, and leaving Erik in charge, he drove them all to Coolya the day after the trucks had left with the latest batch of cattle.

Ella insisted on Skye sitting in front, citing her pregnancy, and Jarrah slid into the driver's seat.

The roadside was blooming after the rain, a blur of colour as they passed, and Ella named some of the flowers for her – fireweed and Australian bluebell and rattlepod. And a little bush with purple bottlebrush flowers that Kelly called lambs tail.

'What does Coolya mean?' Skye asked. 'It's an aboriginal word, isn't it?'

Jarrah smiled and shook his head. 'Nobody knows. It only sounds aboriginal, apparently. Expert opinion suggests either a corruption of a real aboriginal word or possibly a sort of made-up English one. There's a waterhole that might have led to the name – a place where drovers and other travellers could cool down on their way over the old cattle trials. The theory is that after generations of drovers had told each other that when they got to the waterhole "It'll cool ya" the name stuck.' He threw her a sideways glance.

Skye laughed. 'Are you pulling my leg?'

Still looking amused, Jarrah looked at her again, a little longer this time, his lazy gaze passing over her as his eyes crinkled at the corners. 'Would I do that?' he murmured for her ears alone. 'I assure you, I can think of more exciting things to do with your lovely legs.'

Skye blushed and gave him a surreptitious kick.

'No,' Kelly said from the back seat, missing

the aside. 'It's true. I mean, some linguist who was up here studying placenames reckoned that was the only way he could account for it.'

'I'll get you for that later.' Jarrah's eyes gleamed at Skye, and the little face she made at him only made him laugh again.

The township when they reached it looked shabby but freshly washed, the iron-roofed buildings low and modest. There was a long, sleepy-looking pub, a general store and not very much else, but the women spent a couple of hours happily shopping and introducing Skye to fascinated locals.

Jarrah took them to a late lunch at the pub before driving them home again. And the next day he was off with the men for more mustering.

When Skye next visited Mt. Isa for her prenatal check she bought a dozen pot-plants, ignoring Jarrah's muted grumble about flying them home in the Cessna, and arranged them on the balcony outside their room.

The poinsettias and African violets and the little potted fig tree thrived under her care, and Jarrah's mother gave her some seaweed fertiliser and advised her to feed them regularly but not kill them with kindness.

She'd also bought a bassinet, and enlisted Ella's aid in choosing bedding and clothing and all the other things apparently indispensable to babies.

The tomatoes in the garden ripened, and Skye helped to make pickles and sauce and even tomato jam from the surplus. Sometimes the smell of the spicy brews was overwhelming, but she was quite proud of her part in producing the neat rows of filled jars that lined several shelves in the big homestead pantry. She even photographed them.

Nasturtiums and marigolds made bright splashes of gold and red in the garden, and black and white willy wagtails built a nest in the purple bauhinia near the dining room. Skye found a bower-bird's grassy hide, decorated with small treasures including scraps of blue plastic and the bright ring-pulls off beer cans. She lay in wait with her camera, and was rewarded with a splendid snap of the proud owner, a handsome bird with a bright pink marking on his head like a paint splash.

She had begun to find bending and squatting difficult. Ella allowed her to do only the lightest of tasks in the house and garden, and every man around seemed to think she couldn't carry anything heavier than a matchstick. Even Kelly hastened to help her when her increasing clumsiness slowed her movements and made some everyday tasks awkward. The temperature became warmer and the heat made her feel swollen and uncomfortable. She spent most of her time indoors where the air-conditioning had been switched on.

She blessed the swimming pool, where she felt lighter and her movements were easier, but she used it only when the men weren't about, self-conscious about flaunting her ballooning body.

In November the summer storms began. Dry storms, with lightning flickering across a sky sheeted with low purplish clouds but no rainfall. There was a kind of splendid menace about the weather that Skye, using a wide-angle lens, tried to capture on film.

A farm vehicle loaded with water tanks was kept on standby as a fire truck, and Jarrah and Kelly and the two workers patrolled for fires started in the tinder dry grass by lightning strikes. One group of cattle were killed when lightning struck them as they grazed under a coolibah by one of the station waterholes.

'It's time you left,' Jarrah told Skye, and her heart stopped with dread. 'I'll get you a booking on a plane to New Zealand, and you'd better phone your parents.'

The night before she left he took her in his arms and silently made love to her with exquisite tenderness. Afterwards she lay in his arms and he murmured in her ear, 'I don't know how I'll survive the summer without you. I love you – '

'You've never said that before.'

'Of course I have.'

'No.' He had told her she was beautiful, that he loved the feel of her skin, that he went nearly crazy dreaming about her when he was out on the muster, but he had never said the words 'I love you' before. 'This is the first time.'

He was silent for a moment or two. 'You know I do. I adore every bone in your lovely body, every hair on your head. You're all my fantasies come true, and I can hardly believe that you've married me and promised to live with me and love me forever. The first time I saw you I thought you were the most perfect thing I had ever seen – '

'Thing?'

'Being. Woman. The most perfect woman. And you still are. I love your skin,' he stroked her arm and shoulder 'and the exquisite shape of your mouth –' he brushed it with his own, tracing its contours with the tip of his tongue '– the sheen and incredible softness of your hair.' His hand wandered to her breast. 'I love the fact that your body has altered to accommodate our baby, but your legs are as long and slender as ever. I love the way your laugh seems to catch in your throat as though you're trying to hold it back, and this little pulse here,' he placed a fingertip in the hollow at the base of her throat 'that starts beating sometimes when I look at you and you know that I want to leap across the dining table or drag you out of the kitchen and take you to bed.'

He lowered his head and touched his tongue to the spot, and muttered, 'It's leaping about now. I want to make love to you again, Skye. Could you stand it?'

Could she stand it? His words had woken responses that she'd thought already sated. Her body was burning into flames of desire again. She stroked his hair and brought his head up until she could meet his lips with hers. It was their last night together and she wanted it to be unforgettable for them both.

He flew her to Mt. Isa where they boarded a commercial plane for Brisbane airport. At Brisbane he bought her coffee while they waited for her flight to New Zealand to be called, and as he left her at the entrance to the departure gate he said, 'I'll see you before the baby's born.'

'I wish you were coming with me.' She'd been biting back the words ever since he had first told her she would have to go away and she had realized he had no intention of accompanying her. Now they slipped out, too late.

He just smiled at her and said, 'I wish I could.' Then he kissed her lingeringly, and let her go.

All along the carpeted corridor to the plane she wondered if deep down he was glad to be free of the responsibility, at least for the time being. He'd been looking tired lately, his cheeks almost gaunt and his eyes reddened and dulled with fatigue. The relentless round of mustering had taken its toll. But when he saw her freshly bathed and made up and dressed in one of the pretty, floaty maternity dresses she'd made herself, or a silky nightgown with a lowcut neckline showing the new lushness of her breasts, his face lost its grimly preoccupied look and his eyes kindled into appreciative warmth.

Sometimes it had been an effort after helping Ella with the meal to get out of the maternity pants and loose top she usually wore around the house and make herself pretty before the men's return. But it was worth it to see that look on his face. And if he was too tired to talk much, at least she could give him the comfort and stimulation of her body before he fell into an exhausted sleep.

He would miss that, she thought. She would too, of course. But lately she had found herself less eager, wishing that sometimes they could just hold each other quietly. She hid her reluctance from him because he came to her with such passion, rigidly held in check, and he never took his own pleasure without ensuring patiently and surely that she was totally satisfied. So it would be silly to complain. Soon she would have had to call a halt on the doctor's advice, and why should she deprive Jarrah before it was necessary? Especially as she had to admit she always enjoyed his lovemaking in the end.

Yet somewhere inside there was a tiny core of relief as she settled into her seat on the plane and buckled her safety belt.

And, she thought, with her parents she didn't need to feel she must be picture perfect all the time.

Genelle took Skye shopping for baby clothes, although Skye was sure she already had more than necessary, and treated her to lunches in city cafés, to a couple of movies and a concert. And sat in the waiting room while Skye was checked over by the doctor Genelle had handpicked to see her daughter through the remainder of her pregnancy.

Skye was amused at her mother's dedication, but knew it couldn't last, of course – eventually Genelle would be struck by an urge to get back to her painting, a faraway look would enter her eyes, and she'd need to be spoken to twice before responding. If this maternal mood lasted until after the baby was born it would be something of a record.

Sometimes Skye and her father exchanged a glance of laughing affection over her mother's oblivious head. He seemed rather bemused by his wife's mood, and once he said, 'She wasn't like this when she was expecting you or Mark. I had to drag her out to shop for baby things. I don't think she really believed she was having a baby.'

Skye laughed. 'Well, she's making up for it now.'

They visited relatives in another town, and along the way Skye looked out at the lush emerald grass and thick, spreading trees, and thought how everything seemed enclosed in green hills. Of course New Zealand wasn't always like this. There had been droughts that brought the farmers to dire straits. But they hadn't lasted for years on end without a sign of rain, and she didn't think that even the biggest of the sheep runs and cattle stations in the South Island came anywhere near the size of Opal Reach.

After they got home Jarrah phoned, as he did every time he was back at the homestead. 'I'll be flying over as soon as I can get away,' he promised. 'We're almost done mustering the brumbies now.'

'What happens to them?' she asked.

'A few might be broken in and used as plant horses for Opal Reach or other stations, but most of them will become dog tucker.'

She wished she hadn't asked.

That night, without any warning at all, Skye went into premature labour. The doctor and the hospital staff did all they could to persuade the baby to wait a few weeks longer before entering the world, but nothing worked.

With her mother holding her hand and stroking her hair while her father anguished in the waiting room outside, she gave birth to a tiny boy who never breathed.

Afterwards she felt numbed, disbelieving. Genelle cried for her, and for the baby. Even her father had tears in his eyes as he patted her shoulder and assured her gruffly that there was no reason why she couldn't have other babies, perfectly healthy ones.

Skye remained dry-eyed, even when Jarrah arrived at last bearing a bouquet of cut flowers wrapped in purple florist's tissue, his face strained and his eyes bleak, and took her in his arms and held her tightly to him.

'I'm sorry,' he said against her cold cheek. 'I'm so sorry you had to go through this alone.'

'I wasn't alone,' she replied thinly. 'My

mother was with me. It's all right.'

'It's not all right!' He took her shoulders and scanned her face. 'How are you feeling?'

She shrugged under his hands. 'They say I'm okay. There's nothing wrong with me. It was the baby. He . . . they said that some of his internal organs weren't properly formed. That's why he . . . he died. He looked perfect. I saw him. The requisite number of fingers and toes. But . . . he was dead before . . .'

'Yes, I know. Your mother told me on the phone. And I've just spoken to the charge nurse.'

'I'm sorry, Jarrah.' He had really wanted this baby, had married her because of it. 'It was all for nothing.'

'Don't.' Jarrah kissed her forehead, his face drawn in grim lines. 'It was probably for the best. There isn't much they could have done to help him.'

Skye bit her tongue on a blinding unfair rage. Jarrah was doing his clumsy best to find some consolation for them both, and she had no right to lash out at him, when she really wanted to rant and scream at a malign fate. She swallowed hard. 'They asked if we want a funeral for him.'

'Yes.' He looked at her questioningly. 'Don't we?'

She nodded.

'Here?' he asked. 'You don't want to take him back to Opal Reach?'

'That would be complicated, wouldn't it?' There would be lots of red tape, permissions and forms. And how would they transport a tiny coffin across the Tasman and then to Mt. Isa and finally Opal Reach? They wouldn't be allowed to carry it in the cabin, surely. She pictured it stowed in the hold, and irrationally felt that she didn't want her baby there, cold and alone. 'No,' she said. 'No, I want it done here in Auckland. Quietly, just us and my parents.' She added, 'Do you mind?'

'Whatever you want. I agree it's the most sensible solution, the simplest. I'll see to it.'

'How is your mother?' she asked him politely. 'And Kelly and Erik?'

'They're all fine. They sent you their love . . . and sympathy, of course.'

'That's nice of them. My mother is very disappointed. She was looking forward to having a grandchild.'

She still wasn't so sure about his mother. Ella had tried to welcome Skye to Opal Reach and the Kaine family for her son's sake, but Skye felt that Ella's early reservations about Jarrah's marriage had never entirely disappeared. Skye wasn't the kind of wife that his family had expected him to bring home. And now she hadn't even produced the baby that was the whole reason for him marrying her in the first place.

'Everyone's disappointed,' Jarrah said. 'But our main concern is you.'

'I'm all right,' she reiterated. 'A little bit tired.' That was an understatement. She felt drained, totally without emotion.

He held her close, but her arms hung lifeless. She couldn't even make the effort to lift them and hug him back.

He kissed her cheek and eased her carefully onto the pillow. 'Try to get some rest now.'

Jarrah carried their baby's coffin to the gravesite himself, and Genelle cried some more as the minister read a simple service. Afterwards Skye left a posy of white roses on the fresh, pathetically meagre mound of earth, and then they went back to her parents' house.

Jarrah treated her with the utmost gentleness, and she was dimly aware that he must be grieving. They slept in the same bed in her parents' spare room, but when he took her in his arms she stiffened.

'I know we can't make love,' he said. 'But I thought you might like to be held.'

He wanted to comfort her. Perhaps he even needed comforting himself. Skye made a determined effort to relax, but inside her was a deep, hard core of something surprisingly like animosity that she couldn't shake. She said, 'I'm tired, Jarrah. I just want to go to sleep.'

Many times she had fallen asleep in his arms after they had made love. But he didn't remind her of them. He loosened his hold and kissed her forehead. 'That's fine,' he said quietly. 'Goodnight, darling.'

Skye went through the motions of living, and even smiled, and one day to her distant astonishment found herself laughing at a humorous remark of her father's. But inside her something had died with the baby.

Somewhat to her dull surprise, Jarrah stayed on. 'Summer is the Wet,' he explained to Genelle. 'Not a busy time at Opal Reach. We agreed I'd stay until Skye has her six weeks check, and when she's ready we'll fly back home together.'

Home to Opal Reach.

The six weeks dragged by, and the doctor said she had passed her physical check with flying colours. When he asked about her emotional state she put on a bright smile and said she'd been seeing a counsellor since the baby's birth and was coping well. She didn't say she still felt nothing. Perhaps it was unnatural, but she preferred it to being swamped by a grief that she was afraid would overwhelm her.

'It's okay to resume sexual relations,' the doctor told her matter-of-factly, 'but it might be best to give yourself some time before planning another pregnancy.'

She was relieved that Jarrah didn't ask what the doctor had said exactly, just whether everything was all right. That night he gathered her into his arms and said, 'It's over now, Skye. You've had a rough time of it, but we can make more babies. After all, we must be pretty fertile.' A faint thread of humour laced his tone, and she trembled with a surge of sudden, silent anger.

His mouth hovered above hers, but Skye turned her head away. 'The doctor said we shouldn't think of it yet, to give it time.'

'Sure, there's no hurry. Maybe in a few months or so. But that doesn't mean we can't make love, does it?' He kissed her forehead. 'We can take precautions for a while.'

Her voice hard, Skye said, 'Your precautions didn't work before.'

'That's true,' he admitted. 'But there are more reliable ways. Didn't the doctor suggest something?'

He had, and she'd said she would give it some thought. 'I don't have anything yet,' she said. 'I . . . feel it's too soon.'

He stroked her cheek and her hair. 'Okay. I'll content myself with looking at you.'

Every night he continued to kiss her goodnight and move to his side of the bed, not touching her. But within a week he started talking about returning to Opal Reach. And within two they were flying back to Australia.

Summer at Opal Reach was unbelievably hot. And the rain that fell almost constantly made it humid as well. Skye was overwhelmingly grateful for the air-conditioning. She could barely stand the heat outside.

All traces of the preparations for the baby had been removed before she and Jarrah got back. She never asked what had happened to the bassinet, the drawers full of lovingly folded tiny clothes – many of them gifts from neighbours and friends – the stacks of nappies. Presumably Ella and Kelly had stored them away somewhere out of sight.

The stock were largely left to fend for themselves in the wet season. It was too hot to move them about – bad for both animals and humans. But the men were stripping the engines of the farm vehicles in the machinery shed, repairing the damage done by the dust and the rough conditions, and spent a lot of time revving motors and replacing worn parts for another season of rugged use, and carrying out repairs about the house.

They did work shorter hours than in the dry of winter, and came in for meals, including the morning and afternoon smoko. Skye roused herself to help prepare the food.

Ella had looked after the balcony plants in her absence, and Skye continued listlessly to feed and water them, but she'd lost the pleasure she used to feel in watching them thrive. Three of the African violets wilted and died, and she left the pots there and didn't care. She had a strange, almost vindictive desire to let them all die.

One evening when Ella pulled the curtains in the dining room the fabric tore in her hands. She made a disgusted exclamation and said, 'What a nuisance. I knew the sun had faded them, but the fabric's rotting away. We need to get new curtains.'

'You'll have to wait for the winter, won't you?' Skye said. The Cessna couldn't be used because the wheels would have bogged down in the mud on the airstrip, so the only way in and out now was by road, and sometimes the creeks swelled for days at a time, making even that route impassable.

'We can order from a catalogue. One came in the last mail.' Delivery had become erratic, but a bundle had arrived last week. 'Skye might like to choose the curtains,' Jarrah suggested. He looked at her enquiringly.

'No,' she said, afraid that Ella would be hurt or upset. 'Your mother knows what suits the house.'

Ella said, 'I'm sure you have ideas of your own, Skye. And this isn't the only room that could do with a bit of freshening up. Would you like to make some changes in your bedroom?'

'It'll do you good,' Jarrah insisted. 'Give you something to think about besides – '

Skye felt the blood pounding in her head. 'I have quite enough to think about, thank you,' she said, her voice hoarse with the effort to keep it steady and cool. 'You really don't have to dream up things to occupy me.'

She saw the look Jarrah exchanged with his mother, the tiny, resigned shake of Ella's head.

'Ask Beth,' Skye suggested, trying to sound pleasant and interested. 'She showed me a fabric design that she said was based on the colours of Opal Reach. I'm sure it would look perfect here.'

Kelly cast her a look of sympathy. 'Good idea, Skye. Beth's the expert at that sort of thing.'

In their room that night Jarrah said, 'When the road's clear we could go up to Mt. Isa and fly to Surfers again. Would you like that?' He took her in his arms and smiled down at her questioningly.

Surfers Paradise, where they'd spent their

delayed honeymoon, and Jarrah had made love to her with tender passion and shown his delight in the evidence of the coming baby. Where they'd been almost happy. And been closer, perhaps, than at any other time since they had met.

But they could never recapture the past. Now there was only a huge black void where for months there had been anticipation and hope and a measure of joy. Going back would remind her of all that might have been. 'No.' She pushed away from him, went to the dressing table and picked up her hairbrush.

'Skye.' He followed, and took the brush from her fingers and turned her to face him. He bent to kiss her, and she turned her head sharply aside.

There was a strange little silence while they both stood very still. Then he said, 'I want to help you. Tell me what I can do.'

'You can't do anything,' she told him. 'I'm not the first woman to lose a baby. I'll get over it.' She had to believe that was true. No one could go on living forever in this no man's land, feeling as though her heart had died within her. 'We both will.'

Because he wasn't coldhearted enough not to have felt sorrow for his lost son. But it was different for a man. He hadn't established an intimacy with the baby as a mother did, carrying the child inside her own body, feeling its every tiny movement, whispering to it in the sleepless reaches of the night.

Jarrah's arms came around her again. 'Yes,' he said. 'And we'll make other babies. As many as you want.' His lips touched her temple, her cheek, settled on her mouth. He held her tighter, and his kiss firmed and deepened.

Skye had to restrain herself from shoving him away. It wasn't fair to keep him at arm's length any longer. Some time she had to start being a proper wife to him again.

He kissed her, and she forced herself to put her arms about his neck and open her mouth for him.

This was all that was left to him, now his son was gone. And perhaps he was thinking that he needn't have married her after all. Regretting that he'd ever asked her.

Jarrah gave a sigh and slipped the strap of her nightgown from her shoulder, kissing the warm skin. His hand found her breast and caressed it, and Skye gritted her teeth.

He looked up and his hands fell away from her. He heaved in a breath, his complexion fading from the dusky hue of passion to sallow shock. 'I'm sorry. I thought . . .'

'I know. But I'm . . . not ready.' She turned

away from him, going to the bed.

Jarrah hadn't moved. 'When will you be ready?' he asked her. 'It's been months – '

'I don't know! I'm sorry, you've been patient with me, only I feel . . .'

'What is it you feel, Skye?' He came over and slipped into bed beside her but didn't touch her. 'Maybe if you talk about it that will help.'

'Nothing,' she said. 'I don't feel a thing.'

It was the stark truth, and she knew it ought to worry her. But she also knew that it was protecting her from something unbearable, and for that she was grateful.

Jarrah misunderstood. 'If you won't talk to me,' he said, 'is there someone you can open up to? My mother, or . . . do you think you need professional help?'

'A psychiatrist?' she asked him. Where on earth would they find one out here?

'A doctor, maybe.'

The doctor who held the weekly clinic in Coolya was far too busy, she was sure, to spend time trying to counsel a bereaved mother, and the difficulty of getting to him seemed overwhelming anyway. 'I'm not sick.'

Physically she was healthy, and she knew that mentally she'd always been strong. In her career those who needed emotional props soon faltered under the relentless pressure. She had never succumbed to drugs or drink, or the cigarettes that many models chainsmoked, had never needed a personal 'shrink' or even a lover to help her deal with stress, and she had directed her own life and career rather than leave it in the hands of some Svengali-like mentor or manager.

Her mother's absorption in her art had allowed Skye and her brother to develop self-reliance while knowing that if they were in real trouble Genelle would drop everything else to see them through it. Skye had learned early on to deal with her own problems, and she would deal with this, she promised herself. She would.

Knowing she should make some effort, she offered to sew the new curtains, and refrained from snapping at the family when they greeted the offer with exaggerated enthusiasm. Plainly they all thought it would be good therapy for her.

The weeks crawled by and the rain relentlessly continued to fall.

Jarrah said, 'You haven't taken any photos lately, have you?' And Skye took out her camera and found a roll of film and shot off pictures at random of the greening pastures, the dripping trees beside the waterhole, and the pigweed that had spread a lush yellow-flowering carpet about the deserted muster yards when the rains came.

'We could fix you a dark room,' Jarrah said after dinner one night. 'You've still got that book on developing, haven't you?

Skye shrugged. 'Somewhere.'

Erik offered, 'We could convert a corner of the utility room, rip out one of those big cupboards and put in a sink.'

'Are you men stuck for something to do?' Skye asked, meaning to sound lightly teasing, but instead her voice had a waspish note.

There was a small silence, broken by Kelly. 'Did you ever contact that editor about your photographs?' she asked.

Skye shook her head. 'I might,' she said vaguely, 'soon.'

'I'll help you pick some out,' Kelly offered. And because she was insistent, Skye eventually drafted a letter and sent it off with a portfolio.

Most of the horses had been turned out to forage for themselves, but Stardust and a few others remained in the home yards.

The mare seemed to have quietened since losing her foal, and Skye had taken to visiting her often. Perhaps Stardust recalled Skye's voice trying to soothe her during her futile labour. Her dark eyes looked sad, Skye fancied.

Jarrah found her one day talking to the horse, rubbing its nose and murmuring into the twitching ear as Stardust gently blew on her shoulder.

'There you are,' he said. 'I've been looking for you.'

'Why?' Her hand on Stardust's thick coat, Skye turned.

'Do I have to have a reason?' Jarrah came to her side and ruffled the horse's mane. 'Maybe I just miss you.'

He looked down at her but she avoided his eyes, watching the horse instead as the mare snorted gently through wide nostrils.

Jarrah's fingers moved closer to Skye's on the mare's neck. 'Would you like to ride her?'

Skye's hand dropped to her side. 'You said she was too unreliable.'

'She seems to have settled down a bit lately. If I'm with you it should be safe enough.'

'I'd need to learn all over again.'

'I'll teach you. When the winter comes and the ground dries out.'

When the winter came, she thought, he would be too busy.

Jarrah was restless, and spent more and more time either in the machine shed or at the computer in the station office, working on stock projections for the next couple of years.

The faint frown line between his brows had become a permanent fixture. He was short-tempered too, snapping at Kelly and Erik, though never at either his mother or at Skye.

She was miserably aware that his increasingly irritable mood was due to the growing gulf between them that she felt powerless to bridge. If she made one move towards him she knew he would sweep her into bed and make love to her like a man dying of starvation.

Her mind told her she must make the move, that she ought to appreciate his consideration, that it was unfair of her to remain aloof, depriving him of the comfort he might find in making love to her. But she couldn't bring herself to issue the tacit invitation. Her body, like her heart, refused to have any dealings with emotion.

They talked less and less, speaking to each other like polite strangers, and when they were alone the tension was almost unbearable. Whenever she looked up he seemed to be watching her, as if he was trying to assess her every expression, and her eyes would skitter away from him, her heart inexplicably pounding. Skye thought they both knew that some kind of explosion was building up.

An envelope came bearing the imprint of the magazine she'd sent her pictures to, and Kelly, emptying the mailbag onto the kitchen table when the men were in for smoko, pounced on it and insisted that Skye open it first.

'They like the photographs,' Skye said, skimming the first sheet. 'They want me to provide text to go with some of them, and I'm to send the negatives.'

'That's great!' Kelly hugged her.

Jarrah stood up and came over to her chair, kissing the top of her head. 'Congratulations. That's wonderful news.'

'I'm not a writer,' Skye objected.

'Let me see the letter.' Jarrah held out his hand.

She handed it over to him, and after a couple of seconds he said, 'They only want short paragraphs, for a photo-essay. The money they're offering seems quite good.'

'Does it?' She'd hardly taken it in.

'Probably not up to what you earned as a model,' he admitted. 'But it's not bad.'

'Go for it, Skye,' Kelly begged. 'You can do it.'

Once Kelly had got hold of a project there was no going back. The next week's mailbag carried a letter to the editor and several pages of captions that Kelly had printed on the computer. 'We'll tell them they'd better contact you by fax,' she suggested. 'It'd be much quicker.'

Less than a week later the editor faxed an acceptance and a date for publication. Skye tried to look pleased, but she felt the family's elation and Jarrah's professed pride in her, and

Kelly's enthusiastic encouragement to take up the editor's invitation to submit more work, was another attempt to give her 'something to think about'.

The rain stopped at last and the ground began to dry. 'If we want a break,' Jarrah said one morning, coming out of the shower, 'we should take it before the winter. Skye?'

She was standing at their bedroom window looking out at the high ribbons of cloud that were still tinged with pink by the sunrise. A flurry of birds, green and orange and blue feathers flashing in the morning sun, rose from a coolibah tree near the opal pool and spread into the sky.

He came and stood behind her, hooking his arms loosely about her waist and pulling her back to him, his cheek on her hair. 'We need to get away together, have some fun, find each other again.'

'And the muster begins soon.' Then he'd have no time to sort out his marriage. In his life everything was governed by the seasons. He had probably hoped she'd be pregnant again by now. 'All right,' she said wearily. Maybe it would make a difference.

'Good.' He turned her into his arms, kissing her cold lips. 'Where would you like to go? Sydney? The Barrier Reef?'

She didn't care, but said the first thing that came into her head. 'Brisbane, I suppose. Sydney's too far.' She couldn't be bothered making the journey. 'And the Reef is too touristy.'

'Brisbane, then. I'll fix it up tomorrow.'

They stayed at a hotel, but had lunch one day with Dale, and Beth invited them to dinner at her house and said they could have stayed there.

'That's kind of you,' Skye said. 'But . . .'

'I know, it's a sort of second honeymoon, I guess,' Beth said hastily. 'And you don't want family breathing down your necks.'

Skye sat dumb, and Jarrah cut in. 'Skye needs a break, that's all. We just want to relax and enjoy ourselves.'

He seemed determined to fill their every waking moment with all the pleasures offered by the city. He wined and dined her and took her to shows and films. They visited public gardens and shopping malls, art galleries and bookshops, and walked alongside the river that wound through Brisbane. They talked, but about trivial things, not about the baby they had lost. It seemed as if he was pretending it never existed.

They had been there five days when Jarrah took her to a nightclub. She put on the dress that had been Jarrah's favourite before she became too large to wear it, and carefully applied make-up, and told herself she was going to enjoy dancing again.

The lights were dim and the music loud, and when Jarrah took her in his arms she swayed obediently to the music and felt a certain comfort in being held by him. She drank more than she would normally have done, and slowly began to relax, the chronic tension of the past few months easing a little as the alcohol entered her bloodstream. She even managed to smile muzzily at Jarrah and leaned toward him, her cheek brushing his chin.

He held her tighter, and at last said gruffly, 'Shall we go back to the hotel?'

'All right,' she murmured, her head resting now on the shoulder of his jacket.

He kept an arm about her in the taxi, and when they reached their room he didn't switch on the light. Instead he put both arms about her and kissed her, tipping her head back against the curve of his shoulder, parting her lips urgently with his.

Skye was quiescent, glad of his warmth and strength. She felt she'd been living in the cold, and she knew Jarrah had felt the chill of it too. He loved her, he wanted her. She let him carry her to the bed and undress her and with a distant compassion put her arms about him and opened her thighs invitingly to allow him to enter her body, and held him as he shuddered at last within her arms, while she stared into the darkness.

'I'm sorry,' he said when it was over. 'I wanted . . . I hoped that you – '

'Shh,' Skye said, and stroked his hair. 'Don't.'

'Skye,' he groaned. 'Let me – '

'No. Go to sleep, Jarrah. Please.'

He was up before her in the morning, and she only woke when she heard the door of the room close behind him as he went out.

She lay for a while with eyes closed, but sleep would not return, so she got up and had a long shower, washing her hair and drying it in the bathroom.

When she emerged Jarrah was back. 'I brought you some flowers,' he said.

A bouquet lay on the bedside table, pink roses and carnations mixed with dainty sprays of white gypsophila. Baby's breath, it was commonly called.

The heavy, sweet scent of the roses filled the room and Skye thought she'd choke on it. She swallowed. 'Thank you.'

'I suppose we should put them in water,' he said. 'Or they'll die.'

'Yes,' she whispered. 'Yes, they will.'

Jarrah went over and picked up the flowers,

walked to her and smiled, holding them out to her. 'Here,' he said.

Skye stepped back, staring at the flowers with rising horror. All she could think about was a small white coffin with a spray of roses resting on its lid.

'What's the matter?' Jarrah stopped, frowning in perplexity.

'I don't want them.' Her voice was strained with the effort she making to keep it even, and not hysterical.

She wasn't looking at his face, but she saw how his body stiffened, as though he'd flinched. 'I know last night wasn't the greatest success – '

'It has nothing to do with last night!'

'You've always loved flowers. I thought – '

'I don't *want* them!' She felt sick, dizzy. 'Please, *take them away*.'

'Yes, of course.' His voice was clipped. 'I didn't mean to upset you.'

She closed her eyes and heard him go to the door, his muffled voice speaking to someone in the corridor. One of the maids probably. Skye hoped the woman liked roses. And carnations. And . . .

She snapped open her eyes. Jarrah was coming back into the room, his face an expressionless mask. 'Are you all right?' he asked her. For once he seemed to be at a loss.

'Yes. I'm sorry.' Skye swallowed. 'I appreciate the gesture, but . . .'

'They reminded you, somehow. I should have thought, I suppose. It didn't occur to me.'

'You weren't to know.'

They were very polite, but there might have been a wall of glass between them, inches thick. He hesitated a moment. 'I expect they'd like to make up the room soon. Are you ready to go down for breakfast?'

She assented almost eagerly. She wasn't hungry, but anything was better than this agonizing, stilted attempt at normal conversation.

After breakfast they returned to the room, and Jarrah wandered onto the balcony, looking out at the view of the city. The bed had been tidied, smoothed and covered neatly.

Skye picked up a book and listlessly pretended to read. She wondered what jolly activity Jarrah was planning for them now.

He remained there for nearly half an hour, standing perfectly still, his hands in the pockets of his casual slacks. Finally he turned and came inside, and Skye rather warily looked up.

Jarrah stared down at her. 'This isn't working, is it?'

She couldn't pretend to not know what he meant. Closing her book, she gripped it with her hands and said baldly, 'No.'

'Maybe we should go home – '

'No.'

She thought he might be counting. He still hadn't moved from the door, standing just inside it with the bright sky behind him, his face shadowed. 'What do you want to do then, Skye?' He sounded tired, defeated.

'I want to go back to New Zealand.' She hadn't even known it until that moment. She'd spent more of her life living in other countries, but she'd been born in New Zealand and suddenly was inexplicably homesick.

Jarrah was silent for several seconds. 'If that's what you want – '

'Alone.'

This time the silence was longer. 'Do you think that will help?' he asked at last.

'Nothing else has.'

He couldn't argue with that.

So he made a booking for her and phoned her parents and asked them to pick her up at the airport.

She'd scarcely been with them three days before Genelle's worried attention and her father's faintly disapproving concern and probing questions proved too much. 'I need some time alone to sort myself out,' she said with as much tact as she could summon. 'I didn't come here running home to Mummy. Could I rent the beach house for a few weeks?'

They wouldn't accept rent, but of course she could have the house. And she must take their second car, the station wagon – the buses were infrequent, and once there she'd need transport if she wanted to go anywhere at all, even to bring in fresh supplies.

'I'll be better there,' she told Jarrah when he phoned. 'It's quiet and beautiful and I'll be on my own.'

'Is that a good idea?'

'I think so,' she answered him. 'The sea is healing.'

And she had found it so. At least she'd gained a measure of tranquillity and a certain distant pleasure in the salty air and the cold foaming waves, and the dolphins that occasionally swam by, leaping in beautiful glossy curves from the water. Physically she felt fitter and stronger. She had always loved walking on the beach, and watching the endless waves. It took her back to childhood times when life had been blessedly simple and she'd thought that no matter what went wrong her parents would be able to set the world to rights again.

Well, she knew better now. But the sea and the beach still worked their subtle magic. The overwhelming numbness that had assailed her gradually began to fade to a heavy, dull resignation.

Opal Reach and even Jarrah had begun to seem far away and almost dreamlike, something that had happened to her in another lifetime. She knew she would have to deal with it all soon. When she was really recovered, and ready for it.

But now Jarrah had followed her.

CHAPTER 14

Skye half turned away in instinctive flight as Jarrah came up the broad wooden steps. Then she stopped and made herself face him, her hands at the belt of her loose robe, automatically tightening it in a gesture of futile self defence.

He was in the doorway now, and for a moment, with the sun's dazzle on the sea behind him, she saw only a looming figure with broad shoulders and an air of purpose.

When he stepped into the room she discerned the raked lines between his brows, the watchfulness of the darkened eyes. 'What's the matter?' he demanded.

'You sound like some caveman – walking in and announcing that you're taking me home! What are you going to do – drag me by the hair?'

'I didn't think it would be necessary.' He raised a hand to the back of his neck and briefly massaged the muscles, then shoved the hand into his pocket. 'Let's start again. When were you thinking of coming back to Australia – to Opal Reach?'

'Coming back?' Skye realized she sounded as though the thought was new to her. In a sense it was; she'd been living from day to day, deliberately not thinking beyond that. The way Jarrah stiffened, his head jerking upward slightly, gave her an odd jolt of satisfaction. 'I don't know,' she said, gaining a little confidence. 'I'm not ready.'

'And how long do you think it will be before you are ready?'

Thinking she detected sarcasm in his tone, she said sharply, 'I just told you, I don't know!'

For once in his life Jarrah seemed at a loss. He stood staring at her for a few seconds. Then he said quietly, 'Can we talk about it?'

'I'm not dressed,' she blurted out, caught in unreasoning panic.

A familiar curved crease appeared in his taut, tanned cheek. 'I've seen you more undressed than that –' he dropped his gaze over the thick robe '– many times.'

When his eyes met hers again she saw desire in them, and her heart contracted into a small, cold lump. She took an involuntary step backwards and his eyes turned bleak.

'I want to put some clothes on,' she said stubbornly.

'Yeah, maybe you should.' Jarrah made an impatient, defeated gesture. 'Do you mind if I make myself a cup of tea while you're doing that?'

'Help yourself.' She indicated the kitchen and dining area through wide folding doors pushed back to the walls. 'Did you . . . have you driven from Auckland?'

'I hired a car at the airport.' He strode to the kitchen, lifting the lid on the kettle to check the water level before switching it on.

And he must have been in the air or waiting at airports for long hours before that, Skye realized, already on her way to the bedroom again. She closed the door and went to the dressing table, opening a drawer with shaking fingers, dragging out underclothes. Why hadn't he told her he was coming? She could have done with some warning.

She pulled on panties, fastened a bra, her hands clumsy on the tiny hooks.

Had he hoped she'd fall into his arms, welcome him with kisses?

They hadn't even touched.

When she came out, with her hair pinned up in a knot, her body concealed under the loose, soft sweater and her feet thrust into a pair of thick woollen socks over snugly fitted leggings, he was standing at the big windows looking out, a cup cradled in one hand. A gull swooped past, tipped its wings at an angle and glided effortlessly out to sea.

'It's a magnificent view,' he said. 'Peaceful.'

'Not always. Last week there was a storm. White water as far as the eye could see.'

Jarrah nodded. 'I guess that's pretty impressive too.' He turned to face her. 'Want a cup? I made a potful.'

'I'll get it.' Forestalling him, she went to the kitchen and poured herself some tea, adding a smidgen of milk, no sugar. Jarrah liked sugar in his but no milk. He'd spilled a few grains on the counter, and Skye wiped them away with a damp cloth. It wouldn't have taken long for the ants to find them. She put her cup on a saucer and picked it up.

When she rejoined Jarrah he said, 'Can we sit down?'

Skye shrugged and chose one of the armchairs with patterned cotton cushions. Jarrah dropped into the matching two-seater, resting his arm along the back.

'You're looking better,' he said. 'More . . . rested.'

'That was the idea,' she reminded him.

'Your mother's afraid you might not be eating properly.'

Had he called to see her parents before leaving Auckland? Or had her mother summoned him by telephone, telling him she was worried? 'Was it her idea to send you here?'

He regarded her without expression. 'No one sent me.'

'I'm eating perfectly adequately,' Skye assured him. 'Lots of fresh fruit and vegetables.' There was an organic farm two miles away. 'And fish.' Some of the fishermen on the beach were generous with their catches.

'I brought some supplies in case you didn't have enough for us both.'

She'd been looking at the steaming liquid in her cup. Now her gaze flew to his face. 'You're planning to stay?'

'I thought,' he said carefully, 'it might be a day or two before we left.'

Skye lifted her cup and swallowed some tea. It was too hot. 'A day or two,' she repeated. It was probably all the time he could spare from mustering.

'If you need longer – '

'I need longer!' The cup clattered into the saucer on her lap. 'I wish you hadn't come.'

His jaw tensed. 'Well, I'm here now.'

And he wasn't going away again. Not yet. She knew that without asking. 'You could have phoned.'

He leaned over to place his cup on the big square coffee table between them. 'We didn't seem to be getting through to each other on the phone. Did we?'

Skye pressed her lips together, then took another sip of her tea. He was right, of course. He'd phoned every couple of days at first, but she had nothing to tell him, and showed no interest in what he'd been doing at Opal Reach. The cattle station in Queensland might as well have been on another planet. There had been long pauses, and gradually Jarrah had phoned less often. He'd never been good at letters, and Skye hadn't been able to dredge up the will to put pen to paper.

'Skye –' he clasped his hands, between his knees '– you do want our marriage to survive this, don't you?'

She looked at him, a ripple of shock passing through her. Was this an ultimatum? Come home with me now or it's over?

That hard masculine jaw was very evident, and his eyes met hers with sombre demand. '*Do* you?'

Her lips seemed glued together. When she managed to part them she still couldn't speak for a moment. 'I don't know.' Fright stopped her throat. What was she saying? She ought to take back the words, but an unfamiliar, hitherto unrecognized animosity welled inside and kept her silent. He looked so much as he'd always looked – handsome, totally in control, sure of himself. Untouched. While she was an emotional mess. And now he'd decided it was time she pulled herself together and returned to being Jarrah Kaine's wife.

At least she'd shaken some of that unconscious arrogance. He stood up, and she tried not to quail before the controlled anger that emanated from him. 'You won't mind,' he rasped, 'if I go for a walk?'

Dumbly she shook her head. It sounded like a brilliant idea. Give her time to gather her forces, collect her thoughts, plan . . .

Plan? She watched him go out and quickly descend the steps. She hadn't planned anything for months. And what plans could anyone make to deal with a man like Jarrah?

When he had disappeared from view Skye picked up the teacups and paused, staring out at the white-edged waves and the glimpse of sand she could see through the open doorway.

It was only a respite, of course. He had come to take her back to Opal Reach with him, and was determined he wasn't leaving without her. It wouldn't occur to him that she might refuse, that for once he might not succeed in shaping the world to his will.

The first time they met, when he'd surveyed her with that intense grey-green gaze, she'd known deep down that her life had changed forever. Jarrah Kaine had seen what he wanted and with his usual single-minded sense of purpose had gone all out to get it. To get . . . her.

She might as well have rolled over and played dead there and then.

The cups she held chinked against each other. She realized that her hands were trembling, and that she'd been standing there waiting to catch a glimpse of Jarrah walking along the beach. She swung round and hurried to the kitchen to run hot water over the cups, wincing as she scalded her hand. Damn him. Just when she'd convinced herself that she was beginning to come together he had to march in and try to take her over again . . .

It was nearly an hour before he returned, his hair ruffled by the winter breeze, the anger wiped from his expression and replaced with a granite-hard mask that gave nothing away. Even his eyes were neutral, more grey than green.

Skye looked up from the magazine she'd been pretending to read. 'Did you enjoy your walk?'

He took a moment before he answered. 'Enjoyment wasn't the object. It helped put things in perspective, I guess. Have you been on the beach much?'

'Every day. Mostly I jog.'

Something resembling a smile touched his mouth. 'Still a fitness freak.'

Skye closed the magazine and stood up, throwing it on the coffee table. 'I need to get back in shape.'

His head moved very slightly as though he was listening for hidden nuances. 'You look in excellent shape to me.'

'How can you possibly tell?' The loose sweater concealed the new fullness of her breasts, the softened contour of her stomach.

Impatience crossed his features before he smoothed it away. 'That robe you were wearing didn't conceal so much. You're still a very beautiful woman, Skye – '

'You don't have to patronize me.'

'Dammit, Skye! That isn't – '

'All right,' she interrupted. 'I'm sorry. You're doing your best and I had no right to snap at you.'

'You have the right to say whatever you want to me. You're my wife. I'm your husband. For better or worse, until death us do part. That gives you rights no other woman has ever had.'

Skye wrapped her arms about herself and stared down at the coffee table. It was made of recycled kauri planks, the now rare wood still bearing the scars of its original usage as house timber. She focused on a small jagged crack that ran from the edge of the table for six inches along one of the honey-coloured boards. 'I thought marriage was about love,' she said, 'not rights.'

'I love you, Skye. That's why I'm here.' His voice sounded very controlled, almost flat.

She thought about her dream. Thought of his strong arms wrapped about her, and how she had rested her head against him and felt safe and warm. She experienced again the overwhelming longing that had assailed her. One part of her wanted to make the move towards him, take the step that would bring his arms about her in reality.

Her feet stayed stubbornly rooted to the carpet. She went on staring at the crack in the table, old damage from some long-ago accident or failure that could never be restored, although it had been filled with an artificial wood substance and varnished over.

Jarrah gave a sharp sigh. 'I should bring my stuff in. The car's sitting outside in the sun.'

Skye shrugged, spoke around a lump in her throat. 'All right . . . I suppose.' She lifted her head. 'You can have the master bedroom.'

His eyes narrowed very slightly. 'You're not using it?'

'No.' Skye willed herself not to drop her gaze.

She slept in the single bed she had used as a teenager.

His mouth tightened, then one corner dipped. 'Back in a minute,' he said, and strode past her to the door off the kitchen.

He brought in two grocery bags first and placed them on the kitchen counter. 'You might want to put these things away,' he suggested. 'Some of them are perishable.'

He disappeared again outside, and returned carrying a cabin bag.

Skye was listlessly placing a packet of bacon in the refrigerator. A carton of eggs followed. Jarrah went into the bedroom she indicated to him.

Skye stowed a tin of asparagus and a packet of breakfast cereal in the walk-in pantry. Turning, she found Jarrah standing in the doorway, and flinched.

He stepped back. 'I didn't mean to startle you.'

She passed him to take some more food from the bags. A couple of days, he'd said. There was enough here for at least a week. She found a jar of fetta cheese marinated in olive oil and herbs. 'You don't like fetta.'

'You do.'

She put the jar down with a small thud. He'd bought his own favourite too, a wedge of tasty golden cheddar. And a jar of tiny sweet pickled gherkins, the kind she loved to eat like sweets when she felt peckish.

She was still holding the gherkins when she dug her other hand into the bag and found the sugared almonds, a bright red gift box wrapped in cellophane and tied with a jaunty silver bow. She swallowed, her throat hurting.

Behind her Jarrah said, 'I thought of bringing flowers, but . . .'

The last time he'd given her flowers she'd told him to take them away, scarcely restraining herself from screaming the words at him.

'Yes,' she said. 'Thank you.' *Thank you for not bringing me flowers.* She placed the box of almonds carefully on the counter.

'Can I help?'

No one can help, least of all you. 'No,' she said. 'I've almost finished.'

He waited while she put the rest of his groceries away, and when she closed the pantry door again he folded up the bags, not looking at her.

She watched his hands, lean and strong, wondering where he'd got the long, healing scratch on the back of the left one. Maybe he'd snagged it on some barbed wire. But she didn't ask.

He shoved the bags into a corner of the counter and turned to her.

Her gaze skittered away. 'When did you talk to my mother?'

'A few days ago.'

And that was why he was here, Skye deduced. Genelle might not have directly asked him to come, but they'd decided between them it would be a wise move. That was why her mother had asked this morning if Skye had heard from Jarrah, knowing he was probably on his way. 'I keep telling her I'm all right.'

'If you were all right you'd have come home by now,' Jarrah argued harshly.

Skye surprised herself with a short, strained laugh. 'To you?'

The harsh mask of his face didn't crack, but a whiteness appeared along his jawline. When he had unclenched his teeth he said quietly, 'To Opal Reach. And yes, damn it, to me. For God's sake, Skye – we're married. We're supposed to tackle these things together!'

'Yes, well . . .' She turned away from him, wandering blindly into the bigger room because the small kitchen area seemed too confining for them both, he was so big. 'Your way of tackling "these things" doesn't work for me.'

His voice followed her as he too moved away from the kitchen, and she could hear the angry exasperation under its controlled tone. 'Are you going to pretend this has worked for you . . . running away?'

She swung round, taut and defensive. 'I didn't run away. I told you I needed some time to myself. Time to . . . adjust.'

'And I've given it to you – '

'Oh, thanks!' Her arms came across her body, her head lifting. 'And now you've decided not to "give" me any more? To call me to heel like one of your dogs?'

Jarrah's grim composure slipped then. His eyes flashed silver fire and he took a step towards her.

Skye stood her ground, staring at him with cool defiance.

He stopped and stared back at her, his beautiful mouth hardening into a bitter line. 'What have I done,' he asked her, 'to make you hate me so much?'

She had to speak around the huge, hurtful lump in her throat. 'I never said I hated you, Jarrah.'

'You don't need to say it. I can see it in your eyes, in the way you can't bear to stand too close to me. Apparently you can't even stick being in the same country. You put several thousand kilometres and the Tasman Sea between us, and when I turn up on the doorstep you tell me you wish I hadn't come. All that seems a pretty strong indication that your feelings about me have changed since the days – the nights – when you lay in my arms, in my bed, and told me you loved me more than life . . .'

'*Don't!*'

Skye turned from him again, blundering towards the doorway, the bright water blinding her with its myriad dancing starpoints reflecting the muted wintry blaze of the sun.

Jarrah was at her side before she reached the opening, his hand curled about the edge of the door. 'Where are you going?' he demanded. 'You can't avoid this forever, Skye.'

He didn't attempt to touch her, but she backed off from him into the room again, and as if he needed some physical action to vent his feelings, he shifted his hand and gave the door a shove so that it shut with a muffled thud, closing them in together.

'Leave it open!'

He gave her a frowning, baffled look and slid the door back again. But he didn't move away, and if she wanted to go outside she'd have to pass him, probably brush against him. 'Better?' he asked.

Again she detected a thread of sarcasm that brought an answering resentment. But her panic subsided in relief. 'Th-thank you.' She despised the helpless gratitude in her voice.

'You've never been claustrophobic before.'

'I'm not claustrophobic.' It was his presence, being shut in with Jarrah, that had sparked the unwarranted panic. 'It gets stuffy in here without fresh air. And I like to have an unimpeded view of the sea.'

'Ah, the sea.' He took his gaze from her and turned without haste, pushing his hands into his pockets as he studied the view. 'You said it was healing.' He glanced at her over his shoulder. 'Has it healed you?'

He said it as though he didn't really care, standing there with his back to her, his voice so casual he might have been asking if she expected rain.

'It's . . . helped. I've had lots of exercise and fresh air.'

He looked over his shoulder again, and she thought he was going to tell her she could have had that at Opal Reach. But he was silent.

Skye moved back into the room and randomly picked up the magazine she'd discarded, closing it and placing it on the low table, needlessly aligning the edges with one of the corners. When she straightened, Jarrah had abandoned his study of the sea and was watching her.

'You're thin,' he said abruptly.

'I've always been thin. Except . . .'

'Except when you were carrying our child.'

A tremor passed through her. 'Please . . .'

'Maybe you should have had more counselling.'

'I had six weeks of it.' No amount of counselling could change what had happened. And where could she have got it? 'Having more wouldn't do any good. I just need . . .'

'Time.' He looked at her broodingly. 'I'll give you all the time you want, if it's really what you need. But I'm not convinced it is.'

'When did you get your psychology degree?'

'It doesn't take a degree in psychology or anything else to see that you're still in pain,' he told her. 'And still wanting to punish me – '

'I don't want to punish you! I'm not blaming you!' Skye interrupted. 'I never have blamed you. Never!'

'If you believe that,' he said, 'you're not only lying to me, you're lying to yourself.'

'Nothing was your fault,' she said distinctly, her teeth scarcely parting. 'I know that. I don't hold you responsible.'

'If that's true,' Jarrah said with equal deliberation, 'then you and I will share a bed tonight. And we'll make love to each other . . . the way we used to. Won't we?'

CHAPTER 15

'*No*!'

The single word was a slap in the face, a slamming door. Skye's eyes were wide and stinging, and her heart thumped heavily, nearly suffocating her.

The silence that followed her instinctive repudiation was thick with memories and unspoken recriminations. Then Jarrah stirred but didn't move from where he stood. His mouth kinked briefly. 'That's what I thought you'd say.'

The faint note of mockery roused a flare of temper. 'That was so typical!' Skye accused. 'Your answer to every problem.'

'What?' He stiffened, his brows coming together.

'Sex!' she threw at him. 'Every time something went wrong in our marriage – our relationship – you'd take me to bed and . . . and . . .'

'And love you,' Jarrah supplied quietly. 'I don't recall you complaining at the time. You were a very ardent lover yourself, and gave me unimaginable pleasure – '

'Stop it!' Skye put her hands up to cover her ears, whirling round, almost running in her haste to get to her bedroom and away from him. Once there she flung the door shut and, hearing the impact of his open hand on the outside, leaned her body against the wood. 'Go away! Leave me alone!' There was no lock.

The silence on the other side was ominous. With her ear to the cold varnished surface she muttered stupidly, 'Go away.'

There was a soft sound, very like a sigh – his hand sliding down the door. He'd been standing there perfectly still – thinking, presumably. Fuming, probably.

'All right.' His voice was gravelly and, if she hadn't known better, even defeated. 'I didn't come here to harass you, Skye. But we have to talk.' There was a long pause. And at last he said, 'Later, then.'

She knew he'd moved away by the curious emptiness that ensued. She stayed pressed against the door, her eyes jammed shut, hardly daring to breathe.

Of course he wouldn't have gone far away. Had he decided to take another walk? Or was he standing at the outer doorway again, staring at the sea . . . waiting for her to emerge?

When she was sure he wasn't going to change his mind and try to gain entry to her room or coax her out, she backed away and sank down on the bed, her fingers massaging her temples, soothing an incipient headache.

The aspirins were in the kitchen cupboard. She wasn't going out there again. Not for a long while. If she lay down maybe the threatening tightness and throbbing would go away.

She pulled the turquoise-patterned duvet away from the pillow and curled up under its comforting featherlight bulk, her head on clean white linen.

The knot of her hair was uncomfortable. She removed the elastic band and dropped it onto the floor. Her hair fanned over the pillow. Jarrah used to love to see it like that, unconfined and spilling like wanton silk about her shoulders.

He liked to touch it, telling her how seductive he found it, winding it about his fingers, spreading the strands out and letting them fall to frame her face. And often he'd turn on his back, holding her so that she lay on top of him and her hair curtained around them when he drew her head down until his questing mouth met hers.

You gave me unimaginable pleasure . . .

Abruptly Skye turned to her other side, and a sharp jab of pain at her temple warned her to avoid any more sudden movements.

She breathed carefully, tried to make her mind a complete blank.

Unimaginable pleasure. Suddenly she wanted to cry, but although her eyes stung with the effort of keeping them open, of warding off the images that lurked inside her brain, no tears came.

She was riding Stardust, galloping across the red and bleached-gold landscape of Opal Reach, among the bushy grey-green gidgees and rusty mottled bloodwoods. Her thighs hugged the mare's warm, muscular body. The horse's mane streamed in the wind, its hooves beating against the hardpacked earth, and the air was cool on Skye's cheeks . . .

She woke to a brisk tapping on the door, and Jarrah's voice. 'Skye – are you all right?'

She made a small sound of protest at being wrenched from the dream, and he opened the door. It was getting dark. Outside she could hear the waves beating on the sand. Not Opal Reach, despite Jarrah's presence.

She must have slept after all. The headache was a dull, distant throbbing, almost gone.

'I'm all right,' she said. 'I was asleep.'

'Sorry I woke you.' He looked big and dark in the shadowy doorway. 'I was worried.'

'I've been on my own here for weeks, Jarrah.'

He didn't reply to that. 'I've made tea.'

'Tea?'

'Dinner. Lamb chops and eggs, with a salad.'

Suddenly her mouth was watering. She sat up and swung her legs to the floor. 'Thank you. I'll be there in a minute.'

Dismissed, Jarrah withdrew. Skye ran a comb through her hair, and went to the bathroom to rinse her face with cold water. In the mirror over the basin she looked pale, her eyes apprehensive.

Jarrah had set the table for two. He switched on the light as Skye took a chair. 'I hope it's all right.'

She waited for him to sit down opposite her, and picked up a knife and fork to cut off the fatty edges of the two chops on her plate. 'I suppose you learned to cook out on the station camps.'

'Is that a criticism?'

'No, of course not. This looks delicious.' The chops were well browned and the eggs crisp at the edges and a trifle greasy, but the workmanlike salad of fresh torn lettuce, clumsily cut tomato wedges and thickly sliced cucumber was perfectly palatable.

'As long as I have a frypan I can rustle up some kind of tucker. There's more if you want it.'

'I'm sure this is enough.'

They were very polite over the meal. There was no dishwasher, and when they'd eaten Jarrah washed the dishes while Skye dried them and put them away. The mundane task seemed to establish a spurious kind of intimacy. Skye felt as though they were playacting.

'Would you like to read a magazine?' she asked him, and he cast her a sharp glance and after a moment said rather curtly, 'What do you have?'

She went to a cupboard and hauled out a stack of her parents' *Time* and *National Geographic* and art magazines, handing it to him in silence.

Outside darkness had fallen, and the constant thump of the sea on the shelving sand was muted. Skye picked up a book, tried to read for a little while, then said in desperation, 'Do you mind if I put the TV on?'

'Not at all. Something you want to watch?'

She had no idea what was on, but she found the remote control and switched from channel to channel until she found a police drama that seemed marginally more interesting than the other programmes on offer. She had missed the first part and so the plot was difficult to follow, but she made a determined effort all the same.

Jarrah closed the magazine he'd been looking at and dropped it to the floor. The drama was followed by a news backgrounder, and Skye kept her eyes on the screen, not unaware that Jarrah was watching her more often than the TV screen.

Eventually he stood up. 'I think I'll turn in. It's been a long day.'

He'd flown across a time zone, and she calculated that his day had actually been a short one. He'd probably started the trip very early, but he was accustomed to early rising and long days. Perhaps he too was feeling the strain of their less-than-fond reunion.

She looked up. 'You'll need sheets.'

'I'll find them. Just point me in the right direction.'

'It's all right.' She pressed the switch on the remote and the screen went blank. 'I want to go to bed anyway.'

His eyes flickered but he said nothing. Skye turned away and went to the linen closet near the bathroom, pulling out a couple of sheets and some pillow cases, and handing him a folded towel. 'I'll make the bed up.'

'I can do it.' He took the sheets from her. 'Go to bed, Skye. Tomorrow we'll talk.' She shivered inside as if it were a threat.

Skye slept better than she'd expected, but the remnants of dreams remained as she got up quietly and donned her tracksuit and running shoes.

The sea was a silvery sheet with scalloped lace edges, and her feet crunched through the frost and sank into the soft sand beneath. Another set of footprints, larger ones, clearly led from the house to the beach and angled to the right. Jarrah was on the beach somewhere.

Resolutely refusing to look in the direction of the footprints, she swung to the left and began jogging along the firm sand, her breath clouding before her, the cold air stinging her cheeks.

When she came back Jarrah was standing on the sand below the house, patiently waiting.

Skye slowed as she neared him, and stopped a few feet away, eyeing him rather warily.

'You do this every morning?' he asked her.

'Yes.' She pushed a strand of hair from her forehead, willing her breathing to steady.

'It's a great beach. Not many people about.'

'No.' The motorbike had been back again, but the sand was deserted now, except for the two of them. She turned, looking away from him across the sand, because it was rude to brush past him, but she found it difficult to meet his eyes, which were dark and watchful. 'There was a horse yesterday,' she said. 'I saw hoofprints.'

'I noticed a sign on the road when I was driving in.'

'A sign?' Skye glanced at him.

'For a riding and horse-trekking centre. They have horses for hire.'

'Oh? I . . . must have missed it.'

'A few miles back, on the main road.'

She'd been too preoccupied when she drove in to be reading roadside signs, anxious to get to the beach house and shut herself away from the world outside. 'It must be new,' she said. 'Well . . . since I was here last.'

He moved at last, turning towards the house. 'I'll make breakfast while you change,' he offered. 'After that run I guess you'll be ready for it.'

'Thanks.' She felt prickly and uncertain and was afraid her voice betrayed it. 'I'll have a shower first.'

She followed him slowly into the house, locked herself in the bathroom and stayed under the warm water for a long time, hoping it would calm her jumping nerves. Then she dressed in fitting stretch trousers and a bulky sweater over a camisole, and brushed her hair, the ends still damp from the shower, and when she opened her bedroom door was greeted by the aroma of frying bacon.

Jarrah was standing at the stove with his back to her. He couldn't have heard her approach, but he turned anyway and cast her a penetrating glance. 'Ready for your breakfast?'

He had placed a bowl of chopped fresh fruit on the table, and a pottle of plain low-fat yoghurt. It was what she usually had in the morning, followed by a slice of toast. But when she'd eaten it he offered bacon and eggs as well as toast, heaping his own plate with them, and a small laugh escaped her.

'What?' Jarrah looked up.

'A healthy breakfast of fruit and yoghurt followed by bacon and eggs?'

'It wouldn't do you any harm.'

He looked her over critically, and despite the figure-concealing sweater Skye flushed. 'I have enough here, thank you.' She spread a thin covering of marmalade on her toast and cut it in half.

'Enough to feed a bird.'

Skye's hand closed hard about the knife handle. 'I've managed all right for the last couple of months without you monitoring my every move, Jarrah. In fact, I'm very healthy.'

'Good. Then when were you planning to come home?'

Skye didn't answer, staring down at her toast without eating it. She had been living from day to day, not looking ahead at all, intent on getting herself mentally as well as physically fit before she tried to pick up the threads of her life, of their marriage. She'd thought Jarrah would be too busy to bother about her for months yet, according to the pattern of his own life.

Jarrah shoved away his half-emptied plate and said harshly, 'I see.'

Not sure what he meant, Skye looked up at him.

'Are you hoping to get back into modelling?'

Skye blinked, thrown off balance by the abrupt change of subject. 'What makes you think that?'

'Your fitness programme. Your diet.'

'I haven't given any thought to going back to modelling,' she said huskily. 'I'm not in training for it.'

'What *have* you been giving thought to?' he asked. 'Does our relationship figure in your thoughts at all?'

'Yes, of course.' Not that thinking about it had helped very much.

'I know in your world marriage isn't taken seriously – '

'My world?' Her chin lifted. 'If you mean the fashion business, you know damn all about it. You think *I* don't take marriage seriously?' She found she was outraged, trembling with anger.

'Well, do you?' he challenged her. 'Or are you preparing to get rid of excess baggage and move on?'

'What?'

'That's what you told me you're accustomed to doing, remember?'

Dimly she did recall saying something of the sort, if not those exact words. 'I don't discard *relationships* like that, and certainly not a marriage!'

'You didn't seem so certain yesterday.'

Yesterday he'd asked her if she wanted their marriage to survive, and she'd heard herself say she didn't know.

When she didn't answer immediately he said evenly, 'I'd better warn you, I won't let you go easily, Skye. I love you too much not to fight for our marriage.'

Once that declaration would have made her giddy with happiness. Oddly, now it seemed to fall into a void in her soul.

'So,' he pressed her after a moment, 'have you come to any conclusions?'

Skye shook her head. Conclusions, decisions, plans – all of them had been in abeyance. Now Jarrah was tired of waiting and had come with the intention of demanding, probably, all three.

Jarrah pushed back his chair, took his plate and went to scrape the remains of his breakfast into the waste disposal unit.

Skye automatically picked up her toast and bit into it. Her throat refused to swallow, and when she forced the mouthful down it tasted like cardboard. Her hand closed about the cold glass of orange juice that Jarrah had poured for her and she jerkily lifted it and drank some.

He checked the electric kettle for water and switched it on. Making herself finish the toast and marmalade, Skye covertly watched his movements, unusually clumsy for him, as he found tea bags and dropped two into the teapot on the counter. She used to love seeing him do these small, homely chores in her Sydney flat, after they'd spent a passionate night together in her bed. It seemed a very long time ago.

He didn't turn to her again until the tea was brewed and he'd poured himself a cup. And then his face was coolly expressionless. 'Want some?'

'Thanks.' Skye nodded. This was so domestic, it should have been cosy, but the atmosphere was almost explosive. She could feel the tension filling the space between them, thickening the air.

Jarrah placed a cup in front of her and sat down with his, staring into it for several seconds before he began to drink.

He finished quickly and put down his cup. 'What do you do with yourself all day?'

Skye shrugged. But he was making an effort to ease the mood; she could too. 'A couple of exercise sessions, some reading, walking on the beach.' And sometimes just sitting on a driftwood log watching the waves and allowing them to soothe her aching soul.

'All this time?'

'Mostly.' She looked at him defensively. 'I know it must seem like a waste of time – '

'I didn't say that.'

'I've taken some photographs,' she said. Pictures of the sun rising out of the ocean, of the morning fog curling above the incoming waves, of marram grass curving before the wind, and once of a slender silver frost fish lying dead on the sand ripples left by the receding tide.

Sometimes she'd been able to forget for minutes at a time what had happened to her, to their marriage, while she concentrated all her attention on framing and focusing the perfect shot, capturing the moment. The rural delivery van picked the rolls of film up from the mailbox, and delivered them back from the photographic shop in Tauranga within days. More and more often the finished photograph was just as she had seen it in her mind, and she did feel a distant, aesthetic satisfaction in the result.

Perhaps some of her mother's dedication had rubbed off on her after all.

'We saw the magazine with your photo-essay on Opal Reach,' Jarrah said. 'It looked great.'

He paused, 'But I told you that on the phone, didn't I?'

'Yes. Thank you.' He'd put Kelly on the line too, and his sister's bubbling enthusiasm had created a tiny warm spot in the frozen lump where Skye's heart used to be.

'One would almost think you loved the place.'

Skye's fingers tightened about her empty cup. 'Not like you do.'

His quiet voice roughened. 'I guess not.'

Opal Reach was the most important thing in his life. More important than her, than the child they had made together.

Skye stood up, going towards the sink. He was right behind her, and when she put her cup in the sink his brown hand came round and placed his own cup beside it. His breath stirred a tendril of hair at her temple, and she felt suddenly stifled.

When he moved away she almost swayed with relief. Blindly she turned the tap, forgetting that the water pressure here was fierce, and water shot out of it and splashed her sweater.

Jarrah reached across and twisted the tap back to stem the flow as she brushed at the damp wool. 'You okay?'

'It's only water.' She felt flustered and disadvantaged. 'I wish you'd stop hovering! I'll fix these.'

'Why do I frighten you?' he asked.

Skye spun to face him. 'I'm not frightened!' But even in her own ears her voice quivered with nerves.

Jarrah was frowning. 'I've never done anything to make you scared of me,' he said with controlled force. 'Have I?'

'No.' She couldn't explain. Her fear had no physical basis. 'I told you, I'm not frightened of you.'

He stepped back, out of her field of vision as she returned her attention to the sink and hastily rinsed the cups and plates, putting them on the drainer.

She wiped her hands and turned to see him staring out the open doorway of the main room. The sun had risen and made a broad, dazzling path of starbursts on the sea.

Without turning he said, 'I thought you were missing the bright lights. But here you are with not even a streetlamp in sight and apparently quite happy.'

'Happy?' She could almost have laughed.

His shoulders stiffened. He swung round to face her. 'Content. You certainly don't seem to be in any hurry to leave.'

She hadn't been. Even now the thought of allowing him to carry her back with him was alarming, stopping her throat and quickening her breath in inexplicable panic.

When she gave no answer he moved restlessly and she saw him take a deep breath. When he spoke again his voice was calm and even.

'Would you come to the riding centre with me?'

'What?' She stared at him, confused by the sudden change of subject.

'We could hire a couple of horses – '

'Are you missing yours already?'

Her voice sounded sharp, and Jarrah's face stiffened as he looked back at her. 'No. But I thought you enjoyed riding as a kid – didn't you?'

'Yes, I did. But I might have forgotten everything I knew then.'

'I doubt it. And I don't mind coaching you.' When she didn't respond he said, 'Come on, Skye – surely that's one of our problems. We never spent enough leisure time together. I know that was my fault – '

'You couldn't help it,' she said swiftly. 'You had your work.'

Jarrah nodded. 'I'm trying to make up for it. And now that . . . there's no risk, I'd like to take you riding.'

Skye's lips pressed together.

'You don't have to ride if you'd rather not. We could just look around. Or . . . if there's something else you'd rather do . . .'

Anything, Skye thought – wash my hair, read a book, stare at the sea – anything at all that would remove her from Jarrah's disturbing presence. But she doubted he would accept that. And even as her mind shied away from spending time with him, her heart yearned for the months when they'd been happy together, wanting those halcyon days back.

There was no going back, she knew that. But he had come to her and he was trying to bridge the huge gap that had somehow opened between them. She could make some effort to meet him halfway. 'All right,' she said almost inaudibly. At least it would get them away from being shut into the house, which seemed much smaller now that Jarrah was here.

She thought he almost smiled. 'Good. I didn't get the phone number, but we could drive over there later and check out the deal.'

He looked her over and said, 'I don't think you need to change. Shall we take the rental car?'

Skye shrugged, wondering how he'd talked her into this. 'My parents lent me their station wagon.'

'It's in the garage? Mine's easier. I'll get the keys.'

She guessed he wanted to drive. Jarrah always liked to be in control.

'Where's your hat?' he asked when he came back, the keys dangling from his lean fingers.

'It's winter,' she reminded him. 'And this isn't Australia.'

The sun could still get quite hot on a fine winter's day. As he continued to look at her with frowning doubt, she sighed and said, 'All right, I'll get one. What about you?' She hadn't seen a sign of the wide-brimmed hat he usually wore outdoors.

'I don't have your complexion.' He waited while she went and fetched the soft-crowned, stitch-brimmed hat she sometimes wore on the beach, then nodded approvingly and led her out to the car.

The woman who ran the riding centre insisted that they both wear helmets which she provided, anyway, causing Skye to feel a mean little spurt of amusement. She wondered if Jarrah would flatly refuse, but after turning it in his hands with slightly raised brows, he put his on and buckled the strap, while the owner helped Skye to fit hers.

Jarrah had hired the horses for two hours. The woman questioned them about their level of experience, and watched Jarrah help Skye onto the docile dappled mare that he had helped to choose, before he swung confidently into the saddle of a bay gelding with a handsome head. She asked them to ride round a nearby paddock and, apparently satisfied that he'd been telling the truth about his level of expertise, handed Jarrah a sketch map of recommended routes through farmland and quiet country roads, and left them to find their way.

They started off at a steady walk, and Jarrah dealt with a couple of farm gates, taking a trail that led into a stand of cool, damp-smelling bush. Skye knew that he was keeping an eye on her as he rode at her side, adjusting to her pace, but she had quickly settled into the rhythm of the horse and automatically used her hands, thighs and knees to guide her mount, the movements she'd learned as a child easily coming back to her.

They entered the trees and overhead the leaves shut out the sun, and damp ferns and small bushes crowded the edges of the slightly muddy track. Creepers and dense new growth under the tall, shady canopy forced riders to stick to the trail that someone had cut through the bush.

Jarrah was looking about them with interest, and Skye said, 'It's different from your kind of bush.'

Jarrah nodded, and his grey eyes rested on her for a moment. At Opal Reach the taller trees were more open-branched, less crammed together, and even along the creek beds the vegetation was seldom as thick and lush as this.

A fat multicoloured native wood pigeon flew across in front of them, its wings stirring the air with a characteristic whoomp-whoomp sound. Jarrah's horse gave a little start, but he easily controlled it. Skye's plodding mare didn't even blink. Skye leaned over and patted the warm, muscled neck.

They came out again into more farmland, the small paddocks emerald green, a few dark, spreading macrocarpa trees with thick, shaggy bark growing along the fencelines. Fat, glossy black and white cattle cropping the thick grass lifted their heads and stared as the horses crossed their territory. Skye thought how small and closed-in it all must seem to Jarrah. She dug her heels into the horse's side and took it up to a trot, Jarrah following behind until they reached another gate.

He opened it for her and closed it behind them, then they were on a narrow, dirt road, and he said, 'How are you doing?'

'Fine.' Some of the tension that had kept her wound up like a watch-spring ever since he'd arrived had begun to dissipate. She was almost enjoying herself. It was a long time since she'd been on a horse, and now she wondered why.

Suddenly struck by a rare moment of unexpected pleasure, she urged the mare into an easy canter and felt the sun and the wind on her face.

Jarrah let her go, but she knew he was right behind, still watching her – watching over her. They went up a rise and the road ended on a grassy bluff overlooking the sea and a wide estuary cutting into the land. Skye eased her mount to a standstill a few yards from the clifftop fence, and let it lower its head to the long, windblown grass.

Jarrah halted alongside, his gaze on Skye's flushed cheeks and wind-brightened eyes. She looked away from him to the sea breaking along the sand below, and involuntarily said, 'If I'd known about the riding centre I might have done this before.'

'We can do it again. Every day if you like.'

For how long? Skye thought. How many days would he be prepared to be patient, to wait for her to decide to go back with him? She eased back the reins and brought up the mare's head, turning her.

At the head of the estuary a number of houses huddled together on a flat triangle of ground below another bluff, and a few boats were anchored in the water nearby. The little settlement looked tranquil and protected, nestled under the soaring cliffs. 'I wonder how you get to there?' she said.

'Maybe it'll be on the map.' Jarrah pulled the paper from his pocket. 'It's a fairly long way round, but if we rode back along the beach I think we could make it within the two hours.'

He turned his horse, gathering the reins in one strong hand. 'Would you like that?' he queried her.

Skye nodded. 'I think so.'

His searching, slightly sardonic glance emphasized the lack of real enthusiasm in her voice, but he didn't comment. 'This way,' he said, tucking the map back in his pocket. 'I'll lead.'

'Don't you always,' she muttered under her breath. But Jarrah rode ahead as if he hadn't heard.

The trail led in a winding, circuitous route down to sea level, and they took it slowly through scrubby manuka overshadowed by its taller cousin, kanuka, and blade-leaved flax and toetoe. Finally they reached a sandy alluvial flat with a sluggish creek coursing to the inlet, where ripples lapping at the sand heralded the incoming sea.

They rode along the white pumice sand, and the creek widened and divided around several low sand islets. By the time the horses drew level with the settlement on the opposite side of the creek, the islets had disappeared under the incoming tide.

Jarrah drew to halt, and Skye reined in her mount alongside. It was difficult to gauge the depth of the creek at that point. The water lapped at the sand near the horses' hooves, and the gelding moved forward two steps to the edge and then came to a stop, shaking its head and snorting in disapproval. Across the creek the houses dreamed in the cool shadow of the bluff, silent and seemingly uninhabited but tantalizingly close.

'I don't think we can make it.' Jarrah turned to Skye. 'It could be dangerous trying to get across. Unless we go back . . .'

Skye shook her head. 'No. There's no point. We can see it from here.' But she was disappointed. The little settlement looked a haven of peace, a romantic hideaway cut off from the world. But perhaps close up it wouldn't be as attractive, anyway. With a small sigh she turned away, heading towards the beach.

The sea breeze was cool and salty on her face, and the mare sniffed, raising her head and increasing her pace. Skye smiled and let her break into an eager trot.

Although the tide was rising, a broad strip of dry sand remained between land and sea, stretching into the distance. There was no mist about, and the pale winter sky was clear and high, but for a moment Skye was vividly reminded of her dream of yesterday – the big horse rising from the mist, the man on its back galloping towards her.

She glanced about as Jarrah brought his horse level with the mare. His direct, gum-leaf gaze caught Skye's, and something hidden in the depths of his eyes set her heart hammering.

Her whole body seemed to tighten and she felt herself flinch, her gaze sliding from his. Without even thinking about it she dug her heels into the mare's sides and urged her to a full gallop.

CHAPTER 16

The sound of the horses' hooves was subdued by the sand, But Skye knew that Jarrah was a heartbeat behind. Some primal female instinct rose in her, heating her blood and sending it speeding it through her veins. Her eyes and cheeks stung, and the horse's mane streamed in the wind. An errant wave scooted up the beach in a flurry of white foam, and the mare's hooves raised splashes that cooled her hot skin, leaving the taste of salt on her lips.

She thought she heard Jarrah say her name, but her only response was to lean forward and encourage the mare to increase the pace still more, and she felt a shivery adrenalin rush of exhilaration.

Jarrah pulled ahead, turning his head to see her face, and every muscle in her body tightened as she waited for him to catch the mare's reins and slow her down, stop this wild, reckless ride.

She threw him a single defiant look, not slowing down at all, and heard his laughter borne on the wind.

Both his strong hands remained on the reins of his own mount, and he stayed just feet away from her and the mare. Skye returned her total concentration to controlling the mare and keeping her seat in the saddle.

Jarrah was still pacing her, and she knew that he was dividing his attention between her and his own horse. But she kept her eyes on the long ribbon of sand in front of them.

They must have gone for two miles between the rising sea and the sandstone bluffs that gave way to deserted, windswept sandy hillocks before they reached the first of the houses along the shore.

A black dog, its feathery tail rotating madly, dashed from one of the houses across the sand, vociferously barking, but the horses ignored it and soon outstripped it. Jarrah drew ahead, opening a gap between them, and then cut across the mare's path, not too close, but near enough to check the breakneck speed, and as he eased back his own mount the mare slowed too, until the gap closed and the two horses stood heaving and snorting gently, with Jarrah facing Skye, his knee almost touching hers.

Skye leaned across and stroked the mare's

damp, glossy neck.

When she straightened, her glance collided with Jarrah's hard grey stare. 'What was that all about?' he asked her levelly.

'It was about riding,' Skye answered, with the slightest toss of her head.

'Do you think it's wise to go hell-for-leather like that when you've not ridden in years?'

'I was doing fine,' Skye retorted. 'You didn't need to stop me.'

'There could be people about here,' he said shortly. 'It's not safe.'

'I know. I would have slowed down on my own, if you'd trusted me.'

'Would you?' His voice was curt.

The gelding shook its head, snorting loudly, and Jarrah gave it a pat on the shoulder. 'Yeah, I have my doubts too, fella,' he said.

'I'm not stupid, Jarrah!' But the hint of humour in his reaction tempered her exasperation.

'I know you're not.' His head came up and he gave her a look that she couldn't decipher – as though he was thinking something over for the first time. 'Skye – '

'Hadn't we better get these horses back?' she asked, an unaccountable flutter of alarm in her throat.

A slight frown appeared between his brows.

'We've plenty of time.' But after a moment he swung his horse's head around and turned the animal.

They walked the horses the rest of the way to one of the accessways leading to the road, and within half an hour they were trotting up the driveway of the riding centre.

When they reached the yard where they'd mounted, Jarrah was out of his saddle before Skye had freed her right foot from the stirrup. As she gathered the reins and dismounted, she felt hard hands at her waist, sliding under the loose jersey, steadying her and lowering her gently until she stood with both feet on the ground.

She heard the inhalation of Jarrah's breath, felt the warm hardness of his chest at her back, and knew that she had stiffened in every muscle.

'All right?' he said. His thumbs moved over the silk of the camisole she wore beneath her shirt. They might as well have been on her skin, leaving tiny firepoints of sensation.

Dismayed by that reaction, Skye said huskily, 'Yes. I really don't need you . . .'

'Right.' He withdrew his hands without haste, and she looped the reins over the mare's neck, ran a hand over the warm sleek flesh. Confused and obscurely angry, she didn't want to look at Jarrah.

He had turned back to his own horse, and then the owner came out of the office that was attached to the old wooden farmhouse, and asked how they had enjoyed their ride.

By the time they returned to the rental car it was way past midday. Jarrah hung his forearm on the steering wheel and said, 'Are you hungry? We could drive to Tauranga for lunch if you like. There would be places there where we could get a decent meal, I suppose?'

'*You* must be hungry,' Skye guessed. He was accustomed to three hearty meals a day, fuel for hard physical work. 'Tauranga's a nice place, and quite large.'

Apparently taking that for agreement, Jarrah started the engine and headed along the road to the town.

Skye gazed out of the side window, watching the green fields and kiwifruit orchards pass by. Jarrah asked a few questions about farming in the area that she did her best to answer, glad that he wasn't pushing for a more intimate conversation. And when they drove into the seaside town she guided him to the shopping area and they found a place to park the car.

The restaurant he chose was near the waterfront, where civic pride was evident in the plantings and new brick paving. Over lunch Jarrah spoke little, merely remarking on the view and asking if she knew the names of one or two plants, pouring white wine into her glass and teasing her gently when she couldn't finish the Caesar salad she had ordered.

Skye experienced an odd sense of déjà vu; it was so much like many meals they had shared in little Sydney restaurants before she had told him she was pregnant and he asked her to marry him. Imperceptibly she found the nervous expectation that had assailed her since his unexpected advent begin to dissipate.

Jarrah seemed in no hurry to leave, lingering over the last of the wine and then ordering two coffees. He lazed back in his chair, his eyes veiled and heavy-lidded as they studied her.

When they finally left he seemed interested in exploring the town, taking a firm hold of Skye's hand while they wandered along the street windowshopping. She momentarily resisted but when he didn't release her she let her fingers lie inert in his. There was an odd little flutter of some complex emotion in her throat. She was surprised to find a faint, cautious pleasure mixed with alarm at the familiar warm strength of his hand curled about hers.

Jarrah paused outside a florist's shop and turned to her, then without speaking went on walking.

At a secondhand shop, its window crammed

with knick-knacks and genuine antiques, he stopped again. 'This is your kind of place, isn't it?' he asked her.

She recalled taking him to the Paddy's Market in Sydney, spending the morning bargain-hunting, when he'd bought her the woodcut of a pair of Japanese lovers. 'I suppose it is,' she agreed.

He led her inside, and seemed content to browse around the clutter of old furniture, musty books and old glass and china, asking her if she liked this piece, or that, or what she thought of the collection of Edwardian prints in gilt frames that hung on the wall.

When she picked up a tiny, bulbous and long-necked green glass vase, delicately handpainted with a spray of violets, he said, 'Do you like that?'

'It's a little charmer,' she said, and made to put it back, but Jarrah's hand reached out and took it from her.

He turned to the elderly man behind the counter. 'We'll take this.'

'There's no need –' Skye started to protest, but Jarrah took no notice. He dug out his wallet and handed over a couple of notes.

After they'd left the shop he pressed the small tissue-wrapped parcel into Skye's hand. 'Here. At least I know it's something you like.'

He knew he couldn't buy her flowers, Skye

realized bleakly. So this was a kind of substitute. She should be grateful. Instead she felt for some reason infinitely sad, with a lump in her throat that prevented her even saying thank you.

He stopped to buy a newspaper and soon afterwards they headed back to the car and drove to the beach house in almost total silence.

When they got home Skye put the still-wrapped vase on the dressing table in her room, and went to the window. The tide was receding again, the beach wide and wet below the high-water mark. The sun faded with the onset of evening. She took off her jersey and put on a light sweatshirt and pants and padded out to get her sneakers.

Jarrah was dropping the newspaper he'd bought on the coffee table. 'Going jogging again?' he asked her.

'Yes. I'll be about half an hour.'

He nodded, and picked up the paper again.

She expected to find him deep in it when she returned, but instead she was greeted by the smell of cooking. A little later she sat down to steak and chips and a salad. 'I didn't expect this,' she told him, picking up her fork. 'You don't have to cook for me.'

'It's little enough,' Jarrah said. 'Besides, I needed something to do.'

After they'd eaten and cleaned up, Skye

retrieved a book that she'd been part-way through before he arrived, and took it to the deck, switching on the outside light so she could see the print when she had settled herself into a comfortable outdoor chair. It was cool but not unpleasant, and she had put on her jersey again.

She kept expecting Jarrah to force some kind of confrontation, try to make her commit herself to going home with him. The book, she was well aware, was a defence. She hoped he would take the hint.

He did, bringing the paper out and sitting silently on the step to peruse it. She wondered how much of it he'd read before he put it aside to cook the dinner.

Skye turned a page, not taking anything in. She couldn't accuse Jarrah of bothering her, but his silent, apparently absorbed presence was unsettling.

She looked at his bent, dark head, the way his hair waved above the collar of his sweater, and noticed how the broad shoulders flexed under the wool as he turned a page. His hands, strong and steady, folded back the page, and the muscles of his thigh flexed beneath the fabric of his jeans as he shifted his leg to a more comfortable position.

She had always liked watching Jarrah. Even now, among the cold ashes of her feelings, a faint spark of remembered warmth made itself felt. If she reached out a hand to touch him . . .

As if she had, he suddenly looked up, and their eyes met for a breathless, silent moment. A whirring beetle flung itself at the light on the wall, and as though it were a signal, Skye shot to her feet, her gaze still locked with Jarrah's.

Then he stood up too, a deep blaze in his eyes, the paper forgotten, the night breeze lifting a sheet and scudding it across the boards.

'Skye –' His hand moved, going out towards her in an almost pleading gesture.

'I'm going to bed,' she said abruptly, her finger trapped in the leaves of the book. 'I'm not used to horse-riding any more.'

The blaze died, his face going remote and expressionless. 'Of course,' he said. 'You're not sore?'

Skye shook her head. 'Just tired. Goodnight.'

'Goodnight, Skye.' He didn't move, and Skye turned and left him, her heart thudding unaccountably, as if she'd escaped some dire danger.

Which was nonsense, of course. Jarrah was being extremely civilized and patient. Today he'd been . . .

What? she asked herself.

He'd been like the lover she'd known in Sydney, a long time ago when their affair was new and exciting and sweet. It was if he was wooing her all over again. Except that now there were no flowers.

By request. He knew she didn't want flowers. Skye shivered as she stripped off her jersey and bra and fumbled for her night-time T-shirt. Her emotions were all over the place. When Jarrah touched her she went rigid, paralysed by a strange, irrational terror. Yet just now she'd been longing to touch him, feel the warm silkiness of his hair, run her hands over the breadth of his shoulders. And then when he'd looked as though he might let her, she'd run away in panic.

She *knew* he wouldn't hurt her – not physically. And it wasn't as though she didn't already know what it was like to be made love to by him. He was her husband, whom she had promised to love and honour and cherish.

So why couldn't she love him?

She slept better than she'd expected to. Perhaps the horse-riding had that effect. When she got up she was a little stiff, so did some stretching exercises before finding her joggers and going quietly down the steps to the beach.

This time Jarrah didn't appear, but when she made her way back to the house he was leaning on the doorway as if he'd been waiting for her.

'Breakfast?' he said as she came up the steps.

'Thank you, but there's no need for you to make it.'

'I want to. I want to . . .'

She stopped, because he hadn't moved and she didn't want to push past him. 'What?' she asked, staring at the brooding darkness of his eyes.

His mouth twisted strangely. 'Get you breakfast,' he said at last. And stepped inside so she could follow him into the room.

After breakfast Skye fetched her camera from the bedroom, more in order to look busy than for any specific plan. 'I'll be on the beach,' she said.

Jarrah saw the camera in her hands and said, 'I thought I might go for a walk. Do you want anything from the shop?'

Skye shook her head, relieved that for a while at least she'd be alone. It was quite a long walk to the store. 'You'd better lock up,' she said. 'There's a key hanging near the back door.'

Jarrah nodded. 'What about you?'

'I expect you'll be back before me.'

She walked down to the beach and along the sand, and felt some of the tension drain out of her. Yesterday it had almost been lulled into non-existence for a time, but this morning it was back, perhaps because she was sure that beneath Jarrah's apparently laid-back manner he was hiding a deep and dangerous tension of his own.

She walked a long way, snapping a couple of random frames but knowing the camera was only an excuse. Sitting down on a big, half-buried driftwood log, she gazed at the limitless, lazy sea and tried to empty her mind, to banish the perplexing, contradictory thoughts and feelings that seethed inside her. After a long time she almost succeeded, feeling some kind of peace seep into her soul.

Clouds scudded across the sun, and the sea turned dark. Skye got up and walked slowly back along the beach. Jarrah was back, but when he stood up and put aside the book he'd been reading she said, 'I'm going downstairs to do my exercises.'

When she finished that, Jarrah was making lunch. She got accustomed to him preparing meals for her – for them both. And when she started one he would pitch in and help. In the afternoon he suggested they go riding again, and after the barest hesitation, Skye agreed. On horseback it was difficult to sustain a conversation. Skye knew eventually they would have to talk. She wasn't sure why the thought of it stopped her throat with fright. Sometimes she wondered if subconsciously she was punishing him for all the times she had wanted to talk with him and he'd been too busy or too tired, or too intent on making love to her, brushing aside her attempts to deepen their relationship through verbal communication.

Over the next few days they established some kind of routine. He made breakfast while she jogged, then she'd take her camera to the beach, usually they'd have lunch and spend the afternoon riding. Then she'd jog on the beach again before dinner, and afterwards discourage any further discussion by turning on the television or burying herself ostentatiously in a book. Or sometimes they walked together on the beach, in a semi-companionable silence.

She was well aware that Jarrah was being exceedingly patient, that he watched her as if waiting for some signal, looking for a sign that she was prepared to listen to him, perhaps agree to return to his home, be his wife again. He scarcely touched her, only occasionally capturing her hand when they walked, or helping her mount and dismount when they rode. Once when the sky clouded over when they were on the beach, and she shivered, he put an arm about her shoulders and rubbed her arm with his warm palm. She stiffened, and he let his arm drop without comment.

He'd been there five days when after lunch she said, 'Are we riding? I'll get changed.' And Jarrah said, 'No, I think not today.'

She cast him a look, and saw he looked both

wary and determined. He said, 'I thought we might – '

'I'll go back to the beach, then,' she said quickly. 'Take some more photos.'

'You've already taken pictures today.'

'The light's changed. I want to get some more.'

'Then I'll come with you.'

'No. I'd rather be alone. Company's distracting when I'm working.'

Working. She'd never called it that before, but it occurred to her that since being here that was what her photography had become – something she worked at, trying to perfect her skills, develop a professional standard. She'd begun lately to start considering where she could sell her prints, looking at magazines with an eye to market research, even buying some at the store with that in mind. She had no desire to go back to modelling, but the thought of a new career was mildly stimulating.

'All right,' Jarrah said evenly. 'I'll see you when you get back.'

Much later when she pushed aside the door and walked in he rose from one of the chairs by the coffee table.

Walking into the room, she placed the camera on the table.

'You've been a long time,' he commented.

'I don't have to account to you for my time, Jarrah,' Skye said flatly, that unaccountable animosity rising again. 'That's why I came here.' She straightened and faced him across the kauri square. But she'd used all her film ages before, and had spent most of the time staring at the sea and the sky, and thinking. And making a decision.

He'd taken a couple of steps away, nearer to the slider, but now turned to her. 'No one at Opal Reach forced you to do anything.'

'I wasn't implying anything like that.' It was impossible to explain. 'Only I was your wife.'

Jarrah stiffened, his jaw clenching so that she saw the muscles move under his cheek. 'Yes,' he said. 'That was the whole trouble, wasn't it?' His chest lifted, and she saw his fist clench before he shoved it into his pocket. 'I can't tell you how desperately I regret dragooning you into the wedding and burying you at Opal Reach.'

Skye quelled her instinct to turn away, to go on avoiding confrontation. She couldn't run away forever, and he wasn't going to give up. 'You . . . did what you thought was best.' Was his regret for his sake, or hers? Or perhaps for his beloved station? She hadn't been much of an asset to it.

Jarrah stood strangely silent, perhaps expecting her to make some excuse again to escape. And he would let her, she realized, as he'd allowed her to evade his every attempt at a discussion of their relationship since the day he arrived. 'Did you ever mean to stay?' he asked her, his eyes fathomless against the light behind him.

Her breath caught. 'Of course I meant to stay! We were *married!* And there was the baby.'

'I just wondered.'

'*Why*?' Skye discovered she was shaking.

He was quiet for a moment. 'Your flat in Sydney,' he said finally, 'was so . . . it was a home. A place that expressed your personality – vividly. You'd stamped yourself on it. Yet you never seemed the slightest bit interested in Opal Reach. You didn't want to redecorate, or even make minor changes. You never tried to put down any roots as far as I could see. Apart from your books and a few oddments in our room – and a couple of photographs – you've left no mark on the place.'

'Jarrah – I couldn't come into a house like Opal Reach and *change* everything! It's a family home that was built for your mother! You surely didn't expect me to waltz in and take over from her?'

'Not take over,' he said. 'But show some interest – '

'I did show some interest!'

'In a polite sort of way,' he conceded. 'You acted like a visitor.'

'I was *treated* like a visitor! Your mother hardly let me do anything, and you made it very obvious you found me nothing but a nuisance on the station – '

'You weren't a nuisance – just a responsibility,' Jarrah said impatiently. 'One I could do without when I had other things on my mind.'

Skye smiled sadly. 'Yes.' He could do without her very well. Which begged the question of why he was here, why he was so determined to take her back with him, when he had made plain how useless he considered she was to a man like him. In every way but one.

'My mother was doing her best – '

'I know – I'm not criticizing her. She was very kind to me.'

'She tried to make things easier for you. Knowing you were pregnant, and not accustomed to the life on an outback station, she was afraid you might find it all too much. She did everything possible to make it less of a culture shock.'

'Did she tell you that?'

'She didn't need to, but yes, she said something of the sort after you . . . took off.'

'Well, it was . . . good of her,' Skye said

lamely. 'But I think she's probably relieved, actually, that I'm not getting in her way any more.'

'What do you mean? You were never *in the way*.'

Helplessly, Skye shrugged. 'She'd been in charge of that house ever since she was married. It was her . . . her domain. And it must have been hard for her to make room for a total novice who knew nothing and wanted to feel useful. And I know she did try.'

'You think she didn't want to give up the keys to the castle?' Jarrah's voice was dry.

Skye said hastily, 'I'm not complaining about it, Jarrah – '

'Did she ever tell you she's been thinking of moving to Adelaide?'

'Adelaide?' Skye's eyes widened. 'Not because of me?'

'No – not because of you. When we were flying back from there after my aunt's operation she said maybe it was time she got herself an easier life, and that she quite fancied going to live near her sister. She'd almost made up her mind to do it and I'd got as far as looking into hiring a housekeeper. But then I brought you home and she stuck around to help. Because she knew Opal Reach was very different from what you were accustomed to. And she reckons you were pretty game, the way you pitched in to help even when you were feeling rocky.'

'But she didn't think I was cut out for life at Opal Reach. She had doubts from the start, didn't she?'

'Maybe, but she never said so. Naturally she was a bit thrown at first. It was a . . . surprise, our marriage.'

A shock, he meant. He'd never intended to marry someone as unsuitable as herself. Her unexpected pregnancy, which he thought he'd guarded against, had been the wild card that forced his hand.

She said, 'You must have felt cheated when I lost the baby.'

'Cheated?'

'I couldn't even produce a normal, healthy child. After you'd married me because of it.'

Jarrah took a step towards her. It was a moment before he said, his voice oddly hoarse, 'Is that what you think?'

'What else? I'm not saying you didn't love me, in a way, but . . . it wasn't a marrying kind of love, really. Was it?'

He looked almost stunned. 'Skye, you've got it all wrong.'

'You just said you regretted marrying me. You wouldn't have proposed to me if I hadn't been pregnant.'

'Not then,' he conceded. 'But from the first moment I saw you I was in love with you. I could never look at any woman after that without comparing her to you – '

He called it love. But was that what he'd felt for her? She thought of his well-known intolerance of anything short of perfection, his pride of possession. 'You loved my body, and the way I looked, the feel of my skin and hair. You've told me that often enough. What will happen when my skin has lines and my body sags with age and my hair turns grey and thin? When men don't look at me twice any more, and don't envy you having me on your arm?'

'Men will always envy me if they have any sense at all. Provided you're still on my arm.' His eyes searched her face. 'Skye – I know you gave up everything to have my child, and now your career's wrecked and the baby's gone, and all you're left with is me. I can't blame you for hating me – '

Skye's voice trembled. 'I told you, I never hated you.'

'Actions speak louder than words.' He lifted his eyes and looked about, reminding her she'd removed herself from him, from Opal Reach, travelled across an ocean to come here.

Skye blinked, staring at him, with the sea shining behind him, his eyes darkened and his expression angry but controlled, and she tried to explain. 'I wasn't running away from you, Jarrah. Only I needed this time. I . . . suppose I was like an animal, wanting somewhere to hide and lick my wounds.'

'I tried to help – '

'I know. I told you, I'm not blaming you.'

'Not even for not being there?' he asked quietly. When she didn't answer he said, '*I* blame myself, Skye. I've blamed myself day and night since I walked into that hospital room and saw you looking cold and lost and alone. And knew it was my fault.'

CHAPTER 17

A crack shivered through the hard shell Skye had grown around the terrible rift in her heart. Jarrah had never said that before, never hinted at any feeling of guilt.

Of course he had said he was sorry, and she knew he was – sorry for her, sorry he'd lost his son. She knew he regretted that he had been too busy to wait with her in the weeks before their son's birth, that his good intentions had been thwarted and in the end his promise to her had been broken. But she'd had no idea that he had held himself to blame at all. Circumstances and the exigencies of his work had intervened, and she'd tried very hard to understand that, to forgive him for his involuntary defection, to convince herself that it was unreasonable and immature to penalize him for that.

She touched her lip with her tongue. 'You couldn't know the baby would come early.'

'No. And I had to send you away. There was no other choice. But next time – if there is one – I'll be with you all the way, I swear on our baby's grave.'

The crack widened. 'I did . . . resent it,' she admitted, only now realizing how much. 'It's unfair and I tried not to, but you weren't there and I *needed* you –' She had to stop, her throat locking on unshed tears of anger and sorrow and deep, aching hurt.

His face changed, and for a brief moment she saw pain. 'I'm so *sorry*, Skye.' The words seemed wrenched from him. He took another step towards her and then stopped again.

She'd rejected him so many times now, he was wary of touching her. Skye said, 'I know. And I know you must have grieved for our son. But you've never . . . it's never been obvious. You seemed . . . untouched.'

'What was I supposed to do?' he asked hoarsely. 'Of course I grieved – for our son, and even more for you. And for what looked horribly like the slow death of our marriage. But life doesn't stop for grief.'

'I know,' she said again. 'It's stupid and weak and wrong of me, but I think I resent your strength, because I can't match it, I can't . . . live up to it.'

'Live up to it?' He shook his head in quick

denial. 'Skye,' he said despairingly, 'I was trying to be strong for *you*. You were making such a gallant effort to go on living normally, though anyone could see your heart wasn't in it. I don't see how my falling apart could have helped you.'

Skye couldn't imagine him falling apart. 'I felt,' she said, 'that you were writing off our baby . . .'

'Writing him off?' Jarrah sounded shocked.

'You said it was for the best, and gave me flowers, and . . . I know you waited for me while I physically got over it, but back at Opal Reach you just . . . went back to working and living and . . . and expecting us to make love as if nothing had ever happened. As if he'd never existed. And I couldn't . . . think like that . . . feel that way.'

'*Skye* – I wasn't thinking like that either. I could never forget what had happened to you – and to the baby. But if he'd survived his life would have been short and painful. You wouldn't have wanted that for him?'

'No.' She looked down at the floor, fixing her gaze on a smudge of sand that marred the carpet. 'I knew you were right. And of course you had to go on with your life, your job. I knew I wasn't being sensible, or even just. Only . . . I kept thinking maybe you were glad he'd . . . died, because if he hadn't you'd have had a child who was less than perfect.'

When she dared to meet his eyes again she knew she'd shaken him. She could see he was holding back a surge of anger.

'He was my *son* –' Jarrah said at last. 'I would have loved him no matter what.'

Skye looked away again. 'You . . . you put down Stardust's foal without a second thought.'

For a second or two he was silent. Then he burst out, 'For God's sake, Skye! It's not the same thing! And as for that foal – we did the kindest thing we could. It wasn't just some minor fault of conformation. The poor animal would have been crippled – unable to walk, let alone gallop.'

Startled, her eyes returned to his face. 'I didn't know that. You wouldn't let me see.'

'I was trying to protect you!'

'You did a lot of that. Too much, I think.'

'Kelly said that. You look so fragile,' he muttered. 'And cattle raising can be a brutal business. When you nearly fainted at the yards I was terrified you'd find you couldn't stomach it – or me. That you'd be revolted by it all and bolt back to the city.'

'I wouldn't have got dizzy if I hadn't been pregnant. I wasn't expecting what I saw – and the smell. My stomach was sensitive to smells just then. Worse things went on in some of the countries where I lived as a child. And I can hardly be self-righteous about the cattle business unless I give up eating beef.'

She thought his expression lightened a little. 'Can we walk on the beach?' he asked her. 'We have some talking to do – don't we?'

Jarrah wasn't a man who talked easily about his emotions, and he was unused to sitting – or standing – still. He needed some kind of action. With a flutter of hope in her chest, Skye agreed.

He stood back to let her go onto the deck ahead of him. The frost had gone and the sun was a brilliant dish of light. Skye hesitated, and then pulled off her socks before going down the steps and across the short expanse of sparse lawn. Jarrah did the same and followed her.

'Kelly accused me of smothering you,' he told her as they reached the soft sand and headed on a diagonal path towards the waves washing up the beach. 'She said you were a woman, not a china doll, and I couldn't expect to keep you in a box tied up with ribbon.'

'Kelly has a lot of common sense.'

'Hmm.' Perhaps it was a new idea for him. 'I'm afraid I yelled at her. Told her she knew nothing about it and she should mind her own business.'

Skye almost smiled. Kelly would come bouncing back.

'She was right. It seemed to me you wanted to

keep treating me like a mistress, a pretty plaything that you could pick up when you had the time, and leave behind when you had more important things to do.'

'I never thought of you like that.' His tone was curt.

'Not even when we . . . when we were in Sydney?'

'I told you how I felt the first time I saw you. I admit that right then I didn't think beyond seeing you again . . . and again, as often as possible. I knew that your lifestyle, your career path, pretty much precluded anything permanent between us, but I tried to ignore that. What I felt for you was so powerful I just wanted to take all that I could, all that you would let me have of you. That sounds appallingly selfish – but I have to admit I thought you'd . . . be much more experienced, less vulnerable, than you were.'

'You bought into the stereotype,' she scolded mildly. But she supposed it was understandable that he'd expected she would have had other lovers before him.

'I made assumptions,' he agreed. 'After you let me make love to you I figured that in some way I must be more important to you than I'd dared to think. I began to hope – '

They reached the firmer sand and turned to

stroll parallel with the sea. Jarrah scuffed a shell out of the sand with his toe and walked on, his hands thrust into his pockets. 'I knew it was a crazy dream, but the fact that I was the first man you'd trusted with your lovely body gave me some hope for a future together. I didn't fool myself that you'd be willing to give up a wonderful career that was light years from anything I could offer you, but I understand a model's professional life is a short one, and I was willing to wait, and to accept whatever crumbs came my way in the meantime.'

Crumbs? Skye turned her head to stare at him. The salty breeze blew a strand of hair across her face and she pushed it back.

'I tried to close my eyes,' Jarrah went on, 'to the fact that you might hate life in the outback. But I was screwing up the courage to ask you to come and visit Opal Reach if you could make a space for it in your schedule when you sprang the news on me that you were going to America.'

'I had told you – '

'I know, but you hadn't told me when, or for how long. A few weeks, you'd said. And you were so casual about it that day, as if our being apart for two months was nothing –' He bent and picked up a curved stick lying on the sand, hurling it far out into the breakers

Skye bit her lip. She remembered her desperate struggle to keep her self-respect intact, her pride. 'I was hoping you'd tell me it *wasn't* just a casual affair.'

He gave her a glance that held exasperation and humour and indignation. 'You don't know how hard I was biting my tongue. I figured you were laying the conditions, hinting that you didn't want anything too intense in case it interfered with your career. And I was afraid to pressure you in case you called the whole thing off.' Jarrah had halted, and was watching the waves roll in, not looking at her. 'When you came back and broke the news to me about the baby I jumped at the chance to marry you out of hand without giving you time to think. I persuaded myself if you wanted to keep the baby you must love me at least a little. And that it would be enough to get us over any problems. Because I sure as hell loved you.'

'You were right,' Skye said, her voice almost inaudible against the sound of the sea and the high scream of a gull overhead. 'I did love you.'

He gave her a strange look, then began walking again, heedless of a hurrying wave that dampened the hem of his jeans and left foamy kisses on Skye's toes.

'After I'd got you pregnant and messed up your life and your career, you put yourself into my hands with such trust, flew into the unknown so bravely . . . I wanted to make sure nothing harmed you or upset you.' The wayward breeze ruffled his dark hair and he pushed it back from his forehead. 'Then we lost the baby, and you seemed to be going further and further away. I've been terrified since you left that it was the final step. There was no baby after all, and no reason to stay with me. Maybe you could get your old life back. I was afraid that was what you really wanted.'

'I never intended to end our marriage!' she protested. 'It hadn't crossed my mind until that day when you came crashing in, announcing you'd come to take me home and demanding decisions from me.'

'I didn't mean. . . .' He stopped and thrust his fingers through his hair again and glanced at her, then looked out to sea. 'It wasn't my intention to bully you. I just . . .' He cleared his throat. 'I suppose I've got too used to giving orders.'

Maybe he had. She murmured, 'You've been running that huge property since you were barely out of your teens.'

Jarrah nodded jerkily and cast her an odd, almost embarrassed glance. 'The truth is, I was . . . I couldn't bear the thought of leaving here again without you. And when I'm unsure of my ground I compensate with what my little sister calls bloody male arrogance. Not a trait that I'm proud of.'

He didn't sound arrogant now, she thought. Not a bit.

Jarrah cleared his throat. 'We're putting down a concrete airstrip at Opal Reach,' he said, 'so the plane won't be grounded in the Wet. And Erik found a stainless steel double sink unit we could fit in your darkroom if you decide you'd like one. You could make a new career out of your photography, I reckon. You're very talented.'

Disconcerted by the change of subject, Skye took a moment to work out where he was coming from. 'Are you trying to *bribe* me to come back to Opal Reach with you?' She didn't know whether to laugh or cry.

He stopped walking again and looked at her. 'I'm trying to get you come back to *me*.'

He paused, and she saw his chest move with a deepened breath before he added, 'And I've been doing some thinking since I came here. I guess I've been pretty one-eyed about this. The thing is, since I was a kid I'd assumed that when Dad went I'd be in charge at Opal Reach. And after that happened I operated on the principle of leading from the front, never asking anyone to do a job unless I can show willing myself. There's never been anything in my life until now that was as important as Opal Reach, it was a way of life – my way of life – and I never questioned it before.'

Was he questioning it now? 'I don't understand what you're saying, Jarrah.'

A heavy frown creased his brow, as if he was still thinking deeply. 'I'm saying that I realize you felt that I'd put you and our marriage in a corner of my life while I got on with doing what I'd always done. And I'm saying I want to change that. I don't think I could live in the city – I wouldn't know what to do with myself – but we don't have to live at Opal Reach.'

Astounded, Skye stared at him.

'Kelly would love to manage the place. And between her and Erik they'd do it well. You and I could move to one of our properties in New South Wales. The climate's kinder there, and you could spend time in Sydney whenever you like.'

'You'd never leave Opal Reach! You're a part of it – it's part of you.'

His hands were in his pockets, but she thought he clenched them then. 'Don't you understand yet? *You* are the most important thing to me, Skye. Nothing else matters as much as you and the fact that I want to spend my life with you. And I won't do it at the expense of forcing you to live in a place you hate.'

'I don't hate it!'

'No? It's certainly the impression I got when I said I'd come to take you back there with me. Or was it only me you couldn't bear to be with?'

Skye shook her head. 'It wasn't like that. I told you I love you,' she whispered.

He took his hands out of his pockets but quickly halted the movement they made towards her. His eyes glittered. 'Last time you used the past tense.'

'I never stopped,' she said. 'Even when I wanted to feel nothing, after the baby . . . when I couldn't respond to you . . .' finally she put it into words '. . . because I was afraid that if I felt anything at all, like . . . like passion, I'd have to feel the grief too, and I didn't know if I could stand it. Even then, I still loved you. Only I just couldn't . . . tell you, show you . . . because it all hurt too much.'

He did put his hands on her then, and gently drew her to him, his eyes alight with silver fire. 'I wish you'd told me. Just once, it would have helped.'

'I know, and I'm sorry. It was like being in a glass cage that I couldn't break out of.' She raised her hands and laid her palms against his roughened cheeks. 'I do love you, Jarrah. Believe me, I do.'

'And how will you feel about me when I've got lines – sooner than you, with all the sun I've been exposed to – and develop a stoop and lose my hair? Will you stop loving me then?'

'No!'

'Then how *dare* you,' he accused with quiet ferocity, 'suggest that I'm so shallow that I can't see beyond your beautiful face?'

Skye's lips parted in confusion, her eyes searching his and finding anger and a shimmering emotion that brought hot colour to her cheeks.

'How dare you?' he repeated, and dragged her close to him and kissed her with all the anger she had seen in his eyes, and all the passion.

And answering passion rose in a tidal wave that suffused her body and left her stunned and shaken when he lifted his head at last and looked down at her. His arms were wrapped securely about her, and she was glad because she didn't think she could have remained standing on her own.

Jarrah took her hand and tugged her a few steps to dry, soft sand, and drew her down on it and then kissed her again, his warm, muscular thigh intruding between hers.

When he stopped kissing her she was breathing unevenly, her cheeks flushed and her body singing. 'This is a public beach,' she reminded him.

He raised his head and looked in both directions. 'I don't see anyone about.'

'You can't –' She tried to push him away, but Jarrah found her mouth again with his, and she gave up and kissed him back.

His hand was on her breast, and she shuddered and made a small protesting sound in her throat. He lifted his head and grabbed a handful of her hair and wound it about his fist and said, 'Tell me again that you love me.'

'I love you,' she murmured. 'I'll always love you.'

'The hell with this,' he said. 'I'm taking you to bed.' He stood up and hauled her to her feet.

'Jarrah – '

He looked at her stubbornly, then suddenly flushed and dropped her hand. 'I'm sorry. I'm riding roughshod again. Tell me what you'd like to do.'

'I'd like . . .' Skye moistened her lips, her heart erratically jumping about. 'I'd like to go to bed with you.' She held out her hand.

Jarrah swallowed, shut his eyes briefly and opened them again, taking her hand in his hard clasp. 'Thank you.'

They walked slowly and in silence, their feet sinking in the white, gritty sand, but as soon as they'd entered the house he swung her off her feet and into his arms and strode to the master bedroom, kicking the door shut.

He put her on the bed, and drew the curtain against the brightness of the sun, tugging at his belt at the same time. He threw his shirt on the floor and shucked off his jeans and bent over her, and seconds later her clothing and his were mingled in a little heap on the mat beside the bed.

His eyes blazed as he looked at her nakedness, and she pulled the sheet self-consciously over her.

'What's the matter?' he asked, frowning.

'I look . . . different, since the baby . . .' The last time he'd made love to her it had been night-time in the hotel. The dark had covered the changes in her body.

'Skye,' he said quietly, 'I've already seen. And you're no less beautiful to me. You never will be.'

He took away the sheet and his hand shaped the new breadth of her hips. He kissed her breasts with their darkened aureoles, and the few faint silvery blemishes on her belly. 'I hope there'll be other babies,' he said. 'But even if there aren't I'll still love these marks, in memory of our son.' He looked into her eyes and touched her hair, sifting the soft strands through his fingers. 'And I'll love every grey hair and every line and wrinkle you develop. Just don't leave me again. I thought I'd die without you.'

'I wouldn't have stayed away,' Skye assured him, her hand stroking his shoulder. 'I dreamed of you . . .'

His mouth descended on hers, and he kissed her deeply, growling in his throat with pleasure as she kissed him back and wrapped her arms about him.

The waves of desire beat higher and higher, and with a sense of delighted wonder Skye let her emotions go and soared to the dark, whirling heavens locked in Jarrah's strong arms.

When she came down to earth he was stroking her again, whispering into her ear soothing words of love and tenderness.

'I thought I'd never feel anything again,' she confessed. 'I thought I didn't want to.' Her eyes filled unexpectedly with hot tears. 'Oh, Jarrah – our darling little boy!'

'Yes,' he said, and brushed the tears from her cheeks, but they kept coming. 'It's all right,' he murmured to her as she sobbed against his shoulder, and his own tears moistened her hair. 'It's all right to grieve.'

At sunset, dressed in jeans and sweaters, they were sitting on the beach, their arms about each other as they huddled together near the bank. The sea was now faintly streaked with pink and the waves had smoothed out.

'Tell you what,' Jarrah settled her closer against his chest, 'every Wet we could find a beach like this and make love all summer.'

'You'd get bored.'

'Not on your life. Will *you*?'

'No.' She touched his cheek. 'I could never be bored around you.'

'Not even at Opal Reach?'

'I wasn't bored. Just frustrated sometimes that I wasn't allowed to do anything really useful. And I missed you when you were out on the musters.'

He kissed her, and she said, 'How long a break have you taken now?'

'As long as you like. It's up to you.'

'But . . . the muster?'

'I've left Erik and Kelly to run it. It's time they were given a bit more responsibility – and independence. I keep thinking of my brothers and sisters as they were when my father died and I took over the station and the family finances. I'd never been so scared in my life, but I had to hide it for their sakes, and the sake of Opal Reach.'

'Your mother – ?'

'She was the only one who had any idea of my real feelings, but she'd always left the running of the station – the decision-making – to my dad. And she was very careful not to make me feel I couldn't fill Dad's boots.'

'Do you really think Kelly could fill yours?'

'Don't you?'

'I think she's very capable, and someone should give her a chance to prove herself. I was asking what *you* think.'

'I think you're right. Even if we stayed at Opal Reach I could leave Kelly or Erik in charge for the summer, and we could go wherever you want. I'm not indispensable.'

'Only to me,' Skye said softly. 'Jarrah – ?'

'What is it?' He looked down and nuzzled his cheek against her temple, then turned his head and kissed the fine, smooth skin.

'I'll never compete with Kelly – '

'You don't need to! You don't need to do anything you don't want to, Skye. Wherever we live, I'll still hire a housekeeper – we can afford it . . .'

And leave her with even less to occupy her time, Skye thought with wry, loving exasperation. She twisted round and placed two fingers over his lips. 'Suppose I do want to?' she asked him.

'Want to what?' he mumbled, catching her fingers and kissing them.

'Suppose I want to ride to muster or . . . or learn to fly a helicopter or drive a bull-catcher? Would you try to stop me?'

She wanted to laugh, watching the struggle taking place in his mind, reflected in his expression. 'Maybe,' he said at last, forcing himself to honesty. 'But I guess you'd wear me down – if you were determined to do it.'

Skye smiled, and leaned forward and kissed him on the lips. 'I guess I will,' she said.

'But not bull-catching,' he warned, scowling.

She almost let it go, reluctant to spoil their new mood of reconciliation. Then she recalled Kelly's advice. 'Maybe not. But if I wanted to – and don't you roar at me again about who's allowed to do what on *your* station and in *your* station vehicles – '

'I was worried about you.'

'I know. If I wanted to,' she pressed him, 'I'd expect you to discuss it, not just lay down the law and take it for granted that I'd obey.'

'All right,' he conceded. 'I know I overreacted that time. Kelly was ticked off with me then, too.'

Skye smiled. 'You should listen to her more.'

'Yeah?' His eyes narrowed. 'You two going to gang up on me?'

'Probably. I like Kelly. She's the only one who didn't think I needed wrapping in cotton wool.' She wondered if Kelly might stay at Opal Reach after all, now that Jarrah was willing to give her more responsibility. 'How is Stardust?' she asked.

'She's in foal again. Looking very contented.'

Skye looked at the restless water, shot with flame and indigo and silver in the dying day, and remembered the stillness of the waterhole at Opal Reach – the ibis that stalked along the water's edge, the brolgas with their gawky dancing, and the white bark of the ghost gums reflected in the mysterious, fiery depths at sundown.

'I feel contented too,' she murmured. And maybe . . . just maybe she was pregnant again, because when he'd paused in his lovemaking and she'd realized what it was he was searching for, she'd said no, and drawn him fearlessly back to her.

He kissed her temple. 'I'm glad.'

'You must want to go back,' she said.

'There's no hurry.' She felt his silent laughter. 'After all, only a pig-headed, arrogant male chauvinist bossyboots would imagine he was bloody well indispensable.'

Skye smiled. 'A direct quote, I take it.'

'My little sister doesn't mince words. We'll go home when you're ready,' he told her. 'Not before. And home will be wherever you want it to be.'

Skye turned in his arms and kissed him gently, pulling away as he began to return the kiss, his arms hard at her back.

He belonged to a harsh, uncompromising land that had taught him to be tough and hardheaded and not easily bent, but he was human, after all. And he was beginning to learn the art of compromise, to make accommodations for her sake. She could do the same for him.

'I'm ready,' she said softly. 'And my home is where yours has always been, at Opal Reach. Where your heart is.'

His arm tightened. 'You don't have to say that . . . not unless you're sure. My heart goes with you, wherever you are. My heart, and my life, are in your hands.'

'I am sure. Very sure. Take me home tomorrow, Jarrah,' she whispered, looking fearlessly into his eyes. 'Home to Opal Reach.'

PLEASE HELP ME TO HELP YOU!

Dear ***Scarlet*** Reader,

As Editor of ***Scarlet*** Books I want to make sure that the books I offer you every month are up to the high standards ***Scarlet*** readers expect. And to do that I need to know a little more about you and your reading likes and dislikes. So please spare a few minutes to fill in the short questionnaire on the following pages and send it to me.

Looking forward to hearing from you,

Sally Cooper

Editor-in-Chief, ***Scarlet***

Note: further offers which might be of interest may be sent to you by other, carefully selected, companies. If you do not want to receive them, please write to Robinson Publishing Ltd, 7 Kensington Church Court, London W8 4SP, UK.

QUESTIONNAIRE

Please tick the appropriate boxes to indicate your answers

1 Where did you get this Scarlet title?

Bought in supermarket ☐

Bought at my local bookstore ☐ Bought at chain bookstore ☐

Bought at book exchange or used bookstore ☐

Borrowed from a friend ☐

Other (please indicate) ____________________

2 Did you enjoy reading it?

A lot ☐ A little ☐ Not at all ☐

3 What did you particularly like about this book?

Believable characters ☐ Easy to read ☐

Good value for money ☐ Enjoyable locations ☐

Interesting story ☐ Modern setting ☐

Other ____________________

4 What did you particularly dislike about this book?

____

5 Would you buy another Scarlet book?

Yes ☐ No ☐

6 What other kinds of book do you enjoy reading?

Horror ☐ Puzzle books ☐ Historical fiction ☐

General fiction ☐ Crime/Detective ☐ Cookery ☐

Other (please indicate) ____________________

7 Which magazines do you enjoy reading?

1. ____________________

2. ____________________

3. ____________________

And now a little about you –

8 How old are you?

Under 25 ☐ 25–34 ☐ 35–44 ☐

45–54 ☐ 55–64 ☐ over 65 ☐

cont.

9 What is your marital status?

Single ☐ Married/living with partner ☐

Widowed ☐ Separated/divorced ☐

10 What is your current occupation?

Employed full-time ☐ Employed part-time ☐

Student ☐ Housewife full-time ☐

Unemployed ☐ Retired ☐

11 Do you have children? If so, how many and how old are they?

____

____

12 What is your annual household income?

under $15,000	☐	or	£10,000	☐
$15–25,000	☐	or	£10–20,000	☐
$25–35,000	☐	or	£20–30,000	☐
$35–50,000	☐	or	£30–40,000	☐
over $50,000	☐	or	£40,000	☐

Miss/Mrs/Ms ______________________________

Address __________________________________

____

____

Thank you for completing this questionnaire. Now tear it out – put it in an envelope and send it, before 31 August 1998, to:

Sally Cooper, Editor-in-Chief

USA/Can. address
SCARLET c/o London Bridge
85 River Rock Drive
Suite 202
Buffalo
NY 14207
USA

UK address/No stamp required
SCARLET
FREEPOST LON 3335
LONDON W8 4BR
Please use block capitals for address

REOPA/3/98

Forthcoming *Scarlet* titles:

NO SWEETER CONFLICT Megan Paul
When she's sent to interview her 'cousin' Jacob Trevelyn, Florence tries to act with journalistic detachment, and at first succeeds. Until the fact that there's no blood tie between them – *and* her memories of their shared past – start getting in the way!

DANCE UNTIL MORNING Jan McDaniel
Claire Woolrich is used to a wealthy lifestyle . . . drop-out Wheeler Scully isn't at all impressed! They are forced to spend the night together, but surely Claire doesn't need to worry about making a lasting impression on this unsuitable man?

DARK DESIRE Maxine Barry
Dedicated to building up her career, Electra Stapleton has no time for romance. She is particularly wary of handsome stranger Haldane Fox. But Haldane is on a mission which will have an everlasting effect on Electra . . .

LOVERS DON'T LIE Chrissie Loveday
Simon Andrews might be very different from the student she originally fell in love with, but Jenna finds him even more irresistible second-time-around. Trouble is, Simon's now married with a child – isn't he? And with a secret in her past she *must* hide, Jenna *can't* give in to her desires.

Did You Know?

There are over 120 NEW romance novels published each month in the US & Canada?

♥ ***Romantic Times Magazine*** is ***THE ONLY SOURCE*** that tells you what they are and where to find them–even if you live abroad!

♥ ***Each issue*** reviews ***ALL*** 120 titles, saving you time and money at the bookstores!

♥ ***Lists mail-order*** book stores who service international customers!

ROMANTIC TIMES MAGAZINE

Established 1981

Order a SAMPLE COPY Now!

FOR UNITED STATES & CANADA ORDERS:

$2.00 United States & Canada (U.S FUNDS ONLY)

CALL 1-800-989-8816*

* 800 NUMBER FOR US CREDIT CARD ORDERS ONLY

♥ **BY MAIL:** Send US funds Only. Make check payable to:
Romantic Times Magazine, 55 Bergen Street, Brooklyn, NY 11201 USA

♥ **TEL.:** 718-237-1097 ♥ **FAX:** 718-624-4231

VISA • M/C • AMEX • DISCOVER ACCEPTED FOR US, CANADA & UK ORDERS!

FOR UNITED KINGDOM ORDERS: **(Credit Card Orders Accepted!)**

£2.00 Sterling–Check made payable to Robinson Publishing Ltd.

♥ **BY MAIL:** Check to above **DRAWN ON A UK BANK** to: Robinson Publishing Ltd., 7 Kensington Church Court, London W8 4SP England

♥ E-MAIL CREDIT CARD ORDERS: RTmag1@aol.com

♥ VISIT OUR WEB SITE: http://www.rt-online.com